# Murder Dancing

# Murder Dancing

# Lesley Cookman

Published by Accent Press Ltd 2016

ISBN 9781783756926

# Acknowledgements

The first acknowledgement I have to make is a sad one. *Murder Dancing* was inspired by Matthew Bourne's ballet company, New Adventures, and in particular Jonathan Ollivier, whom I saw dance The Swan in 2014. Sadly, not long after starting this book, Jonathan was killed in a motorbike accident, aged only 38.

To more cheerful things – I apologise to the Police Forces of Great Britain for using and abusing them, as usual. They would never hold an investigation like this, and if I could get away without the police, I would. However, I have learnt that there are many readers who are secretly in love with DCI Connell, so perhaps I shall leave them in.

Unusually, the idea for this book did not come from my son Miles. The next one, however…

As always, thanks to my patient editor, Greg Rees.

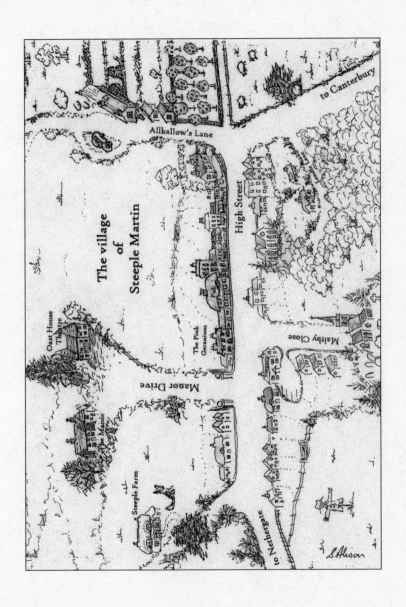

The village
of
Steeple Martin

Allhallow's Lane

to Canterbury

High Street

Maltby Close

The Pink
Geranium

Oast House
Theatre

Manor Drive

The Manor

Steeple Farm

to Nethergate

S. Alison

# WHO'S WHO IN THE LIBBY SARJEANT SERIES

Libby Sarjeant

Former actor, sometime artist, resident of 17, Allhallow's Lane, Steeple Martin. Owner of Sidney the cat.

Fran Wolfe

Also former actor, occasional psychic, resident of Coastguard Cottage, Nethergate. Owner of Balzac the cat.

Ben Wilde

Libby's significant other. Owner of The Manor Farm and the Oast House Theatre.

Guy Wolfe

Fran's husband. Artist and owner of a shop and gallery in Harbour Street, Nethergate.

Peter Parker

Ben's cousin. Freelance journalist, part owner of The Pink

Geranium restaurant and life partner of Harry Price.

Harry Price

Chef and co-owner of The Pink Geranium and Peter Parker's life partner.

Hetty Wilde

Ben's mother. Lives at The Manor.

DCI Ian Connell

Local policeman and friend. Former suitor of Fran's.

Adam Sarjeant

Libby's son.

Sophie Wilde

Guy's daughter.

Flo Carpenter

Hetty's oldest friend.

Lenny Fisher

Hetty's brother. Lives with Flo Carpenter.

Reverend Bethany Cole

Vicar of Steeple Martin.

Reverend Patti Pearson

Vicar of St Aldeberge's.

Anne Douglas

Librarian, friend of

Reverend Patti.

Ali and Ahmed        Owners of the eight-til-late in the village.

Sir Andrew McColl        Acclaimed theatre actor.

## Tobin Dance Theatre (TDT to its friends)

Max Tobin        Company director and choreographer.

Owen Talbot        Max's partner and director of the Tobin School.

Damian Singleton        Composer of *Pendle*.

Stan Willis        Stage and company manager.

Sebastian Long        Company assistant stage manager.

## Cast of *Pendle*

Dan Washburn        Roger Nowell
Phillip Newcombe        Alizon Device
Jonathan Chandler        Demdike
Will Davies        Abraham Law
Tom Matthews        Chattox
Alan Neville        Elizabeth Device

| | |
|---|---|
| Lee | John Law |
| Paul | Ensemble |
| Jeremy | Ensemble |
| Bernie | Ensemble |
| Paddy | Original Demdike |
| Gerry | Original Abraham Law |

# Chapter One

'The Pendle Witches?' said Libby Sarjeant. 'A ballet?'

'Sounds interesting,' said Fran Wolfe. 'But played by men?'

Sir Andrew McColl, dapper in a tweed suit and highly polished brown brogues, sat back in his armchair and crossed one elegant leg over the other.

'The Witches in *Macbeth* have often been played by men,' he said. 'And this is called "Dance Theatre", rather than ballet.'

'And you're talking to us why?' asked Fran.

'Max – the director – has been having some ... er ... trouble during rehearsal.' Andrew looked at his nails.

Libby scowled suspiciously. 'I said I'm never getting involved again.'

Andrew raised innocent eyebrows. 'Did I ask you to?'

'You were going to,' said Fran, amused.

'Yes, well.' Andrew returned to his nails.

Ben Wilde, Libby's significant other, sighed and got to his feet. 'Another drink, anyone?'

The pub was quiet on this weekday lunchtime. Andrew had arrived, out of the blue as he often did, booked into the pub and then asked if he could meet Libby, Ben and Fran for a drink.

'Tonic water, thank you, Ben,' said Andrew.

'Coffee, please,' said Fran, who was driving.

'A half, please,' said Libby, who wasn't.

'Will you come back for dinner tonight, Fran? You and Guy?' asked Andrew. 'I've booked a table at Harry's for eight thirty.'

'How can I resist,' said Fran with a smile. 'I haven't eaten at the Pink Geranium for weeks.'

'Bribery,' said Libby, with another scowl.

'So,' said Ben, arriving back at the table with a tray of drinks. 'What is it this Max wants? And who exactly is he?'

'Max Tobin. He's the founder and choreographer of the company. They're only small, so far, but they're gaining a good reputation.'

'And what problems has he been having?' asked Fran.

'He's not sure what the reason is, but he's had two of his principal danseurs leave and the others seem very jumpy. None of them will explain it.'

'Danseurs? Is that a posh way of saying "dancers"?' asked Libby.

'Male dancers,' said Fran. 'Put simply.'

'Ah. And they're uncomfortable about something?'

'That's what Max says.' Andrew uncrossed his legs. 'I was telling him about what led up to our concert last Christmas – he was in the audience, you see. And then he told me.'

'And,' said Ben again, 'what does he want?'

'Libby and Fran to look into it,' said Andrew, and took a sip of tonic water.

Fran and Libby looked at each other.

'And how exactly are we supposed to do that?' asked Libby. 'If they won't talk to their boss, they certainly won't talk to a couple of middle-aged amateur sleuths.'

'I said you wouldn't want to,' said Andrew. 'And you don't want to go trailing up to London to the rehearsal rooms.'

'Not particularly,' said Libby.

'So he had another idea.'

They all looked at him suspiciously.

'Well,' said Libby after a moment. 'What?'

'He'd like to hire the theatre for a trial run.'

Libby sat back in her chair, surprised.

'Good God,' said Ben.

'Well, it's logical,' said Fran.

Andrew smiled. 'Yes, it is. Then you'd be among them. They'd talk to you.'

'Would they?' Libby looked dubious.

'They're a small company. If you'd let them the rooms in the Manor, Ben, it would work very well.' Andrew finished his tonic water and stood up. 'I'll leave you to think it over and see you tonight at Harry's.'

'What do we think?' asked Libby, when Andrew had left the bar.

'It would depend when they want to come,' said Ben. 'We don't want to run into panto time.'

'And we've got a few one-nighters,' said Libby.

'What about the end of October?' asked Fran. 'That would coincide with Halloween, just right for Pendle Witches.'

'Bloody witches again,' said Libby. 'I've had enough of witches.'

'They're only fake witches, though, Lib,' said Ben. 'And Fran's right. As long as they don't want to come for too long we could do the last couple of weeks of October and the first in November. I'm assuming he wants to rehearse down here as well.'

'Well, we could hardly get them to talk to us if all they were doing was performing, could we?' said Libby. 'Do you think Hetty will mind having them at the Manor?'

'Of course she won't, but I'm not letting her supply them with food. They can forage for themselves.'

'I expect Harry will put on special arrangements for them,' said Fran. 'He'll love having a pack of male dancers tittuping around.'

'True.' Libby finished her half pint of lager and stood up. 'Now I'm going home to read up on the Pendle Witches. I saved all the information we found before.'

Libby and Fran had become entangled with local groups of witches before. In both cases the so-called rites were little more than a cover for unsavoury activities.

'I'll go home and toss up with Guy who's going to drive tonight,' said Fran.

'Stay over,' said Libby. 'You can always get up early to get back and open the shop.'

'Right,' said Ben. 'I'm going up to the estate office. I'll check the theatre bookings and text Andrew some dates. Then he can get on to his friend Max before we meet this evening.'

At eight o'clock, Libby, Ben, Fran and Guy opened the door of The Pink Geranium, the restaurant owned by Harry Price and Peter Parker, and run by Harry as *chef patron*. Libby's son

Adam, doing duty as a waiter, met them in his long Victorian apron and showed them into the left-hand window where Andrew awaited them on the deep sofa, accompanied, to their surprise, by a very tall man in a very sharp suit.

Andrew rose gracefully and took Libby's hand.

'This is Max, my dear,' he said.

Max Tobin also rose and bent over Libby's hand.

'Delighted to meet you,' he said, in a voice like smooth gravel.

When introductions had been completed all round and Adam sent off for drinks, Max spoke again.

'Andrew has told me you've very kindly made some time available for our Witches at your theatre.' He looked at Libby. 'And you'll see if you can get anything out of my dancers about why they're unhappy?'

'I don't promise,' said Libby, looking uncomfortable. 'They won't know me, or Fran.'

'I thought of a secret weapon,' said Andrew with a smile. 'After Ben had sent me the dates and I confirmed them with Max, I called Harry.'

'You said at lunchtime you'd already booked the table,' said Ben.

'Ah, but Max said he wanted to come down, so I needed to add to my booking. And it occurred to me that Harry would make an excellent agony uncle.' Andrew beamed round the table.

'And I will.' Harry, tall, blond and slightly raffish, appeared beside them flourishing bottles. 'Pete, of course, will be standing guard over me like a bulldog.'

'He's more Afghan than bulldog,' said Libby.
'Peter's my cousin,' Ben explained to Max, who was looking faintly bewildered, 'and Harry's partner.'

'In life, dearie,' sighed Harry, 'and in all things. Right, who's having what?'

Harry departed with the orders, and Max laughed.

'I remember him, of course,' he said. 'We came here after your concert, didn't we?'

Andrew smiled. 'We did. And that brings us back to why

4

you're bringing *Pendle* down here. Tell them all about it.'

Max picked up his gin and tonic and swirled it absently round the glass.

'I suppose it started when I took a group of my boys to see a revival of Matthew Bourne's *Swan Lake*.'

'Oh, bliss,' said Libby.

'What's that?' asked Guy, frowning.

'Matthew Bourne has a ballet company called New Adventures, and one of his ballets is a version of *Swan Lake* danced by men,' explained Andrew.

'Oh,' said Guy.

'Anyway,' Max went on, 'we talked about it, naturally, and they were very enthusiastic, all of them expressing a wish to do the same. I said we couldn't do *Swan Lake*, but we could possibly do something similar.'

'And you thought of the Pendle Witches?' said Fran.

'No, actually, it was one of the boys.' Max smiled slightly. 'He grew up "in the shadow of the hill" as he put it, and the whole area is a rather grisly tourist attraction. And he pointed out that these days the witches are often played by men in –' he glanced at Andrew.

'The Scottish play,' the company chanted.

'Exactly.' Max smiled at them. 'So we began to workshop it. The storyline and so on.'

'What about music?' asked Fran.

'We workshopped without. Our rehearsal pianist extemporised a bit, and then offered to write it.'

'Really? Is he experienced as a composer?' asked Libby.
'He's written a lot, although it's not often performed. He's very young, but he's been a rehearsal pianist for long enough that he knows what we need. And he's just modern enough for it not to feel too classical and to be more accessible.'

'So it all fell into place?' said Ben.

'It seemed to. We began proper rehearsals and it was all going well.' Max shook his head. 'Then my principal dancer – playing Demdike – started arriving late and behaving oddly. Eventually when I took him aside, he said someone had been playing tricks on him.'

5

'What sort of tricks?' asked Guy after a pause.

'Leaving odd messages in his locker, that sort of thing.'

'Messages about what?'

'Oddly, they were all quotations from that play. From the Three Witches speeches, and Banquo's description of them.'

'Oh, yes,' said Andrew, turning to the others. 'Remember? "What are these/So wither'd and so wild in their attire," and then it goes on "You should be women/And yet your beards forbid me to interpret/That you are so." That helps us see that the creatures could be either male or female.'

'How did you call that up so quickly?' asked Libby, admiring.

'I've played Banquo a couple of times,' said Andrew with a grin.

'I played Maria in *Twelfth Night* three times and I'm not sure I could spout anything but "By my troth Sir Toby" and then it all goes blank.'

'There's nothing particularly threatening in that, though,' said Fran.

'What, Maria?'

'No, idiot, Banquo's speech.'

'But there is in the witch's description of what she does to the sailor,' said Max.

'Ah,' said Andrew. 'She makes him impotent.'

'Does she?' said Guy. 'And what sailor?'

'It's sometimes cut,' said Andrew, 'it's at the beginning of act one, scene three, before they meet Macbeth. The first witch describes what she will do to a sailor to punish his wife. Not relevant to the story as a whole, so, as I said, it's occasionally cut.'

'And that was one of the messages?' said Fran.

Max nodded. 'And after that, apparently, there were dead frogs. And a snake skin.'

'The fenny snake!' said Libby.

'From the witches' song,' explained Andrew.

'Oh, is that "Double trouble, cauldron ... something"?' asked Guy.

'Nearly,' said Andrew. 'I won't correct you.'

6

'Oh, no, you mustn't quote, must you?' said Ben.

'But you already have,' said Libby, looking at Andrew. 'Banquo's speech.'

'So I did.' Andrew's cheeks grew pink above his neat beard. 'Unwarrantable showing off.'

'So what happened after the fenny snake?' asked Libby.

'He left.' Max sighed. 'Pity. He was shaping up so well. He's gone back to West End ensemble now. Better paid, of course.'

Adam arrived to show them to their table. When they were settled, Max resumed.

'I thought that was it, and we would carry on as before. I recast Demdike, and then Chattox began experiencing the same sort of thing.'

'Is Chattox another witch?' asked Ben.

'Demdike and Chattox, as they were known, were the two most famous, along with Anne Redferne, Chattox's daughter, so they are my three principals. Demdike and Chattox are the main two, of course.'

'Was it the same?' asked Libby. 'Messages and frogs?'

'At first. But what came next was really shocking.'

'What?' Fran asked.

'He found a disembowelled cockerel in his locker.'

# Chapter Two

'That's serious stuff, then,' said Libby.

'You said "he". Who did you mean? The new Demdike?' asked Fran.

'Sorry, no. My Chattox.' Max sighed. 'And of course, the whole troupe got the wind up.'

'They would,' said Ben. 'I'm surprised they didn't walk out en masse.'

'I think they would have, but Chattox happens to be a very strong, no-nonsense, unsuperstitious person. Not at all the sort who would give in to this sort of pressure. In fact it made him rather ...' he paused.

'Bolshie?' suggested Libby.

Max smiled at her. 'Exactly.'

'Sort of "no one's going to push me out of this part" feeling?'

'Spot on.' Max turned to Andrew. 'You told me she was good.'

'Oh, don't tell her that,' said Adam, appearing with their first course. Max once more looked startled.

'That's my son,' said Libby. 'Don't take any notice.'

'So what happened next?' asked Fran.

'I called them together after a rehearsal and asked them what they thought about it. If any of them wanted to pull out, or if they thought we should stop altogether.' Max thoughtfully selected a cheese-smothered nacho from the plate. 'They all wanted to carry on.'

'All of them?' Libby raised her eyebrows.

'Well, there were a couple who didn't look too keen, but when they realised that everyone else was all for carrying on they agreed to do so, too. I'm pleased about that, as one of them is playing Roger Nowell, who was the chief prosecutor.'

'Has anything else happened since then?' asked Guy.

'No. That was when Andrew and I came up with the plan to – well, to enlist your support,' Max finished lamely.

'Rehearsals are quite advanced, are they?' asked Libby.

'They are. Which is just as well, because we haven't given you very much notice, have we?'

'When exactly are you coming?' asked Fran.

'The weekend after next. We'll have a week rehearsing in the theatre, then four or five days culminating in a final Halloween performance on the Saturday. We'll clear out on the Sunday. Some of the boys have got panto this season, but they won't need to start that for a few weeks.'

'You don't have to go on the Sunday,' said Ben. 'We've got nothing booked in until the end of the week, and that's only a one-nighter. Unless you have another venue to get to, of course.'

'No, because this will be a trial. I'm getting a few people down to have a look, and we'll see where we go from there.'

The conversation turned to more general aspects of theatre, and particularly pantomime, until Harry emerged from the kitchen to join them, carrying a bottle of brandy and followed by Peter, who was introduced to Max.

'I can see I shall have to keep an eye on my boys if they're going to be eating here,' said Max, eyeing the brandy with amusement.

'Oh, I don't dish this out to everyone,' said Harry, swinging a chair around and sitting astride it. 'Only favoured guests.' He bent a darkling glance on Libby. 'Sometimes.'

'Exactly how many of you will be coming?' asked Ben. 'I'll have to warn my mother.'

'Your mother?'

'Ben and his mother own the theatre and the Manor, where you'll all be staying,' said Andrew. 'If there's room for you all. If not, the pub, as you know, has a couple of rooms, and there's always Anderson Place if you want to be really exclusive.'

'There are ten dancers, me, the composer/pianist and our stage manager. We could bring our own stage crew, unless the theatre can provide them?'

'What about lighting?' asked Peter, who specialised in what was known as FX, or sound and lighting effects.

'We can supply our own techies, unless you're prepared to do that, too,' said Max. 'It's a question of how many you can actually accommodate.'

Peter and Ben looked at each other.

'We've got twelve rooms in the Manor,' said Ben, 'and there are a couple of rooms here at the pub if they're free.'

'And we would have had the flat upstairs if Adam hadn't moved back in,' said Harry.

'He could move back in with us for the fortnight,' said Libby with resignation.

'Are you only using piano for the performances?' asked Fran.

'No, we're having the music recorded by a small orchestra,' said Max, 'so technically, our composer needn't be here for the run, but we'll need him for some of the rehearsals, and he rather regards it as his baby.'

'So that's thirteen essentials,' said Ben.

'Unlucky,' said Libby, pulling a face.

'Oh, Lib, really,' said Harry.

'How many rooms are there at the pub?' asked Guy. 'Is it really only two?'

Andrew stood up. 'I'll pop next door and ask. Shall I book whatever they've got free at the time?'

'I think we can provide backstage and tech crew,' said Peter after he'd gone, 'as long as your stage manager doesn't mind. And I'm happy to do lighting design and operate.' He gazed at Max thoughtfully. 'In fact, I shall look forward to it. At least it's different from lighting one-nighters and pantomime.'

Andrew re-appeared. 'Three!' he said triumphantly. 'I've booked them all.'

'There!' Libby looked round the table delightedly. 'The ten boys in the Manor and three top bods in the pub.'

'Top bods is putting it a bit high,' said Max, with a laugh, 'but yes, it works. And the boys, as you call them, will probably be happier with me staying somewhere else.'

'Good, that's settled then,' said Ben. 'I'll tell Mum

11

tomorrow.'

'And we'll organise a work party to get the rooms ready,' said Libby.

'It's all very informal.' Max looked at Ben and Libby. 'Thank you.'

'Are we a bit too informal?' Libby asked Ben later as they got ready for bed. 'As far as the theatre goes, I mean.'

'I suppose we are a bit. But I'll issue Max with a contract tomorrow, and do all the paperwork. After all, there's no one looking over our shoulders, is there? The theatre belongs to us, lock, stock and barrel. As long as we comply with health and safety and council regulations, we're fine.'

'And declare it to the tax people.' Libby climbed into bed. 'I'm glad I don't have to do any of that.'

'So am I,' said Ben. 'I'd never hear the last of it.'

By the time Max arrived, a day ahead of his company, Ben had discovered he needed no extra backstage support and Libby had helped Hetty and a small army of village ladies give all the rooms at the Manor a good airing. The whole place smelt of lavender polish and pine disinfectant.

'Never mind, gal, it'll go off,' said Hetty, casting a gimlet eye over the seldom-used large sitting-room, which she was turning over to the guests for the duration of their stay. 'Now you get off and see to this Max.'

Ben was showing Max over the theatre, which he had prepared according to the instructions sent down by the stage manager. As Libby entered the foyer, Peter appeared at the top of the spiral staircase which led to the sound and lighting box.

'Our musical genius is here. Want to meet him?'

'Ssh!' Libby looked round frantically. 'Where is he?'

Peter grinned. 'Sitting in there with headphones on. Completely oblivious.'

Libby climbed the staircase and squeezed into the lighting box behind Peter. The young man sitting hunched over the control desk didn't move.

'Damian,' said Peter. The young man still didn't move. Peter tapped him on the shoulder.

12

'Eh? What? Oh!' The young man swung round and re-focused large, blue eyes on Libby.

'This is Libby Sarjeant,' said Peter, 'one of the joint owners of the theatre.'

Libby sent him a startled look.

The young man removed his headphones, swept thick, straight, pale hair off his forehead and gave Libby a singularly sweet smile.

'Hi – I'm Damian Singleton.'

Libby shook the proffered hand. 'And you're the composer?'

'Well ...' Damian looked awkward. 'You could put it like that.'

'That's how Max put it,' said Libby, amused.

'That was nice of him,' mumbled Damian, looking at his feet.

Libby and Peter looked at each other and shrugged.

'Were you listening to your music?' asked Libby. 'How does our sound system stand up?'

'Oh, it's excellent.' Damian looked up, now enthusiastic. 'I was actually wondering if I could be up here during the run.'

'You can, of course, but there won't be anything to do. It'll be switched on and then run on its own,' said Peter.

'Well, in case, you know, something happens ...' Damian turned and looked wistfully at the desk.

'Like someone falls over and they have to start again?' suggested Libby.

Damian turned back, shocked. 'Oh, no! That would never happen.'

'I don't suppose it does,' said Peter. 'What happens if someone twists an ankle or lands badly after a jump?'

'They carry on. As far as they can, of course.' Damian looked back at the control desk. 'Do you mind if I ...?'

'No, you carry on,' said Peter, and watched with amusement as Damian resumed his headphones and sat down again, once more oblivious to the outside world.

'Is he listening to his score?' asked Libby, as she and Peter descended the spiral staircase.

'Yes. They only finished recording it the day before

yesterday, and he hasn't heard it through a proper sound system until now. He's in a state of high excitement – and very nervous.'

'Where are Ben and Max?'

'Somewhere backstage.' Peter pushed open the auditorium doors. 'Go and have a look.'

The stage was hung with shaded grey gauze, which drifted slightly in an undefinable breeze in front of an impressionistic depiction of Pendle Hill, also in shades of grey. The company stage manager had sent them down and all Ben had to do was hang them from barrels in the flies. There were no changes of scene, merely changes of lighting, which Peter was to work out with Max and the stage manager that afternoon.

Ben appeared on the stage and peered into the auditorium. 'That you, Lib?'

'Yes.' Libby advanced to the edge of the stage. 'How's it going?'

'Fine. Everything meets with approval. Apparently the SM is driving the company bus down with costumes and props and should be here soon. Then he'll take it to meet the dancers at the station tomorrow.'

'Any more incidents since we last heard?'

Ben turned and called over his shoulder. 'Max! Libby's here.' He turned back. 'I haven't asked. And he hasn't said.'

Max appeared looking far more workmanlike than he had last time Libby had seen him. He grinned and came down to the front of the stage.

'Your old man's done us proud,' he said, squatting down on his haunches. 'The boys are going to love it. I'm going across to the Manor in a minute to meet Hetty.'

'Good,' said Libby. 'Are the boys looking forward to coming down?'

'Yes.' Max looked doubtful for a moment. 'Well, mostly. Some of them do have a rather London-centric attitude, I'm afraid.'

'Think it's the next thing to death here in the sticks?' said Ben.

Max grinned ruefully. 'I'm afraid so. But they're all up for

14

the piece, so that's all right.'

'And no more incidents?' said Libby lightly.

'Except for one of the witches ending up in hospital, no.'

# Chapter Three

'What?' Libby gasped.

'Hospital?' said Ben.

'Oh, it was nothing sinister.' Max stood up. 'Over-indulgence more likely. Although the hospital did suggest food poisoning.'

'Poor thing. Is he better now?'

'Oh, yes. Pale and complaining, but a lot better and inclined not to eat seafood for the foreseeable future.'

'So nothing to do with the other incidents?' said Ben.

'Not unless someone coerced the restaurant staff.' Max looked up into the flies. 'Did you manage the robotics and the Kabuki?'

'The what?' Libby peered upwards. 'What are they?'

Ben looked down at her and grinned. 'Aha! You wait till you see!'

'FX?' Libby looked over her shoulder at Peter. 'Are you in on this?'

'Of course. You just wait and see.'

'When do you want to try it out, Max?' asked Ben.

'We won't rehearse tomorrow, they'll be too tired. Or fractious. So on Monday, if that's all right? And I'll warn them it's a tech. They've never worked with this before, although they obviously know it's going to happen –'

'But what's going to happen?' Libby broke in.

The three men laughed.

'Just an effect, Libby,' said Max. 'Honestly, it would be better to wait and see.'

'Oh, all right,' grumbled Libby.

The auditorium doors crashed open.

'Hello?' came a muffled voice. 'Am I in the right place?'

Libby spun round to see what appeared to be a mountain of

fabric hovering above the back row of seats.

'Stan!' Max jumped lightly down from the stage and made his way up the central aisle. 'Give me some of those.'

Slowly, a small man with large glasses was revealed behind the fabric. He beamed towards the stage. 'Hi! I'm Stan Willis. Which one of you's Ben?'

'Me.' Ben grinned back and followed Max up the aisle.

Max took some of the costumes and Stan was further revealed. He was younger than his name suggested, very slim and neat.

'Hello,' he said holding out a hand to Libby. 'Are you Libby?'

'I am. And this is Peter.'

Peter shook hands. 'I'm the one up in the box. Your composer's up there now testing our sound system.'

Stan rolled his eyes. 'Oh, God. I do hope he isn't going to interfere.'

Peter looked amused. 'So do I!'

'I don't know why he had to be here at all,' said Stan testily, with a sulky glare at Max, who laughed.

'It would be most unfair to deny him the chance of being at the debut of his first public piece,' he said, 'and anyway, he might be playing for rehearsals.'

'How demeaning,' said Stan with a sniff.

'Are you moaning about me?' a voice shouted from above.

Everyone looked up to see Damian grinning down from the lighting box.

'Yes, he was,' said Max. 'Come down here and give us a hand.'

'Well,' said Libby, 'if you don't need me for anything, I'll get out of your way.'

'So will I,' said Peter. 'We can go through the lighting plot on Monday, can't we?'

Stan looked slightly bewildered. 'Not tomorrow?'

'It's Sunday,' said Peter.

'Stan,' said Max in a warning tone.

Peter grinned amiably. 'We're not pros, you see, Stan. Purely amateur set-up.' He set off towards the back of the auditorium. 'Coming, Lib?'

Libby followed him outside into the little garden, where he flung himself into one of the white, wrought-iron chairs.

'I've never heard you claim that we're an amateur set-up,' she said. 'He annoyed you, didn't he?'

'He did, rather. Strikes me as one of those stage managers who despise every other discipline in the theatre.'

Libby sat down opposite him. 'We had one of those once. He also did design and construction and refused to have pictures hung on the walls of his precious sets as it spoilt them. And the actors messed them up.'

'Like those old-fashioned nurses who complained that the patients made their wards untidy,' said Peter. 'Yes, just like that. And our Stanley also strikes me as someone who expects everyone to do exactly what he wants, when he wants it.'

'So do I gather we don't offer to do anything?' asked Libby with a grin.

'Other than what we've agreed to. I've already said I'll do lighting, so I'm stuck with that, and Ben offered to crew, although it doesn't look as though there's much to do backstage.'

'Just that Kabuki thing, whatever it is.'

'Oh, Stan can do that on his own.' Peter shook his head. 'And no, I'm not going to tell you what it is.'

Libby went home.

Ben joined her a couple of hours later.

'How did it go?' Libby moved the big kettle over to the Rayburn hotplate.

'OK, I think.' Ben sat down at the kitchen table. 'That Stan is a bit pernickety.'

'Peter thinks he's one of those people who expect all productions to revolve around them.'

'I suspect he's right.' Ben sighed and shook his head. 'I'm glad I won't have to crew for him.'

'You won't? I thought you'd offered?'

'He's got someone coming down, apparently, and there's hardly anything to do anyway.'

'Except the Kabuki thing,' said Libby hopefully.

Ben grinned. 'Oh, no, you're not getting me that way!'

'So have we got room for this new person?'

'He's sharing with Stan.'

'Oh?' Libby's eyebrows shot up. 'He didn't strike me as someone who would welcome sharing with anyone.'

'I believe they're partners,' said Ben. 'That's the impression I got. Max seems fine with it and ignores Stan's little foibles as far as I can see.'

'What about Damian? Did he come down to the stage?'

'Yes. He and Stan seem to enjoy baiting each other. Some of the things they were saying to each other were outrageous.'

'Golly,' said Libby.

The rest of the *Pendle* company were due to arrive at the Manor at around two o'clock on Sunday afternoon. Max had booked them all in at the pub for dinner, so there was nothing for Hetty to do except welcome them; nevertheless her regular Sunday roast had been put back to dinner time. Libby and Ben went up to the Manor to be on hand should they be needed, and Ben wandered into the theatre to switch on lights in case anyone wanted to look round.

'I needn't have bothered,' he said, as he returned to Libby and Hetty in the huge Manor kitchen, 'Damian's already in the sound box listening to his bloody score again.'

'How did he get in?' asked Libby.

'That Max came up with 'im,' said Hetty. 'Went in the minibus to fetch the dancers.'

'They'll be here any minute,' said Ben looking at his watch.

'If the train isn't late and they haven't had to get on replacement buses,' said Libby, this being a regular feature of the line into London.

On cue, the sound of an engine coming up the drive announced the arrival of the company. Libby, Ben and Hetty went outside.

The minibus came to a halt, the doors opened and Max jumped down from the near side.

'Here we are, dears,' he said. Libby and Ben exchanged raised eyebrows. This was the first time they'd heard Max slip into theatrical camp.

A flood of young men followed him out on to the drive, chattering like sparrows. Max held up a hand and they fell silent.

'Boys, these people are your hosts. Libby here and Ben own and run the theatre, and Hetty is your hostess at the Manor.'

'Hello,' said Libby, Ben and Hetty together. There was a chorus of replies and a couple came forward to shake hands.

'Nice to meet you,' said the blond giant who was shaking Libby's hand enthusiastically. 'I'm Dan Washburn. Not that you'll remember us all by name!'

Libby beamed up at him. 'I'll try. And you're very tall!'

'I'm too big, really,' said Dan, with an answering grin. 'But I can do lifts like billy-o.'

'I bet you can,' said Libby. 'Have you got your bags? We'll start showing you your rooms.'

Hetty retreated to the kitchen and Ben and Libby began to lead the dancers to their rooms. They were all delighted that they didn't have to share.

'You wouldn't believe some of the digs,' confided a slight, dark young man, as Libby showed him into a room overlooking the private garden at the back. 'This is luxury.'

'Oh, I would,' Libby told him. 'I was in the business myself.'

'You were?' Delicate eyebrows were raised. Libby laughed.

'Acting, not dancing. Though of course I had to learn the basics.'

'You had to learn to move.' The dark young man sounded slightly scornful.

'And did you have to learn to act?' asked Libby.

'Ah.' He broke into a deep and surprising guffaw. 'Got me there.' He put his case on the bed and stuck out a hand. 'I'm Phillip Newcombe.'

'Pleased to meet you, Phillip. Are you a witch?'

'I'm Alizon, Demdike's granddaughter.' He put his head on one side. 'Do you know the story?'

'The official version – vaguely,' said Libby. 'Isn't Alizon the one who's accused of killing the pedlar?'

Phillip grinned, delighted. 'That's the one! John Law, he is.'

'I'm looking forward to seeing it,' said Libby. 'Are you enjoying it?'

'Loving it.' He clasped his hands together and cast his eyes up to the ceiling. 'Praise whoever's up there.'

Amused, Libby left him to it and went back to see if anyone else needed shepherding to their rooms. After half an hour she joined Ben, Hetty and Max in the kitchen.

'All safely stowed,' she said. 'They seem a nice bunch. If I can get them all sorted out.'

Max laughed. 'A bit overwhelming all at once, aren't they?'

'They're fine. No one complained. They all seemed very pleased with the accommodation.'

'That's what one of them said to me. Told me I'd be surprised how awful some digs were!'

'Did you put him right?' asked Max. 'Which one was that?'

'Phillip. Your Alizon, he told me.'

'Ah, yes, Phillip. Can be a little wasp, but in general quite amusing.'

'Who does Dan Washburn play? He seems very big for a dancer.'

'Dan's our Roger Nowell, the magistrate. Yes, he's big, but did you get a good look at the others? Most of them are. And strong.'

'Didn't you say your Nowell was one of the people who weren't keen on continuing after the incidents?' said Ben.

'That's right,' said Max.

'He doesn't seem the type to get frightened off,' said Libby.

'His wife's just had a baby and he gets worried about being away from her for too long and in case anything happens to him. He's less – what would you call it? – venturesome than some of the others.'

'Sensible, you mean,' said Hetty. 'Want a cuppa?'

Max declined, saying that he must check on his flock, as did Libby and Ben on the grounds that they were going to have a quick Sunday lunchtime drink at the pub.

'We'll see you later, Mum,' said Ben. 'What time?'

'Six o'clock. Time for a glass before dinner. Tell Pete and Harry.'

Harry was still serving lunches in The Pink Geranium, so Ben just put his head round the door and asked the current waitress to give him the message. Meanwhile, Libby ran back to Peter and Harry's cottage and delivered the message to Peter.

'We're just going for a quick one at the pub,' said Libby. 'Coming?'

'No, I've got some stuff to get off this afternoon. I'll see you at Hetty's this evening. Did all the little darlings arrive?'

'Yes, all settled. Very butch, most of them.'

'Oh? Shows you, you shouldn't stereotype people. See you later.'

Ben was already in the pub.

'Look out,' he muttered, 'Stuffy Stan's coming our way.'

'Stuffy –?'

'Hello, you two.'

Libby turned to see Stan Willis and Damian Singleton behind her.

'Oh, hello.' She smiled weakly.

'All the lads settled in?'

'Yes, thank you,' said Libby. 'I didn't see you up there.'

'Oh, I got away as quickly as I could. I knew Damian was here having lunch, so I joined him.'

Damian smiled benignly, pale hair flopping over pale forehead as he nodded agreement.

'We'll leave you to it, then,' said Ben firmly turning from the bar with two glasses in his hand. 'Lib, Flo's beckoning us from the other bar.'

'See you later,' said Libby, hoping she wouldn't.

Flo Carpenter, Hetty's best friend since childhood, was indeed in the other bar with Lenny, Hetty's brother, who lived with her.

''Oo's that?' she said before Ben and Libby had even sat down. 'One of them dancers?'

'No, the stage manager,' said Ben. 'Shhh, Flo.'

''E looks familiar.' Flo was frowning. 'Where've I seen 'im before?'

'He lives in London as far as I know,' said Libby. 'Where would you have seen a London-based stage manager?'

''T'isn't 'im,' said Lenny suddenly.

'Eh?' said Flo.

'You're thinkin' it's old Wally Willis. Can't be 'im, 'e's dead.'

# Chapter Four

'Wally Willis?' echoed Ben and Libby together.

'That's Stan Willis,' said Libby.

'There, see?' said Flo triumphantly. 'Said I knew 'im.'

'You don't,' said Lenny. 'That ain't Wally.'

'Must be 'is son, or grandson,' said Flo.

'Who is Wally Willis?' asked Ben.

'Cor, don't you ever read yer newspapers?' said Lenny.

'Not these days, Lenny,' said Libby with amusement. 'Well-known, was he?'

'Yeah, and not for the right reasons,' said Flo. 'Come from round our way, 'e did – younger'n us – 'e worked for some of the biggest names … well, you know.' She nodded portentously.

'Criminals?' said Libby. 'Well-known criminals?'

'The best,' said Lenny.

'Worst,' said Flo.

'Not – *them*?' whispered Libby, her eyes round with wonder.

'Never 'eard of the Cat Club shootin'?' asked Flo.

'Vaguely,' said Ben.

'They reckoned that was Wally,' said Lenny.

'And Stan looks like him?' asked Libby.

'Just like,' said Flo. 'Even down to the specs. Little bloke, very neat. Never think of 'im as – well, you know.'

'If it's true,' said Ben, 'why hasn't Stan changed his name?'

Flo shrugged. 'Not many remember.'

'You thought we should have,' said Libby.

'Yeah, well.' Flo looked uncomfortable.

'So, did he get caught?' asked Ben.

'Reckon 'e did. Never 'eard of 'im after – when was it, Len?'

'Early seventies? Don't think they 'anged 'im, though. Too

late for that.'

'Golly!' said Libby, looking at Ben. 'Wouldn't you just love to ask him!'

'No, Libby,' said Ben. 'I wouldn't. And neither must you.'

Flo began to struggle to her feet. 'Got to 'ave me nap before we goes up to Het's. Come on, Len.'

'Oh, you're coming, are you?' said Libby.

'Wants to 'ave a gander at them young boys!' said Lenny with a wink. Flo hit him on the arm.

As they left, Libby looked after them and nonchalantly waved.

'Stan's still there with Damian,' she said as she turned back to Ben.

'Well, they are both staying here,' said Ben. 'Perhaps we'd better go, too. I don't want to talk to him, particularly now we know about his possible grandad.'

'Are you afraid I'll let the cat out of the bag?' said Libby.

Ben laughed. 'Of course I am.'

At six o'clock on the dot, Ben and Libby joined Peter and Harry at the door of the Manor. Harry peered up at the first floor windows.

'Will we see any of them?'

'They won't come into the kitchen,' said Ben. 'We might hear them.'

'Are you feeding them during the week?' asked Libby.

'Max has arranged a group discount for them, but they don't have to eat with me. They can eat at the pub if they like.'

'They don't have much of a choice, do they?' said Peter.

'What will they do the week of the show?' asked Libby. 'They won't want to eat before.'

'No idea.' Harry shrugged. 'Not your problem, petal.'

Ben pushed open the heavy door and they followed him down the passage and into the kitchen where Flo and Lenny already sat at the table with glasses of red wine in front of them. To their surprise, so did two of the dancers.

'Met Will and Jonathan, didn't you?' grunted Hetty, turning from where she was taking the huge rib of beef out of the Aga.

'Er, yes,' said Ben. 'Hello.'

The tall, dark dancer stood up and grinned deprecatingly.

'Sorry,' he said in a distinctly northern accent. 'Will and I both wanted milk for tea, so we ventured down and – er – got invited.'

'I invited 'em,' said Flo with an evil grin.

Will, smaller and sandy-haired, also stood. 'We didn't mean to intrude,' he began.

'Don't be silly,' said Libby. 'Do sit down and finish your wine. This is Peter and this – Harry. He's the owner of the restaurant where you can eat during the week if you like.'

Jonathan held out a hand to both Peter and Harry, and Will followed suit.

'Vegetarian, isn't it?' said Jonathan. He grinned. 'That'll suit Will.

'It started that way,' said Harry, 'but I do a few meat dishes now. Oh – in a separate kitchen, of course.' He went round the table to kiss first Hetty's cheek, then Flo's.

'I thought we'd supplied tea and coffee in the rooms?' said Ben, filling extra glasses from the open bottle of Cabernet.

'We both wondered if there was any chance of fresh milk,' said Will. 'A bit cheeky, sorry.'

'Can't leave fresh milk out,' said Hetty. 'You can come down here and fetch it. I'll order extra.'

'So you came down for milk and got wine,' said Libby, lifting her glass. 'Cheers.'

'I brought it,' said Flo. 'You be quiet.'

Everyone laughed, while the two dancers looked bewildered.

'Don't worry about it,' said Ben. 'All just one big happy family.'

'Tell me, who do you play?' asked Peter. 'I'm not terribly familiar with the story.'

'I'm Demdike,' said Jonathan. 'Promoted from Abraham Law.'

'And I've taken over Abraham,' said Will.

'Funny names,' said Flo. 'Why was you promoted? First one no good?'

'He left,' said Jonathan, looking uncomfortable.

'Ah.' Flo nodded wisely. 'Temp'rament, was it?'

'Er – not exactly,' said Will.

'I think it's a company thing, Flo,' Libby interposed hastily. 'I'm really looking forward to seeing a rehearsal tomorrow.'

'It's a lovely theatre,' said Will. 'We went over there earlier. You're very lucky.'

'My Ben,' said Hetty suddenly. ''Is idea.'

Libby was surprised to see Ben go bright red.

'Well, it was sitting there doing nothing,' he said in a strangled voice.

'And he's an architect, so he drew up the plans,' said Harry.

'And he used to be in the business when he was young,' said Peter.

'And Libby's ex-pro,' concluded Ben.

'So there you are,' said Peter. 'Our own theatre.' He noticed the dancers' raised eyebrows. 'Oh, yes, and I'm family, too, so Ben, Libby and I run it between us.'

'Fancy having your own theatre.' Will was gazing at Peter as if spellbound and Harry began to fidget.

'What time are you meeting Max at the pub?' asked Libby.

'Oh, not until seven,' said Will.

'But I think we ought to leave these people to their dinner,' said Jonathan, standing up again. He bowed to Flo. 'Thank you for the wine.'

'Oh, OK,' said Will reluctantly. 'Thank you for the wine. Oh – and the milk!' He raised a small china jug.

'So what was that about promotion?' asked Flo, when the dancers had left. 'You didn't want me to ask.'

'The first dancer left because of an incident,' said Ben repressively.

'Bad boy, was 'e?'

'No, Flo. Something was done to him, he didn't do anything.' Ben went to help his mother lift a dish of roast potatoes to the table.

'Well, if yer don't want to tell me …' Flo shrugged.

'Not ours to tell, Flo,' said Libby.

'That Jonathan's a nice boy,' said Hetty, surprisingly. 'Good manners.'

'He's at least as old as I am,' said Harry, a trifle pettishly.

'And Will obviously took a fancy to Pete,' said Libby wickedly.

'Did he?' Peter sounded surprised.

'Yes, he did,' said Harry, 'so you keep your hands off.'

Peter smiled and patted his arm. 'It's usually you they fancy, isn't it, dear heart? Jealous?'

Harry sniffed and got up to help Hetty.

'Now, now,' said Libby. 'Little birds in their nests agree.'

'All the same,' said Ben later, as they all strolled back down the Manor drive, 'they could be a disturbing bunch to have around for a fortnight.'

'We'll keep out of their way,' said Peter, draping an arm across Harry's shoulder.

'Except when they come to the caff,' said Harry.

'I shall come in every night to protect you,' said Peter.

'And I suppose I'm going to have to mingle with them, aren't I?' said Libby.

'Eh?' Harry stopped and looked at her. 'Why?'

'We've almost forgotten, haven't we? That's why they're here. Max wants me to see if I can find out what's behind all these strange goings on.'

'Well,' said Ben as they resumed walking, 'you already got those two this afternoon talking. I don't see why you shouldn't do the same with the others.'

'Yes, but what excuse do I have? I can't just sit through rehearsals every day.'

'Do they have a lunch break?' asked Harry.

'I suppose so,' said Libby. 'Why?'

'How about if I supply a bit of a buffet lunch and take it up and serve it in the Manor. That would give you the excuse to come in and mingle, wouldn't it? Are they using that big sitting-room again?'

'That's a genius idea, Hal. But how will you find time?'

'I prep up for lunch every day except Monday, don't I? Won't be a problem. I'll tell Max, don't worry. I won't charge him much.' Harry grinned.

'You could tell him now,' said Ben. 'They'll all still be in the pub, won't they?'

'Oh, no, I couldn't face them all now,' said Harry with a shudder. 'I'll send him a text.'

Libby and Ben continued towards Allhallow's Lane.

'So who have we met so far?' said Libby.

'How do you mean?'

'Well, characters in the play – I mean dance. Jonathan who is the new Demdike.'

'Will Davies who's Abraham Something.'

'Law,' said Libby. 'I wonder who he was before?'

'Before?'

'He was promoted, too, wasn't he?'

'I doubt if that was a motive for frightening off the original Demdike,' said Ben.

'And we've got to remember it's started again with Chattox now.' Libby frowned. 'Anyway, to go on with the cast, we've met Demdike and Abraham, who else?'

'The people you spoke to earlier.'

'Oh, yes – Roger Nowell, the magistrate and Alizon, Demdike's granddaughter. So we haven't yet met Chattox, who is a very determined character, according to Max.'

'Then there's Stan Willis and Damian the composer.'

'And we haven't met Stan's assistant,' said Libby. 'I thought he would have come down today.'

'Never mind, I'm sure we will.' Ben took out his key to let them into number seventeen. 'Now, make me a cup of tea, woman!'


Monday morning Max had called his company for ten o'clock. Ben and Libby opened the theatre at nine thirty and waited to see who would arrive.

Stan Willis came fussing in five minutes later, followed by a shortish, squarish man with red hair and an equally red face.

'This is Seb,' said Stan. 'Seb, this is Ben, our stage manager, and Libby, our … um…'

'Hostess?' suggested Libby sweetly.

'Hostess. Yes.'

Seb and Libby shook hands.

'Now, I really must go up and check the robotics.' Stan sped away into the wings and Seb turned to Ben.

'Has he been driving you mad?' he asked.

'Er – no, not really,' said Ben, surprised. 'We haven't done much really. I just set everything up as he'd requested, and now I'm leaving it all to him, I think.'

'And me,' said Seb, gloomily.

'Ah!' said Libby. 'You're his – what? ASM?'

'Dogsbody,' corrected Seb. 'That's me.' He grinned. 'At home and away.'

'Oh, dear,' said Libby. 'Well, there doesn't seem to be much to do, stage-wise.'

'There's the Kabuki,' said Seb. He turned to Ben. 'Have we –?'

'Not yet. We're trying it this morning before rehearsal.'

People began drifting in. Those Libby had met raised their hands to her, but they were all obviously preoccupied with the coming rehearsal. Hetty had reported that most of them had eaten very light breakfasts, and Libby only hoped they had the stamina to get through to lunchtime. Backpacks and sports bags were dumped in the aisles and on seats, and contorted positions taken up on the stage. At ten o'clock, Max appeared from the wings and clapped his hands.

'Clear, please, everybody. We're going to test the robotics and the Kabuki.'

'Here you are, dear heart.' Peter's voice sounded in Libby's ear. 'Now you can see and wonder.'

'So can I.' Harry's voice was in her other ear. 'Exciting, isn't it.'

'I'm off to the box to dazzle you,' said Peter and slipped out of the auditorium doors. Libby and Harry settled in the back row as the house lights went down.

'Now! Sound, please,' called Max, and there was an immediate blackout as music erupted into the auditorium. Suddenly, along the top of the proscenium arch flashed blue lights and the backdrop Libby hadn't realised was there disappeared in front of her eyes, revealing the lowering form of Pendle Hill.

There was a gasp from those watching, then applause as the

music stopped and the house lights went up.

Max, beaming, came to the front of the stage.

'Did any of you realise you were looking at a cloth?' he asked.

Discussion broke out among the dancers, and Libby looked at Harry. 'Impressive.'

'It was. One minute it was there – the next it wasn't. How'd they do it?'

'Classic misdirection, I should think,' said Libby.

Harry looked at her. 'Really? Like the three card trick?'

'Sort of.' Libby poked him in the ribs. 'Don't put me on the spot. Go and make those boys their lunch.'

# Chapter Five

Harry's buffet lunch, supplemented with energy drinks supplied by Libby, who had raided the eight-till-late, went down very well. So did Harry.

Peter, watching with amusement as several dancers crowded round his beloved, murmured, 'He should be able to get anything out of them, shouldn't he?'

Libby laughed. 'As long as they don't get *him* out of anything!'

She moved across, ostensibly to check that everything was all right, in reality to rescue Harry.

'Libby, this is heaven.' Phillip Newcombe was at her elbow.

'Really? Which particular bit?'

'All of it.' Phillip waved an expansive arm. 'The theatre, the rooms here, the food … Couldn't ask for more, could we?'

'Well, let's hope the run of bad luck didn't follow you down here,' said Libby.

'Run of …?' Phillip's dark brows drew together. 'Oh, you mean all those nasty little tricks.' He shrugged. 'I bet it was someone who didn't get into the company and was jealous. Don't you? And they'd still be in London, wouldn't they.'

'I suppose that's possible,' said Libby, wondering if it was. 'Wasn't the Kabuki curtain stunt good?'

'Oh, is that what it was? Fabulous. Can't wait to see it in the actual piece, although I won't, I suppose. Only from the back.'

'Someone will film it, though, surely?' said Libby.

'Oh, I expect so, even if it's only for Max to make us sit through it and point out where we went wrong.'

He is waspish, thought Libby, and went to ask Max if Phillip's theory was possible.

Max was thoughtful. 'He could be right. We did hold auditions when we realised we didn't have quite enough people in the company to put this on, and there were several who were disappointed. But not to the extent of sabotaging the production.'

'No, I thought it was a bit unlikely. And whoever it was had to know all about the rehearsal arrangements and the lockers. An auditionee wouldn't know.'

'Unless they were close to a company member,' said Max. 'Have you talked to any of the others yet?'

Libby was taken aback. 'Give me a chance! I've got to get to know them a bit better first. Tell me, who's your Chattox? I've met Demdike.'

'Tom Matthews. He's over there.' Max nodded towards a group of dancers clustered round the table where Libby and Hetty had set up the coffee pots.

'Which one? I've met Dan – is it? The Roger Nowell.'

'Talking to Dan now,' said Max. 'That's Tom.'

Libby eyed the tall, well-muscled young man appreciatively. 'Very nice.'

Max smiled at her. 'He is, isn't he? And tough as old boots.'

'Yes, you said he wasn't fazed by the cockerel.'

'I think maybe you should go and check the coffee pots,' said Max with a wink. 'They may need refilling.'

Libby grinned at him and wandered over to the table.

'Hello – Libby, isn't it?' said Dan Washburn.

'That's me,' said Libby. 'Just checking the coffee pots.'

'I think there's still plenty,' said Tom Matthews, and stuck out a hand. 'I'm Tom, by the way.'

'Ah, yes – the Chattox.' Libby shook his hand. 'And are you all OK – your rooms are all right?'

'It's great,' said Dan. 'Such a lovely set-up. And this food is wonderful.'

'Mexican street food, apparently,' said Libby. 'Harry over there has a Mexican restaurant in the village.'

'So we've been told,' said Tom. 'With a special discount for us if we eat there.'

'Indeed.' Libby smiled brightly. 'We're all family, you see.'

'You are?' Tom looked at Harry and back at Libby.

'Well, extended family. My partner Ben owns the Manor and

the theatre, which he designed, being an architect, with his mum, Hetty, who's over there talking to Peter, who is doing your FX. Peter is her nephew and Ben's cousin, and is married to Harry.'

The group of men laughed.

'I might need that disentangling,' said the third in the group, a slim boy who looked as if he might be perfect casting for Puck.

'Oh, this is Alan who plays Demdike's daughter Elizabeth,' said Dan.

'Is that Alizon's mother?' asked Libby, shaking hands again.

Alan pulled a face. 'Yes. And he's older than I am.'

The other two laughed.

'Well, if you don't need more coffee, I'll start collecting plates,' said Libby. 'Can you all dance after all that food?'

'It was fairly light,' said Tom. 'Your Harry knows what he's doing. I think a lot of us are sorry he's spoken for, though.'

Libby grinned. 'Thought you might be!'

The dancers began to drift back towards the theatre. Most of them called out 'Thank you' to Hetty, Harry and Libby.

'He's not going to do that every day, is he?' asked Max, following Libby into the kitchen.

'Isn't he? He said he was going to talk to you about it.' Libby put the stack of plates by the sink.

'He did.' Max was frowning. 'He suggested bringing a lunch up every day, but I thought he meant just some sandwiches or small snacks.'

'Did he give you a price?' asked Libby.

'Oh, yes. It's not expensive.'

'Well, this is what you get, obviously. He's doing these things in the regular menu, now, so I don't suppose it's that much effort. Probably won't want to do it at the weekend, though.'

'Oh, they're getting part of next weekend off. We'll see how it goes, but a full day's rehearsal on Monday and Tuesday. Have you seen the publicity?'

Libby grinned. 'Couldn't miss it! All over the local media – and national, too, I understand?'

'Oh, yes.' Max's colour was rising. 'People have been very kind.'

'People like Sir Andrew?' asked Libby slyly.

'Yes.' Max was now obviously uncomfortable.

'You don't like charity, do you?'

'No, and I know people do these things because they are genuinely nice, but …'

'I know.' Libby patted his arm. 'Now, go and bully your poor boys and leave Hetty and me to finish clearing up.'

'What's up with him?' grunted Hetty, as she began to load plates into the dishwasher.

'He thinks people are being too kind to him,' said Libby.

'Silly bugger.'

Libby looked down at Hetty's grey head with affectionate amusement. 'Exactly.'

When the sitting-room and kitchen had been restored to order, Libby looked into the theatre and wasted a few minutes admiring the perfect male physiques displaying themselves on the stage, before leaving and going to find Harry.

The Pink Geranium's door was locked, but Harry heard her knock and came to let her in.

'How did it go?' he asked, leading the way back to the kitchen.

'Wonderful. They all told you so, didn't they?'

'Well, yes. What did Max think?'

'That you'd spoilt them. He was expecting something far more ordinary – and not as much.'

'Oh!' Harry took his hands out of the sink and looked at her. 'Is that what he wants?'

'I think he's just uncomfortable with people being nice to him. As far as I can see, Andrew's paid for advertising and media coverage and he doesn't like that, either.'

Harry frowned. 'What's wrong with him?'

'I expect he feels he doesn't deserve it.'

'Proud,' said Harry, returning to the sink. 'He didn't query the price of the lunches, you know. Just said was I sure that was enough.'

'Do we know how he started the company? Or why? Has

36

Andrew said anything to you?'

Sir Andrew and Harry had a special relationship, of which Peter was occasionally jealous.

'Not a word. Why?'

'I just wondered. Presumably he was a dancer himself. Or maybe still is.' Libby absently picked up a tea towel.

'Don't do that!' snapped Harry.

'Do what?'

'Dry these dishes. They have to air dry.'

'Why didn't you do them in the dishwasher then?'

Harry sighed. 'Have a look at them, dearie.'

'Oh,' said Libby. 'They're a bit old, aren't they?'

'Just a bit, petal. My mum Millie's best china.'

Millicent was Hetty's younger sister and Peter's mother, now residing in a very expensive home for the bewildered.

'Oh, OK. Why did you use them for the dancers?'

'Because I didn't want to use the caff's stuff. Looks a bit you know – what's the word?'

'Utilitarian?'

'If you so say so. Now. Glass of wine before you go? Or are you going to be good?'

'I'm going to be good *and* have a glass of wine,' said Libby.

Harry brought a bottle of red into the sofa corner and sat down with a sigh.

'Did you get anything out of them at lunchtime?' he asked.

'No, did you?'

'Too early,' said Harry. 'They were all a bit flirty, you know?'

'Peter and I saw,' said Libby, accepting a glass.

'Oh, bugger. Was he jealous?'

'No, he seemed fine. Did any of them chat?'

'Oh, yes. All very complimentary about the digs and the theatre. And the food of course. I picked up a little bit of gossip among themselves, though.'

'Oh?'

'Who's Stan? He's the stage manager, isn't he?'

'Stage and company manager, I think.'

'I thought Max was the company manager?'

Libby shook her head. 'No, he's the director. And choreographer. The company manager does all the mundane stuff.'

'That explains it,' said Harry. 'They were grousing about him trying to make trouble regarding the Manor.'

'He what?' gasped Libby.

'He was complaining, apparently. Saying it should have been left to him.'

'Well, theoretically, it should,' said Libby, 'but Max arranged this as a package through Andrew. Doesn't he realise that?'

'Don't ask me, petal. I'm just reporting what they were saying. I don't think they like him much.'

'No,' said Libby thoughtfully. 'You don't think he would sabotage the production, do you?'

'Me? I don't know the bloke, do I? And why the hell should he? It pays his wages, doesn't it?'

'I suppose so. I don't know much about the set-up, really.' Libby gazed into her wine glass. 'I think I'd better try and find out a bit more. I expect there's a website.'

'Do you think it might be to do with the company rather than the dancers?' asked Harry.

'It could be, couldn't it? One of the boys suggested someone who had been turned down at audition.'

'And so upset he left a dead cockerel in a locker? Nah. Besides, it has to be someone who knows the rehearsal rooms and the whole set-up, doesn't it?'

'That's what I said to Max. He did say it could be someone who was close to one of the company, though.'

'And did he make any suggestions?'

'No, I think it was just a random thought.' Libby drained her glass. 'Oh, well. I'll go home and do some research, then I'll pop up and mingle a bit more when they've finished for the day.'

'What about Fran? When's she coming up?'

'I don't know. I expect she'll ring.'

But she didn't. She arrived.

# Chapter Six

'I didn't know what you were planning to do, so I thought I ought to come and find out.' Fran followed Libby into the kitchen.

'I don't think I'm planning anything,' said Libby. 'I went up at lunchtime, but I didn't manage to get any confidences. Sit down and I'll tell you what's been happening over the last couple of days.'

By the time Libby had finished and they had both drunk two large mugs of tea, Fran was looking thoughtful.

'So nobody seemed unduly worried?'

'No, I suppose they didn't. Do you think Max was over-reacting?'

'We don't know about the two people who left. Has anything been said about them?'

'No!' Libby was surprised. 'No. Even when Jonathan – the new Demdike – told me he'd been promoted, he said nothing about the previous one. That's odd, isn't it?'

'If you introduce me to the people you've actually met, I can do a bit of gentle questioning, can't I? Are you going up this afternoon?'

'I thought I would. I'll see if they want tea in the sitting-room. Although I don't know how long Max intends to work them for.'

Fran looked at her watch. 'Let's wander up about four. We can always watch rehearsal, can't we?'

It appeared that Max was sticking to a strict ten-to-five routine.

'Can't tire them out too much,' he told Fran with a grin. 'They get stroppy.'

Fran raised her eyebrows. 'What happened to show-fitness?'

'Oh, they're all as tough as old shoe leather, really. But they like to moan.'

'Do they want tea in the sitting-room?' asked Libby. 'We didn't know. They've all got kettles in their rooms.'

'Don't worry about that,' said Max. 'They might congregate in the sitting-room for a chat, but they'll all wander off to their rooms eventually before going down to the pub for dinner. I think Harry might find himself inundated tomorrow night.'

Libby and Fran repaired to the Manor, where Hetty presented them with two huge Victoria sponges.

'Thought they might like a bit o' cake,' she said gruffly and disappeared into the kitchen.

Libby looked at Fran and giggled. 'I hope none of them are watching their weight.'

As they crossed the hall towards the sitting-room, the first dancers came in.

'Ooh!'

'Look at that!'

'Is it for us?'

'Can we have some?'

Followed by a sweaty clutch of male bodies in an assortment of T-shirts, shorts, jogging bottoms and leggings, Libby and Fran bore their cakes aloft into the sitting-room, where Hetty had provided knives and paper plates.

'So you're Demdike?' said Fran, serving Jonathan a large slice. 'Why did the previous one leave? I would have thought this was a great – do you say part in dance theatre?'

'Yes, well.' Jonathan took his paper plate. 'There was an incident.'

'Oh, like Chattox's cockerel?'

'Oh, you know about that?'

'Max warned Libby and Ben. Just in case anything else happened.'

'I'm sure it won't.' Jonathan sounded confident. 'Now we've left London.'

'Why? What difference does that make?' asked Fran.

'Well –' Jonathan looked confused for a moment. 'I suppose I assumed that whoever was behind all this stuff was in London. He won't have followed us here.'

'You said "he",' said Fran. 'Do you know who it was?'

'No, of course not. I'd have said if I did. It's just – we're all men. It won't have been a woman.'

'Could have been.'

Fran turned to see a large, blond man holding out a plate.

'Hi, I'm Dan. Could I have another piece?'

Fran laughed. 'OK. But what did you mean "it could have been"? A woman?'

'Well, yes. A couple of people have been a bit – well – a bit … *surprised* that we're danseurs playing women.'

'Really?' Fran handed over the cake. 'Not unusual, is it? Apart from recent pieces, what about *La Fille mal gardée*? The famous clog dance.'

Jonathan and Dan both sighed and rolled their eyes.

'Why does everyone know that?' Jonathan shook his head. 'And I bet most people couldn't tell you what the hell the ballet is about.'

'It's a bit of a hotch-potch, isn't it?' said Fran. 'The general public only know the Frederick Ashton version, I would think.'

Dan and Jonathan looked at her with respect.

'Sorry,' said Jonathan. 'I sounded rude.'

'Don't worry about it,' said Fran. 'I suppose the people who object are those who only view witches as women with hooked noses and tall hats.'

Dan snorted. 'Fairy tale witches.'

'Arthur Rackham witches,' said Jonathan surprisingly.

'Well, yes, though his were scary,' said Fran. 'But it was the Victorian view, wasn't it? All witches were female, when, in fact, they weren't.'

'The Pendle witches were female, though,' said Dan.

'So you're saying that a woman could have been scandalised enough to play nasty tricks on the company just because the piece is danced by men?' Fran looked doubtful.

'It does sound a bit naff, doesn't it?' Dan sighed. 'Oh, well, just a thought. My wife actually thought of it. She says women have much nastier minds than men!'

'Not all men,' said Jonathan. He looked round the room, his eyes resting suggestively on Stan Willis and Seb, who, as usual, was looking gloomy.

'Who are they?' asked Fran.

'That's Stan Willis, the stage manager,' said Jonathan.

'And company manager,' added Dan.

'And that's Seb with him. He's Stan's partner.'

'And ASM,' added Dan.

'Which is which?'

'Stan's the one with the glasses, and Seb's the miserable looking one with red hair.'

'Doesn't he like being the ASM?' asked Fran.

'I don't think he much likes being Stan's partner,' said Jonathan with a giggle.

'So which of them has the nasty mind?' asked Fran. 'You implied that one of them had.'

'Oh, Stan, of course.'

'Shhh, Jon!' Dan nudged Jonathan sharply. 'Don't stir anything else up.'

Fran raised her eyebrows, but nothing more was forthcoming. She went across to join Libby, who introduced her to Phillip Newcombe and Will Davies.

'I must say I'm finding all these names very confusing,' said Fran, 'especially when everyone has a character name, too!'

'Oh, don't worry about it,' said Phillip. 'We're all interchangeable. Just a load of poofy dancers to the general public.'

Fran looked shocked.

'Don't take any notice, Fran,' said Libby. 'I've only known Phillip a couple of days and I've already decided he's the wasp of the company.'

Phillip beamed delightedly. 'Darting around hither and yon seeing whom I can sting.'

'I see you were making friends with Jonathan and Dan,' said Libby.

Fran nodded. 'Jonathan said he thought whoever had been playing tricks on the company would still be in London.'

'Unless it's one of us,' said Will.

'Why would one of you do something like that?'

'Perhaps it's Jon himself. To get to dance Demdike.' Phillip eyed the two women with glee.

'I shall consider you seriously,' said Libby.

'You will?' Phillip looked taken aback.

Libby grinned. 'Not really. But it must have been rather upsetting for you all. What actually happened?'

Phillip looked at her sideways. 'Why do you want to know?'

'She's nosy,' said Fran. 'Always has been.'

'Our beloved leader will tell you. You're friendly with him, aren't you?' Phillip picked up his bag from the floor. 'I'm off to have a shower.'

Will watched him weave his way through the other dancers and pause to have a word with Stan Willis.

'I don't know why he was like that,' he said. 'He's one of the biggest gossips in the company.'

'Doesn't matter,' said Libby. 'I don't suppose many of you want to talk about it.'

'Why wouldn't we?' Will looked surprised. 'We all talked about it all the time. Especially when Paddy and Gerry left.'

'Was one of them the original Demdike?' asked Fran.

'Yes – Paddy. He was very good. I've worked with him before. Well,' he gave a shrug, 'I've worked with most of them before, either in Max's company or in the West End.'

'Which do you prefer?' asked Libby. 'This is more straight ballet, isn't it?'

'Nearer to it, anyway,' said Will. 'And of course I prefer this sort of thing, but it doesn't pay as well. I expect I'll be doing panto by Christmas.'

'Why?' said Fran. 'It's nearly the end of October. You'd know by now, wouldn't you?'

Will shrugged again. 'Normally, yes. But this production was supposed to run right up to and past Christmas, and none of us thought we'd need panto.'

'Then what's changed?' asked Libby.

'The atmosphere. It's just too tense. It's a good show, but it's looking – I don't know – fated.'

'Had you got a theatre?' said Fran.

'Off Broadway.' Will grinned. 'If you know what I mean. But yes, we have. If we go in.'

43

'But what on earth could be nasty enough to stop the show?' asked Libby. 'I got the impression from Max that the cockerel was the worst event.'

'Physically, yes.' Will perched on the arm of a chair and rubbed a hand over his face. 'It was the letters.'

'Letters?' said the women together.

'We all got at least one.'

'*All*?' gasped Libby.

'Most of them were just nasty little digs about being gay, which is a laugh because half the company aren't gay. Then a couple of people got second letters accusing them of all sorts of things, and finally Paddy and Gerry both got really threatening letters.'

'Threatening to do what?' asked Fran.

'Burn them.'

'*Burn* them?' said Fran.

Libby burst out laughing. 'That's absurd. You can't burn people these days.'

'It quoted quite graphic examples,' said Will. 'True ones.'

'And they would be burnt why?'

'It was more or less along the lines of "if you carry on pretending to be witches you'll be treated like them." Only worse, if you know what I mean.'

'So the complaint seems to be against – what? The portrayal of the witches by men, or the portrayal of them at all?' said Libby.

'There was a lot of balls about it being against nature.' Will shook his head. 'I didn't see Paddy's and Gerry's, but that's what it said in some of the earlier ones.'

'Seems rather odd,' said Fran, staring fixedly at nothing in particular.

'That's an understatement,' said Libby.

'No, odd in that none of it seems coherent. It looks as though someone is trying to stop the production and doesn't really care how.'

Libby and Will looked at her in surprise.

'Actually stop the production?' echoed Will.

'Well, what other reason is there?' Fran was reasonable.

'Nothing seems directed at one individual, does it? And what's against nature? Dancing? Theatre? Men dressed as women?'

'Don't forget there was some animosity against gays,' said Libby. 'Even if it was misdirected.'

'Well,' said Will, standing up, 'I'm just glad we're out of London and we can all forget about it.'

'I'm not so sure of that,' murmured Fran, as Will wandered out to the hallway.

'What?' said Libby.

'That it's all over. After all, Max asked us to look into it. Why?'

'What do you mean, why? To find out what was going on, of course.'

'Because he thought there was a threat to the production, obviously.'

'Oh! Yes, I suppose so.'

'And he brought them all down here.' Fran was looking thoughtful. 'Why?'

'To talk to us,' said Libby, beginning to feel worried.

'That's a hell of an expense just to get two nosy women to talk to his troupe, isn't it?'

'You think there was more to it?'

Fran looked at her friend. 'Don't you?'

Next morning, they found a rat, suspended by its neck, hanging in the middle of the stage.

# Chapter Seven

Sebastian, who had opened up the theatre in advance of the company, called Max and then Stan. Max called Ben, who called Hetty and Peter.

'They're not to go into the theatre,' Ben told Libby, as he drank a hasty cup of tea before going to join a council of war. 'Sebastian's been told to go over to the Manor and hold them all there.'

'I'll go up and help,' said Libby. 'Seb will be needed at your council of war, and Hetty won't cope on her own.'

'All right.' Ben gave her a quick kiss and left. Libby sighed, put the mugs in the sink and went to get dressed.

As soon as she set foot inside the sitting-room at the Manor, she was surrounded by anxious dancers.

'What is it?'

'What's going on?'

'Seb wouldn't tell us a thing!'

'It's another incident, isn't it?' Alan Neville's voice came from the back of the room. The others fell silent.

'I believe it is,' said Libby. 'I'm sure you'll be told all about it in due course, but in the meantime, does anyone want any more coffee or tea?'

She escaped into the kitchen and explained to Hetty what was going on. Hetty shook her head.

'Brought trouble, that's what,' she muttered, manoeuvring the huge kettle onto the Aga hotplate.

Libby eyed her nervously. Hetty's relationship with the theatre had been ambivalent in the past.

'I'll go and collect cups,' she said.

As she crossed the hall, Ben appeared in the doorway.

'They can come across now,' he said. 'Sebastian got the thing down, but Max is furious. Will you bring them across? I've got to go and wash.' He disappeared to his estate office where there was a convenient shower room.

Libby went back to the kitchen.

'Cancel the tea and coffee, Hetty. I've got to shepherd them all across to the theatre. I'll come back and help clear up in a bit.'

'You carry on, gal,' said Hetty. 'I'm all right on me own.'

Libby went back to the sitting-room, where disconsolate dancers were sitting or lounging with boneless grace.

'OK, you can come over, now,' she said, and stood aside as they all made for the door.

In the auditorium, Max asked them all to sit down. He stood on the stage, while Stan fidgeted at the side, and Sebastian sat alone on the edge looking miserable.

'As I'm sure you've all guessed we've had another incident,' Max began. 'It has been dealt with and has caused no harm to anyone, but it was unpleasant.'

'What was it?' called someone.

'A rat,' said Stan. 'A hanged rat.'

Various expressions of disgust quivered round the auditorium.

'Someone must have got into the theatre during the night,' said Max. 'Apart from Ben, Peter and Libby, the only people who have keys are Stan, and Sebastian and me. None of us was responsible, so I'm asking now if anyone here knows anything about it.'

'None of them will admit it if they are,' Peter murmured in Libby's ear. 'Can't make it out myself.'

As expected, no one in the auditorium had anything to say.

'Very well,' said Max, 'then we will carry on with rehearsals. Warm up on-stage in five minutes please.'

He strode off into the wings, followed by Stan. Sebastian stayed on the edge of the stage. Libby went and sat beside him.

'You found it, didn't you?'

Sebastian nodded. 'Horrible, it was. I felt so sorry for it.'

'I wonder how they caught it?'

'I expect they found it.' Sebastian shuddered. 'Whoever "they" are. I just can't understand why.'

'No, neither can I. Did you think it would stop when you came down here?'

'I suppose I did. Stan said the show was doomed, but he's never exactly a ray of sunshine.'

Libby regarded him with interest. 'Do you actually *like* Stan?'

Sebastian grinned. 'No, actually I don't. And before you ask why the hell I'm shacked up with him, I'll tell you. I owe him. He got me out of a bit of trouble a year or so back, and he's kept me around like a pet bloody monkey ever since.'

Libby diplomatically didn't ask about the trouble. 'Were you already in the theatre?'

'Stage Management degree. But I buggered up. Stan – ah – rescued me. And here I am.'

'Well, it's quite a good start,' said Libby cautiously.

'Suppose so. But I want to do proper theatre.' He turned to her hastily. 'Not that this isn't a proper theatre …'

Libby laughed. 'I know what you mean. Drama?'

'Yes.' A dreamy look came over Sebastian's face. 'I'd love to work at The Globe.'

'Wouldn't we all,' said Libby. 'Come on. We'd better get off the stage or we'll get trampled.'

She wandered to the back of the auditorium, where Ben was now standing with his arms folded and a scowl on his face.

'What's up?'

'They've messed up the bloody lanterns.'

'Oh. Did they hang the rat from one of the barrels?' The barrels were the bars on to which the stage lights, or lanterns, were attached.

Ben nodded. 'And young Seb had to move everything to get the rope off.'

'Why didn't he just cut it?'

'He did, but we still had to get the rope off. It was wound round one of the lanterns. Now we've got to re-set and probably re-plot.'

'Oh, dear.' Libby left him glowering at the stage and crept up the spiral stairs to the lighting box.

'Is it as bad as Ben's made it sound?' she asked Peter.

'Oh, we can re-set, that's no problem, but obviously we can't do it while they're rehearsing.'

'So that means what? Tonight?'

'Suppose so.' Peter looked across at Damian, who still sat with earphones on gazing at the stage.

'Does he ever take them off?' whispered Libby.

'Not when he's up here.' Peter shook his head sadly. 'Musicians, eh?'

Libby went back to the Manor, collected more dirty cups from the sitting-room and took them into the kitchen.

'I hope we don't get any more so-called incidents,' she said to Hetty, as she piled them next to the dishwasher.

'What d'yer make of it, then?' asked Hetty.

'What do *I* make of it? I've no idea!'

'Bit odd, if you ask me.' Hetty turned and leant back on the sink, folding her arms. 'Don't follow, some'ow.'

'What do you mean?'

'Like that business when we opened the theatre.'

'*The Hop Pickers*?' Libby was bewildered. 'How?'

'Different things, weren't they? The murder weren't nothing to do with it.'

Libby stared and Hetty turned to the Aga with a shrug.

*The Hop Pickers* had been written by Peter based on events in Hetty's family background and was the opening play at the Oast Theatre. A murder had somewhat marred proceedings, and various other incidents had complicated matters. Hetty obviously had the idea that the situation regarding the Tobin Dance Theatre was similar.

Libby called Fran as she walked home down the Manor drive.

'Why would she think that?' she asked. 'I don't get it.'

'Neither do I. There hasn't been a really awful incident, has there?'

'The worst was the cockerel, I should think. Although the rat this morning wasn't pleasant. There hasn't been anything really dangerous, either. Not like *The Hop Pickers*.'

'Perhaps it's simply all the small things adding up, and Hetty thinks it's all going to erupt in something nasty.'

'I suppose so, but there's no indication of that, is there? And I must admit I thought they would have left it all behind in London.'

'Have you talked to Max?'

'No,' said Libby. 'I expect he'll want to have a chat later, though. I don't think I can tell him anything. I'm wondering exactly what he thought we'd be able to do.'

'He thought the company might talk to us, didn't he? Well, some of them have.'

'Not to any purpose.' Libby sighed and kicked a pebble. 'Oh, well. I'll wait and see what happens. Ben's in a mood because the rat-hanger disturbed all the lights and they've all got to be re-set.'

'Oh, dear. So it's actually disturbing the production now, not just the dancers?'

'Oh, yes! I didn't think of that. I suppose they'll be poking round the set every day now, looking for traps.'

Libby made herself a sandwich for lunch, wondering if Ben was going to come home. As he didn't, she took the sandwich into the conservatory and tried to summon up some enthusiasm for the painting which sat, barely started, on an easel. So far, it consisted of a shakily sketched horizon line and an even shakier cliff edge. As usual, it was to be a view of Nethergate to sell in Guy's shop/gallery. Again as usual, she seemed to have no appetite for it. Instead she found herself idly doodling what looked like a stage set, with floating figures skimming over the sea which had turned into a stage.

'Witches!' she muttered to herself, just as the landline began to ring.

'Libby? Sorry to disturb you. Max here.'

'Hello, Max. Everything all right?'

'Well – you were there this morning, weren't you? I thought I saw you.'

'Yes, I came up to help at the Manor, but it all seemed to be dealt with very speedily.'

'Yes, it was.' He paused. 'Look, I wonder if it would be convenient to have a word? We've broken for lunch, and Ben's taken the opportunity to re-set some of the lanterns, so I've got

51

an hour or so.'

Here we go, thought Libby. 'Yes, of course,' she said aloud. 'Would you like to come here? Do you know where I am?'

She gave him directions and went to move the kettle on to the Rayburn. Hoping he wasn't too London-sophisticated to reject her instant coffee, she set out mugs and went to light the fire in the sitting-room. It was nearly the end of October, and feeling distinctly damp and chilly.

'Tea or coffee?' she asked when Max arrived.

'Oh – tea, please.' He smiled a little diffidently. 'I'm not much of a coffee drinker actually. Disgrace to the glitterati, me.'

Libby beamed. 'Excellent. We'll have proper tea made in a proper pot, then.'

'What did you want to talk about?' she asked, as she carried the tray into the sitting-room.

'I wanted to know if any of the boys had talked to you – or to Fran – since we arrived. If you'd managed to form any sort of opinion?' He took a mug from her.

'We've talked to a few of them. None of them seem averse to talking about it, but the rat came as a surprise. I think they'd convinced themselves that all the trouble had been left behind in London. I rather thought that myself.'

Max nodded. 'I was hoping that was the case. But now I'm not so sure.'

Libby leant forward. 'My mother-in-law – Hetty, you know – has a theory that the incidents in London had nothing to do with the one this morning.'

Max looked startled. 'What? How? Why does she think that?'

Libby sat back. 'It's not really logical, simply based on experience.' She explained about *The Hop Pickers*. 'And she could be right. If someone has a grudge, they could simply be copying what happened in London.'

Max shook his head. 'That doesn't make sense. That would mean two people with a grudge against the company, the work, or the individual dancers.'

Libby sighed. 'Yes, that does seem unlikely. Oh, and you

didn't tell us that there had actually been threats to harm anybody.'

Max looked up. 'Who told you that?' he asked sharply.

'Apparently, there were threats of burning.' Libby regarded him with interest. 'Why didn't you tell us? You wanted us to poke around.'

He tried a half-hearted laugh. 'Oh, that was ridiculous.'

'So ridiculous that two of your principals left?'

Max sighed. 'All right, yes. So you've heard about all the little notes, I suppose?'

'Most of them. I don't know exactly to whom they were sent, except to Paddy and – Gerry, was it? – who left, but the consensus now seems to be that it isn't an individual, but the production itself that's being threatened. Fran and I were trying to work out what it is that's "unnatural", as one of the notes apparently said. Witchcraft? Men dancing women? Dance or theatre itself? What?'

Max looked up uneasily. 'Homosexuality?'

Libby shook her head. 'There were accusations of homosexuality, I gather, but rather blanket ones – and not true, for the most part. It's a common and often erroneous assumption about dancers, although why the hell it should matter, I can't think.'

Max smiled. 'You sound as though you're on a podium.'

'It happens to be one of my bugbears, sorry.' Libby smiled back. 'Don't you agree with me?'

'Of course I do. But if someone has some kind of objection to the production on the other grounds – which are archaic – they could just as easily be objecting to homosexuality.'

'That's true.' Libby nodded thoughtfully. 'Stan thinks the whole thing's doomed, apparently.'

'Did Seb tell you that?'

'Yes. I don't think he's that happy with Stan, to tell you the truth. He seems to be under some sort of obligation to him.'

Max sent her a quick look. 'You *have* been finding out a lot.'

'I thought that's what you wanted.'

Max sighed. 'Yes, of course. But have you found out if any

of them are really unhappy?'

'Only Stan, and he hasn't said that to me. All the others seem OK, and they like the theatre. No one seems scared or anything. As I said, I think they all thought the trouble had been left behind in London.'

'And no one said anything about the – the rat?'

'I haven't seen anyone since you asked them all into the theatre and told them about it. I know Ben was cross about having to re-rig and possibly re-plot the lights, but that's about it.'

Max drained his mug. 'That was a lovely cup of tea.' He stood up. 'Well, if you haven't heard anything, I suppose there's nothing we can do.'

'If I had heard something, what would you have done?'

He scowled. 'I don't know.'

'Are you going to carry on with your rehearsal now?' Libby also stood up. 'May I come up and watch?'

'Of course. We're going to see how the transformation scene works.'

'Oh – the Kabuki curtain? That's so impressive.'

'You ought to congratulate Ben about that. It was mostly his idea.'

'Was it?' Libby was surprised. 'He never told me!'

'He and Peter came up with it after Stan told them what effect we wanted for the transformation to Pendle Hill.'

'Is that what it is? From where?'

'From inside Malkin Tower, where Demdike and Alizon live. Alizon goes straight out and meets John Law.'

'That's the pedlar she curses, isn't it?'

'That's right. Been reading up on it?'

Libby laughed and carried the tray into the kitchen. 'Certainly have.'

Together they walked up the Manor drive under the grey October sky.

'You feel the seasons more in the country, don't you?' said Max with a shiver, pulling his long, woollen scarf tighter round his neck.

'I suppose so,' said Libby. 'It's so long since I lived in town that I've forgotten.'

In the auditorium the dancers were draped across the seats like discarded washing. Max clapped his hands and they metamorphosed into lithe young men. Ben was standing with Peter at the back.

'All done?' asked Libby.

'Oh, yes.' Ben pushed a weary hand through his grey curls. 'We had Seb up the ladder in the end, while we re-set from up top.' He indicated the lighting box. 'I'm going to watch for a while, just to make sure it's all OK.'

'Yes, I asked if I could watch, too.' Libby took a seat on the back row, just as Peter went upstairs and lowered the house lights. Ben sat down beside her as the first notes of the music rang out eerily across the auditorium and dim lighting illuminated the inside of Demdike's house.

Then Jonathan as Demdike was pointing Phillip, as Alizon, outside and suddenly there was a blue flash as the Kabuki disappeared, revealing the menacing view of Pendle Hill. And the screaming started.

# Chapter Eight

The dancers froze. Ben jack-knifed out of his seat and he and Max raced each other to the stage. Over it all, the music continued.

Libby stood slowly, her heart pumping madly. She and the dancers seemed to be incapable of movement, until suddenly Phillip sat down on the stage with a thump and put his head in his hands.

Ben appeared from the wings, his phone to his ear. Libby's legs decided to work and she moved down the auditorium. As she reached the stage, Ben ended his call and smiled down at her.

'Nothing too dreadful,' he said. 'Sounded a lot worse than it was.'

'But *what* was it?'

'There was something inside the Kabuki.'

'What do you mean – inside? How could it have been?'

'You know Stan has to pull it into the wings? There's a specific way to do it, and exactly where Stan has to grab it there was an open Stanley knife.'

'Goodness!' Libby's hand flew to her mouth. 'How bad is it?'

'It missed his wrist, which it could have caught, but it's right across his palm. He's laid out in the wings looking very pale at the moment. That young doctor over the road is on his way. We didn't think it was worth calling an ambulance.'

As he was speaking, the doctor himself pushed through the auditorium doors and joined them by the stage. Ben took him into the wings.

'I heard.' Peter was standing behind her. 'Two incidents in one day. Whatever it is, it hasn't been left behind in London.'

Max emerged from the wings frowning.

57

'This is ridiculous.' He pushed a hand through his hair and addressed his company, all of whom were sitting tense and worried. 'All of you go back to the Manor for the time being. I'll come across and tell you what's happening when I've worked out what to do.'

'I'll go and organise coffee,' said Libby. 'Hetty was going to make some earlier, so I expect it will all be prepared.'

'You haven't got decaf, have you?' asked Max with a wry smile. 'I don't want them more het up than they are already.'

'Believe it or not, Hetty got some in specially,' said Libby. 'It was her sop to sophistication!'

The dancers had trailed disconsolately out of the theatre and Libby followed them and went to the Manor kitchen. Hetty was standing, hands on hips, at the kitchen table behind two urns.

'What's happened now?'

Libby told her.

'Saw that young Dr Peasegood rushing up. So I got the coffee back on.' Hetty shook her head. 'Something goin' on over there.' She cocked an eyebrow at Libby.

'Yes, Het, looks like it.' Libby heaved the first urn on to the trolley. 'I'll take this through. They're all in there looking like a wet week of Mondays.'

'Decaf,' she announced, pushing the trolley into the big sitting-room, where the dancers were draped in attitudes of extreme depression all over the furniture. They certainly knew how to express their feelings with their bodies, thought Libby, beginning to fill coffee cups. When she brought in the second urn, the atmosphere had lifted markedly.

'News?' She raised an enquiring eyebrow.

'Yes.' Sebastian appeared from the midst of a group of dancers. 'Max says we're to carry on from where we left off when we're ready.'

'What about Stan?'

'The doctor's taken him off to the surgery, and said he's to rest today. I can do whatever's necessary for rehearsal and your Ben's said he'll help me. We've got to check over the Kabuki at some point, too.'

'Is Stan happy about that?'

Seb's face darkened. 'He's not happy about anything.'

'Same person that fixed up the rat?' asked a quiet voice in Libby's ear. She turned to see Jonathan frowning at Seb.

'I don't know. What do you think?'

'Got to be. Can't have been two people fooling about with the barrels in the watches of the night, can there?'

Libby nodded. It seemed an age since the morning's discovery of the rat.

'It's odd, though. The rat wasn't meant to harm anyone, was it? But the Kabuki definitely was.'

'And it was definitely Stan,' said Jonathan. 'He's the only one who operates it.'

'Could the production go on without him?' asked Libby.

'Oh, yes. He would say no, but as Seb just said, he can do everything needed with perhaps a bit of help.'

'So injuring Stan wouldn't put paid to the whole thing?'

'No – but neither would the rat.'

'Hmm.' Libby was thoughtful. 'But whether or not the Kabuki was aimed at Stan, both events were aimed at undermining the production. Just as the events in London were.'

'You think that's it? Someone really doesn't want us to go on?'

Libby shrugged. 'The events are so random. Although people have been targeted, the minute they go or shrug it off, it starts somewhere else. And I'm sorry, but it has to be someone in the company.'

Jonathan stepped back, looking at her with horror in his face. 'It can't be!'

'Why not?' asked Libby reasonably. 'It's followed you down here. And the only people here are company people. And none of us support staff, as it were, were there in London. So where does that leave you?'

Jonathan nodded gloomily. 'I suppose so. Oh, God. Now I'll be looking over my shoulder all the time.'

Libby made up her mind, mentally crossing her fingers.

'Look. You seem a sensible sort of person. Who else would you say is?'

Jonathan shook his head, looking bewildered. 'God, I don't

know! Tom, I suppose. He can be a bit gung-ho, but he's very down to earth.'

'Right. Then at some point I want to have a chat with the two of you about the rest of the company.'

'Why?' Jonathan was suspicious.

'Because –' Libby hesitated, 'because Max wanted my friend Fran and I to look into all this weirdness.'

'You?'

'Yes. We've done it before, and Max's friend Andrew McColl recommended us.'

Jonathan was staring at her as if she was mad. Libby sighed. 'I know it sounds weird, but ask Max if you don't believe me. And now you'd better go and start being Demdike again.'

The room was emptying slowly and, with a last incredulous look at his hostess, Jonathan followed his fellow company members. Libby put the urns back on the trolley and wheeled them back to the kitchen.

'This is more difficult than I thought, Het,' she said. 'And look at the time! Max wanted them to carry on where they left off, but it's already half past four. They won't get much done now.'

'Leave 'em to it, I would,' grunted Hetty from the sink. 'You go and get me those dirty cups, gal.'

Libby trailed back to the sitting-room with a tray and began to load cups. All she had to do now was persuade Jonathan and Tom Matthews to talk to her about the other dancers, and it sounded as if that might be a hard job. They wouldn't want to rat on each other, she thought, and then berated herself for the inadvertent pun.

After she'd finished loading the cups into Hetty's dishwasher, she sat down at the kitchen table, took out her phone and rang Fran.

When she had finished relating the events of the day, there was a short silence.

'I think you've done the right thing,' said Fran eventually, 'if you can persuade them to talk. When you've done that, tell me when and I'll come, too.'

'What I was thinking, actually,' said Libby, 'was if I *can* persuade them, I could bring them down to Nethergate in the evening. Get them away from the others.'

'Might work,' agreed Fran. 'Have a go and see what happens.'

Libby didn't have to wait long. Just over half an hour later Jonathan put his head round the kitchen door.

'Sorry to disturb you,' he said to Hetty. 'Could I have a word, Libby?'

Libby winked at Hetty and followed him out into the passage, where Tom stood leaning against the wall. He grinned at Libby.

'Jonathan explained,' he said, 'and actually Max had already mentioned something. At your service, Mrs Investigator.'

Libby looked at Jonathan. 'You weren't keen.'

Jonathan looked sheepishly at Tom. 'I didn't want to talk about anyone.'

'I told him it was our duty.' Tom assumed a self-sacrificing attitude, with hand on breast. 'I mean, someone got hurt today. It's not a joke any more.'

'It never was,' said Libby seriously. 'But look. Did Max say anything about my friend Fran?'

'He said you and your friend who's a bit of a specialist.' Tom's face showed intense curiosity. 'That's your friend who was here the other day, isn't it? What's she a specialist in?'

'She helps the police sometimes,' said Libby vaguely, 'but the point is she said how would you two like to come with me down to where she lives in Nethergate? Then you'll be right away from here.'

'Sure. When?' asked Tom.

'Will Max mind?' asked Jonathan.

'No, but I'll ask him. How about this evening?'

Jonathan looked at Tom. 'Will we have time?'

'Do you like Indian food?' asked Libby. 'Only there's a terrifically good restaurant in Nethergate. We could go there for supper.'

'Sounds good. When would we go?' asked Tom.

'I'll call Fran now and go and tell Ben and Max,' said Libby.

'Max won't be with us?' said Jonathan in horror.

'No, but I said I'd tell him, didn't I? You two go into the sitting-room and I'll come and tell you what I've organised.'

Max was all for the expedition, but did show a tendency to try and accompany them. Ben declined, saying Libby and Fran would be better without his interference. Libby grinned.

'All set,' she told Tom and Jonathan five minutes later. 'I'll pick you up in half an hour. OK?'

Appealed to, Fran had agreed to book a table at The Golden Spice and meet them there at a quarter to seven. Guy also declined an invitation.

The journey to Nethergate in the Range Rover was enlivened by anecdotes from the world of dance from Jonathan and Tom, which kept Libby laughing all the way there. There were some scurrilous attacks on well-known figures but she understood that essentially these two were neither malicious nor cruel.

Fran greeted them from a table in the window and they were immediately presented with menus by a bowing waiter. When they had ordered drinks and food, Fran opened the meeting.

'What we want to know,' she began, 'is why any member of your present company might wish to harm either the production or an individual.'

Jonathan and Tom looked at one another.

'We've all been asking ourselves that since London,' said Jonathan.

'Not quite,' said Tom. 'We were thinking of the production, not individuals.'

'So you didn't think it was directed specifically at anyone? Not the two who left, Paddy, was it?' said Libby.

'And Gerry. No,' said Jonathan. 'After all, it was Tom who got the worst of it.'

'The cockerel?' said Fran.

'Yes,' said Tom, 'but at least I wasn't threatened with burning.'

Fran leaned her elbows on the table, clasped her hands and rested her chin on them. 'So you felt there was nothing personal in the attacks.'

'Well, no.' Jonathan looked uncomfortable. 'Not exactly.'

'There were very random accusations,' said Tom cheerfully.

'And I got the impression it was more against the staging of the piece, but not why: because we were taking the piss out of witches, we were men, or we were homosexual.'

'Which a lot of you aren't,' said Libby.

Tom shrugged. 'It's a popular perception.'

'Oh, I know. Just as all actresses were considered to be whores in the good old days.' Libby shook her head. 'And old perceptions can stay alive and dormant for years, more's the pity.'

'But,' said Jonathan reasonably, 'no member of the company could have felt like that.'

'No.' Fran was thoughtful.

'Fran?' Libby peered across the table at her friend.

'I was just thinking ...' Fran fell silent.

Tom and Jonathan looked at Libby, who sighed.

'She's rather good at – um – seeing beyond the obvious.' Libby squirmed a bit. Fran hated her so-called psychic gift, even though it had on occasion saved lives. 'One of the reasons Max ... called us in.'

Jonathan narrowed his eyes. 'You don't mean what I think you mean, do you?'

'I don't know what you think,' said Libby.

Tom was watching Fran. 'Does Max believe it?'

'Sir Andrew does, anyway,' said Libby, wishing Fran would deal with this herself.

Fran looked up. 'I don't know what it is,' she said. 'I do know that most people are sceptical, as I am myself. But it's been useful sometimes.'

Once again, Jonathan and Tom exchanged glances.

'All right,' said Fran. 'Let's get back to the known facts. You can't think of anyone in the present company who would have perpetrated all the practical jokes, or whatever they were, in London?'

Both men shook their heads.

'And were they all directed at particularly sensitive people?'

'No. One was directed at me.' Tom grinned. 'I am known as the most insensitive of the lot.'

'So who is it?' said Jonathan. 'Who would hang rats up and

63

actually hurt poor old Stan?'

'Oh, it's not the same person,' said Fran. 'No, that's somebody quite different.'

# Chapter Nine

Libby, Tom and Jonathan gaped. Fran looked surprised. It was at this spectacularly inappropriate moment the waiters arrived with the food.

'Well, it can't be, can it?' said Fran when they had departed.

Libby found her voice. 'Why can't it?'

Now Fran looked confused. 'Actually, I don't know.'

Libby sighed. 'Here we go. What did you see?'

Jonathan looked alarmed. 'See?'

'I didn't see anything. I was just sure it wasn't the same person. And there was a different motive.'

'How can you possibly be sure of that?' Tom was sceptical but interested.

'I don't know.' Fran shook her head. 'I've told Libby before, things appear in my head as if I've always known them as facts. I have no idea how it happens. But I'm not unique.'

'Most people would be turning that into a money-spinner,' said Jonathan, even more sceptical than Tom.

'Well, she did work for Goodall and Smythe,' said Libby apologetically.

'The estate agents?' Tom's eyebrows rose. 'Selling houses?'

'No, investigating them. They used to send her in to properties to see if anything had happened there that might put prospective purchasers off,' explained Libby. 'Ben used her occasionally, too.'

'*Ben* did?' said Jonathan, as though this was a step too far. 'What for?'

'Building sites,' said Fran succinctly.

The two men looked at each other and shook their heads.

'Anyway,' said Fran, 'what it suggests to me is that someone within the company, or just possibly without, but with a connection to it, wanted the production to fail in London, but

65

here – I don't know, it's more personal.'

'Couldn't it just be that the attempts didn't work in London so they've upped the ante?' suggested Libby.

Fran shrugged. 'Maybe. I'm just telling you what I – feel.'

'OK,' said Libby, 'but meanwhile, we want to know about the members of the company. Let's ignore the possibility of two different – er – protagonists at the moment. What can you tell us about everyone?'

'You start,' said Jonathan.

'OK.' Tom settled himself more comfortably in the chair. 'Starting with Max, who can't possibly be under suspicion. He would hardly sabotage his own production.'

'He's one of the best,' agreed Jonathan. 'Always willing to take a chance on a young dancer, and very innovative. He's got his own school, you know.'

'Has he?' said Fran. 'How does he manage to do that as well?'

'His partner runs it and he has teachers,' said Tom. 'All trained by him, of course. They hold Saturday classes for kids from thirteen upwards and prepare them for ballet school entry if they want it, or they stay on as apprentices in the company. Sometimes he has to tell people they simply aren't suited, but more often than not the dead wood dies off through natural selection when they're young.'

'I came up that way myself,' said Jonathan. 'I did go to ballet school, but I applied to come back to the company when I graduated.'

'So there are people who could be jealous of him?' said Libby.

Both men nodded. 'Oh, yes. There's a lot of jealousy in the profession. And Max has helped to make dance popular with the general public who wouldn't have thought to go to see *Swan Lake* or *Coppelia* before,' said Jonathan.

'But no one in the company?' asked Fran.

'No,' said Tom. 'And we already discounted the guys who were turned down at audition. They couldn't have got into the rehearsal rooms.'

'Go on to the others, then,' said Libby. 'Damian, for

instance.'

'Damian?' Both men laughed.

'Never!' said Tom. 'He's been our rehearsal pianist for years, and he plays when we do small shows at arts festivals and so on, and this is his big chance. He composed *Pendle* out of the improvs we were doing when we workshopped it. And it's bloody good.'

'It is,' agreed Jonathan. 'And he's *so* proud of it. He'd never jeopardise his chance of being noticed.'

'Dancers, then,' said Fran. 'People who didn't want to come down here.'

'Dan, I suppose, but that was because of his baby. And he's come down anyway,' said Tom.

'Phillip?' suggested Libby. 'He's a wasp, Max says, and I agree with him, although I quite like him.'

'Oh, he's all right,' said Jonathan. 'Makes everyone laugh, actually. And he's very dedicated. He teaches for Max, too, when he's not dancing.'

'So very unlikely to undermine anything,' mused Fran. 'Who else?'

'Will and Alan are the only two I know,' said Libby.

Jonathan shook his head and Tom said, 'No. They're both so delighted to be out of panto this winter they'd never do anything to upset the apple cart.'

'Who else, then?' said Fran again. 'There aren't many others, are there?'

'Four. All younger than we are. One came up through the school, the other three auditioned,' said Tom.

'What are their names?' asked Libby.

'Lee is our boy,' said Jonathan. 'I taught him and so did Phillip. It wouldn't be him.'

'Paul, Jeremy and Bernie are the other three. We don't know much about them except they're all from Manchester, but I can't see what motives they'd have.' Tom peered gloomily at his plate as if searching there for the answer.

'Jeremy's a bit of an activist,' said Jonathan. 'Gets very annoyed about what he sees as injustices. He's probably up in arms about all this. But he shouts about it. He wouldn't be underhand.'

'What about Sebastian? He doesn't like Stan very much,' said Libby.

'He's told you, has he?' Jonathan looked interested. 'He hardly speaks to any of us. Do you think it could be him?'

'He doesn't like Stan but he seems to be tied to him,' said Libby. 'He says he buggered up a stage management degree and Stan helped him out. He didn't say how he buggered it up, though.'

'I didn't know that.' Now Tom, too, was looking interested. 'So he could have rigged the Kabuki. In fact, he's the perfect person to have done it. Didn't he have to get that rat down this morning? He could have done it then.'

'I think he'd have been seen,' said Libby doubtfully. 'Ben and Max were watching him do it. Come to that, so was Stan.'

'What about Stan?' asked Fran. 'He's a bit of a wasp, too, isn't he?'

'He's a pain in the arse,' said Tom firmly. 'Sorry, girls, but he is. The trouble is, he's a good designer and a very organised company manager. In fact, I don't know where we'd be without him.'

'Unpaid, probably,' said Jonathan.

'How does he manage all that?' asked Libby. 'Does he run the school, too?'

'No, as I said, the school's run by Max's partner,' said Jonathan. 'But Stan pays us, organises appearances, accommodation –'

'Not this time,' put in Tom.

'And tells us what to do,' continued Jonathan.

'Isn't that Max's job?' said Libby.

'Yes, but Stan's always muscling in.'

'How did he come into the business?' asked Fran. 'Was he a dancer?'

'No, he went to drama school to do stage management. Probably the same one young Seb went to,' said Tom. 'That may be how they met. I know he goes back to give occasional talks.'

'Is there much difference in stage management for drama

and for ballet?' asked Libby. 'There isn't for musicals.'

'It's useful to be able to read a score,' said Jonathan. 'In opera you have to. Especially for lighting.'

'Oh, yes,' said Fran, nodding. 'You can't follow a script for cues, can you? But you can get to know the moves, I suppose.'

'The choreography, darling,' said Jonathan, striking a pose.

'Oh, sorry.' Fran grinned back.

'So where did we get to?' said Libby. 'Everyone, really. The four newbies, Seb, Stan, you lot, Damian and Max himself. It doesn't look like anyone, does it?'

'But it must be,' said Fran. 'Unless someone's smuggled him or herself down here in a suitcase and is hiding somewhere.'

'That's a possibility,' said Libby. 'After all, we've had people hiding out on the estate in the past.'

'You have?' Jonathan looked worried, Tom interested.

Libby explained about the Hoppers' Huts, left over from when The Manor was a working hop farm.

'People get into them, and they're so far from the main house we don't know about it.'

'Could that be it?' Tom looked anxiously at Libby.

'I'll check the huts tomorrow,' said Libby, 'but I doubt if there's anyone there. They've all had new locks since last winter, and there's a security light and camera on the end of the block now.'

'Is there? I didn't know that.' Fran put aside her knife and fork. 'So whether you like it or not, the culprit – or the most recent one – must be one of you. There isn't another option.'

Tom and Jonathan looked at each other uncomfortably. 'What about this first one?' asked Tom. 'If you say they're different.'

Fran shrugged. 'I think they are, but I can't be sure of course. There's a much wider field back in London. Far more people can have access to the rehearsal rooms, for instance.'

'But no one could have got in without us knowing,' objected Tom.

Libby regarded him pityingly. 'How many people do you know who've been burgled?'

'Even while they're asleep in the house?' added Fran.

'But –' began Tom.

'No, they're right,' said Jonathan. 'Burglars can get in anywhere they want unless there's a very high-tech security system.'

'But this wasn't a burglar,' said Tom. 'This was a malicious – er – a malicious …'

'Prankster,' Libby finished for him.

'With the same motive as the one down here?' asked Jonathan. 'This is all very confusing.'

'Tell me,' said Fran. 'Was Stan the only person who would have been harmed by that thing this morning?'

'Yes, it's his job to operate it,' said Jonathan.

'So he could have been targeted deliberately?'

'I don't know,' the dancers said together, looking bewildered.

'If so,' said Libby slowly, 'then it's against Stan, not the company. And the incidents in London were fairly random, weren't they?'

'But all were attacks on the dancers,' said Tom.

'Maybe the next incident will be against someone else,' said Libby. 'Maybe whoever it is is working his way through the company.'

'In that case we're back to motive again,' said Fran. 'And you're both convinced that nobody has one.'

'Well, somebody has,' said Tom, 'but not against the company or the ballet. Not that I can see.'

'Perhaps someone has a deep-seated hatred of witches,' said Libby.

'In that case they wouldn't have wanted to be part of the company, would they?' said Fran.

'Or of someone taking the piss out of witches?' said Tom.

'We thought of that one earlier, but the same thing applies,' said Libby.

'Except that they might join the company to sabotage the production,' said Fran.

'Which is what they, or he, is doing anyway. It isn't personal. It's against the company or the production. And in the end they come to the same thing.' Libby finished her wine. 'I suggest we go back. I don't think we've arrived at any sort of conclusion really, do you?'

# Chapter Ten

'So we didn't really get anywhere,' Libby told Max the following morning.

'I think the bloody thing's cursed,' said Max gloomily.

'Don't let anyone hear you say that,' said Libby. 'They'll start thinking all sorts of superstitious nonsense.'

Max stared at the stage, empty except for Stan wandering around making a great deal of his bandaged hand, which reposed in a pristine white sling. 'Does Fran really think there are two different people behind it?'

'It makes sense, if you think about it,' said Libby. 'Well, in so far as it *could* make sense. In London, it could have been anyone and it did look as if it was a ploy to stop the production. But it came down here, and –'

'It still looks like it's a ploy to stop the production,' Max butted in.

'Oh.' Libby was crestfallen. 'Yes. When Fran was talking about it, it made sense.'

'Do you think it's to do with the subject matter? Someone who's obsessed with witches or witchcraft?'

'Honestly, Max, I have no idea. But if the boys talk to one another, it will soon be known that you've asked us to look into it and may deter any more attempts.'

'They knew before,' said Max. 'I left them in no doubt that I was extremely annoyed and wanted it to stop. And you two investigating isn't really likely to stop someone who's determined, is it?'

'Two middle-aged biddies, one of whom is supposed to be psychic. No, I suppose not,' said Libby gloomily. 'I wish we could get the police involved.'

'No.' Max was firm. 'Not unless something really awful happens.' He hesitated. 'Well, more awful.'

Libby cast him a cynical glance. 'Like someone gets killed?'

He looked sick. 'Not that bad.'

'I don't think there's anything else Fran or I can do. We've talked to them and found nothing. Jonathan and Tom don't suspect anyone, in fact they don't think there's a single person connected with the company who would sabotage it.'

'I wouldn't have thought so either,' said Max. 'But there it is. Someone has. And really badly. They've hurt someone.'

Libby patted his arm ineffectually. 'Let's hope they stop now. Ben and Peter are checking the theatre now to make sure there are no nasty surprises lurking in corners.'

Ben and Peter reported that all was well and Libby went back to the Manor to help Hetty clear up after breakfast. Although originally this was not going to be provided, Hetty would not allow anyone staying in her house to go unfed, and provided toast and cereal on long tables in the sitting-room.

'After all,' she pointed out, 'them as is staying in the pub get breakfast, don't they?'

Unable to refute this impeccable logic, Max had agreed, forbearing to say that those staying in the pub didn't have to dance their way through the mornings on full stomachs. However, the dancers appreciated their cereal and fruit juice and were beginning to treat Hetty like a surrogate mother.

Tuesday passed quietly. Harry again provided lunch and spent time chatting, the results of which he gave to Libby when she called in to the restaurant on her way home in the afternoon.

'But there's nothing,' he said. 'They're all mystified. And a bit scared, too.'

'I wondered about that,' said Libby with a sigh. 'They've got a right to be, I suppose.'

But Tuesday night turned into Wednesday without incident, and on Wednesday evening Ben and Libby decided to join their friends Patti Pearson and Anne Douglas, who were on their regular Wednesday date at The Pink Geranium. Several of the dancers were also in there, and Patti and Anne were keen to know who they were.

'So you see,' said Libby, when she'd finished relaying the events of the past few days, 'we're no further forward. They're all a bit scared, really, although nothing's happened since Monday morning.'

'Are you going to tell Ian about it? Or have you already?' asked Anne.

'Max doesn't want the police involved,' said Ben. 'Which is why he asked Libby and Fran.'

'Really?' Patti raised her eyebrows.

'In a way.' Libby felt her cheeks going hot. 'You remember Sir Andrew? He told Max about what happened with the ukulele player last year – Max had been to the concert – and that Fran and I had been involved in, er, *things* before. And he thought it would be a good idea to bring the show here for a try-out. Which it was.'

'Is it on all next week?' asked Anne.

'Barring accidents, Wednesday to Saturday,' said Libby. 'But funnily enough, almost sold out. They did all the marketing in London, and it's still ongoing, so they've got masses of people coming down for it. I believe Anderson Place is practically booked out for the week.'

'Could we get tickets for Wednesday?' asked Patti. 'I'll ring up in the morning, shall I?'

'I'll find two for you,' said Ben. 'You don't mind the subject matter?'

'Witches?' Patti's eyes slid to meet Libby's. 'Let's face it, I have more knowledge of them than most, haven't I?'

Patti, the vicar of St Aldeberge along the coast from Nethergate, had fallen foul of a so-called coven of witches some years before. Libby and Fran had helped unmask them.

'Everybody's wondering if it's something to do with witches. The campaign, or whatever it is,' said Libby.

'Disapproval of same?' asked Anne, finishing off her glass of white wine and waving at Harry, who was flirting madly with a table full of dancers.

'Well, yes,' said Libby. 'I mean, they're terribly disapproved of in the church, aren't they?'

'The modern church doesn't believe in them,' said Patti. 'Or at least, not as the church in 1612 did.'

'You believe in evil,' said Anne, fixing her friend with a

steely eye. Patti blushed, and Libby wondered what the subtext was beneath this exchange.

'Anyway, the church would hardly disapprove of a play, or a ballet, about the Pendle Witches,' said Patti, also finishing her wine.

'More wine, I take it?' said Harry, appearing behind them. 'Sancerre, again, Anne?'

'We'll have a bottle,' said Anne recklessly. 'Patti can help me drink it at home if we don't finish it tonight.'

Harry's lips twitched. 'Yes'm. But may I ask if you're going to the pub from here? Because they won't be too pleased if you wander in clutching an open bottle of wine.'

'Ah.' Anne looked at Patti and giggled. 'Didn't think of that.'

'You have much more and you'll fall out of your chair,' said Harry. 'I shall give you one more glass.'

Anne shimmied her wheelchair left and right to demonstrate her fitness to control it and grinned at Libby. 'Isn't he bossy?'

Libby laughed. 'On occasion. But very helpful.'

'Returning to Ian,' said Patti, when Harry had refilled their glasses, 'are you going to tell him?'

'Do you think he'll be in tonight?' asked Ben.

Detective Chief Inspector Ian Connell had been a friend for some years and often popped into the pub on Wednesdays to join them all for a drink.

'He might be,' said Libby, 'but I'm not sure I ought to say anything to him if Max doesn't want me to.'

But when Ian appeared in the pub an hour later it was obvious that he already knew at least part of the situation.

'How do you know, then?' asked Libby, as he accepted his coffee from Ben and sat down.

'I went in to see Harry and found him surrounded by male dancers.' Ian grinned and nodded over to the other bar. 'And they're in there with some others, I see.'

'Oh,' said Libby. 'Patti wanted to know if we'd told you the story, you see.'

'Tell me now,' said Ian. 'Harry wouldn't say much in front of his adoring followers.'

So, between them, Ben and Libby gave him the outline of the problems besetting Max's Pendle Witches.

'Did he report this in London?' asked Ian when they'd finished.

'Do you know, I never thought to ask,' said Libby.

'It doesn't sound as though he did.' Ian gazed thoughtfully into his coffee cup. 'I can't do anything unless he tells me, I suppose, but I don't like the sound of this knife attack.'

'Would you call it a knife attack?' wondered Libby.

'What would you call it? A playground prank?' said Ben. 'Of course it's a knife attack, and very accurately aimed, too.'

'You mean at this stage manager person?'

'Stan Willis, yes,' said Libby. 'Apparently, so Flo tells us, he's the image of Wally Willis.'

'Who?' said Ian, Patti and Anne together.

'A London villain from the sixties and seventies.'

'And Flo knew him?'

'Flo and Lenny. He was a bit of a well-known character in London.'

'So is this his son?'

'Son or grandson,' said Libby. 'Stan's only in his thirties, I should think.'

'It isn't a reason to go to so much trouble to slash his hand, though,' said Anne. 'Sins of the father and all that.'

'Don't you believe it,' said Ian. 'In London gangland they take it out on anybody. Or they used to. Things have changed a lot now with so much corporate crime.'

'You're not going to do anything about it, are you?' asked Libby. 'I'd feel I'd betrayed Max.'

Ian raised an eyebrow. 'And you're quite happy about being asked in to look into something possibly dangerous *instead* of the police?'

Libby looked uncomfortably round the table. 'Well, not exactly,' she said.

'Would anyone like another drink?' asked Patti, standing up. 'My round.'

Ian declined, but Anne, Libby and Ben all nodded.

'Well, Libby – you do have the local monopoly on charmers,

don't you?' Phillip Newcombe had approached silently from the other bar and was beaming at Ian.

'Hello, little wasp,' said Libby. 'Everybody – this is Phillip Newcombe who is playing – I'm sorry, *dancing* – Alizon, one of the principal witches. Anne and Ian, Phillip. Oh, and this is Patti.'

Everyone murmured greetings.

When it became apparent they were not going to ask him to join them, Phillip cocked his head on one side at Libby and began to turn away.

'I don't know if it's my imagination or not,' he said over his shoulder, 'but I'm pretty sure I got the whiff of the constabulary just now in Harry's lovely caff. And here, too. Strange, isn't it?'

He twinkled off and Ian swore.

'I was talking to Harry about a consignment of wine that has mysteriously gone missing. I had hoped no one had overheard.'

'No harm done, I suppose,' said Ben, 'but as Libby said, he's a wasp. Likeable, but definitely a wasp. He'll spread that around.'

'And on cue,' said Libby, looking doleful, 'here comes Max.'

'We'll go,' said Patti, standing up and grasping the handle of Anne's chair.

'No need,' said Libby.

'No, it's best,' said Ian. 'Thanks, girls.' He went to open the door for them and saw them through.

'They left their drinks,' said Libby miserably. 'Oh, bugger all this.'

Max arrived at their table, not looking angry, thought Libby thankfully.

'Hello,' she said. 'This is our friend Ian. You've just missed Patti and Anne.'

Ben looked at her as though she was babbling.

Ian nodded as he came back to the table. 'They've gone back to Harry's. We'll collect them later.'

Libby's eyes flew up into her hairline. 'That's nice of you.'

'I can be, sometimes,' said Ian and turned to Max. 'You're Max Tobin, I understand, and something tells me you want to ask me some questions.'

'I – er – I –' Max was floundering.

'Do sit down,' said Ian, the height of urbanity. 'And before you ask, no, Libby has not reported anything officially to the police. In the same way that your dancers gathered I was a policeman, I gathered that there is something going on within your company.'

Max looked from Ben to Libby and back to Ian. 'How ...?' he began.

'I'm a friend.' Ian's eyebrows quirked. 'Policemen can have friends, you know.'

Max was still looking wary and Ben lost his patience.

'Max, things have been going on in your company. Not just criminal damage but actual harm to someone. I really think you ought to tell Ian.'

Max sighed.

'We won't make it official,' said Ian. 'Unless, of course, it becomes necessary.'

'How much do you know?' asked Max, capitulating. When he had finished his story, Ian looked thoughtful.

'There is, in fact, sufficient evidence for you to report this to the police and for us to investigate.'

'I would rather ...' began Max.

'I know you don't want to. May I ask why?'

Max looked uncomfortable.

'You don't want to upset the company, is that it?' asked Libby.

'Partly. And I don't want it to get out.'

Ian was now looking scornful. 'So you're prepared to risk further incidents to avoid bad publicity?'

Max went down like a pricked balloon. 'Sounds awful when you put it like that.'

'It's more for the boys than for Max himself,' Libby tried to explain. 'A lot of it is their own work.'

'How?' Ian was frowning.

'They workshopped it. Didn't one of them suggest the story?' Ben said.

'That's right.' Max nodded. 'It was Alan, after we'd seen

*Swan Lake*.'

Ian was now looking confused, so Libby explained Matthew Bourne's innovative *Swan Lake*.

'And Damian, the company pianist, devised the music, so he'd hardly do anything to harm the production. You see, I really can't think any of them would do this sort of thing.' Max stared earnestly at Ian.

'You'd be surprised how many people swear that their best friend or partner couldn't kill a fly and then discover they're a bestial murderer,' said Ian.

'I know.' Max sighed gustily. 'But could we leave it until tomorrow? I'd like to discuss it with my company manager first.'

'Company manager?' asked Ian.

'Stan Willis,' said Libby. 'He's also the stage manager and the victim of the Kabuki curtain assault.'

'Surely he will be in favour of going to the police?' said Ian.

'I should think so,' said Ben. 'He was certain someone was out to kill him after the attack.'

'Oh? What did he say?' asked Ian.

'I don't remember exactly, but it was sort of "They'll get me next time, you see if they don't". None of us took it seriously.'

'Hmmm,' said Ian, more thoughtful than ever. 'That sounds as though he believed it was definitely an attack on him, doesn't it?'

'I'll ask him,' said Max with resignation. 'He's staying here, as I am, so I'll knock on his door when I go up.'

'He isn't in the bar with the others?' said Libby.

'No. Damian and Seb are there, but they said Stan had gone up.'

Libby explained to Ian who Sebastian and Damian were in case Ian had got muddled with all the names.

Max stood up. 'I'll go up, then. I'll be in touch tomorrow.' He nodded at Ian, smiled sadly at Libby and Ben and went towards the stairs.

Ben stood up. 'I'll go and fetch the girls, shall I?'

'Yes, please. They've still got drinks to finish,' said Libby.

'Well?' she said to Ian when Ben had gone. 'What do you

think? Storm in a teacup?'

'I think it's more dangerous than that,' said Ian. 'If your friend Max won't report it formally I shall force his hand. I'm not sure I shouldn't also force him to cancel the production.'

'Oh, Ian, no!' gasped Libby. 'All that work!'

'And suppose something worse happens?' said Ian.

'What if it has?' said Ben, appearing behind them. 'Stan isn't in his bedroom. And it's been ransacked.'

# Chapter Eleven

Ian was out of his seat so fast he was at the door before Libby could even stand up.

'What?' she said to Ben.

'When I got into the hall Max was practically falling down the stairs. I left him there and came to get Ian. I don't know any more than that.'

'Oh, bloody hell.' Libby shook her head. 'Why was Max nearly falling down the stairs?'

'He's got the wind up. He was worried by Ian's attitude.' Ben sat down. 'He was trying not to think any of it was really serious and he's realised he can't ignore it any more.'

'You never made it to collect the girls,' said Libby after a moment. 'I'll go and get them.'

Ben nodded and Libby left the pub, avoiding the reception area.

Harry and Peter were sitting with Anne and Patti in the left-hand window, the one with the comfortable sofa and chairs, a bottle between them on the coffee table. Libby quickly told them what had happened.

'I came to fetch you,' she said at last. 'You left drinks on the table.'

'I think we'd be better keeping out of the way,' said Patti. 'Harry's treated us to the wine, so we're quite happy.'

Just then, the door opened and Ben stuck his head round.

'Pete, Hal, could you come and give us a hand?'

'What's happened?' Peter stood up.

'Ian's worried about Stan, and as we can't raise him on his phone, he wants to go and look for him. I'll have to open the theatre in case he went back there, and Ian thinks we should have a look round outside. He doesn't want the dance crowd involved.'

'That makes sense,' said Libby, but with a sense of foreboding. 'Shall we stay here?'

'Yes.' Ben came and patted her on the shoulder. 'You'd only get plagued by the company if you went back to the pub.'

The men left and Patti, Anne and Libby sat and looked at each other.

'What shall we do now?' said Anne. 'I feel useless just sitting here.'

'I think Ian's over-reacting,' said Libby. 'He's making much more of it than the rest of us did. I don't know why he's so worried.'

'He's a lot more experienced than any of us,' said Patti. 'He must have spotted something that got past the rest of you.'

'Or perhaps he knows something we don't,' said Anne. 'Or rather, you don't.' She shifted impatiently in her chair. 'I feel so useless.'

'You've already said that,' said Patti. 'There's nothing we can do anyway. And we don't know any of the people concerned.'

Anne smiled. 'I know. I'm just over-reacting to the situation like Ian. I think I tend to dramatise things because I can't do anything about them.'

Libby looked at her with sympathy. 'I think I know what you mean. But I can't think anything's really happened. Far more likely that Stan stayed behind at the theatre to fiddle about with the set or something. Or even check his accounts. Oh, I don't know.' She picked up the wine bottle. 'Do you think I could have a glass of this?'

'Course you can. Shall I get you a glass?' said Patti.

'No, I'll go.' Libby went over to the counter and found a glass. Patti poured them all more wine and they settled down in silence to wait.

'But his room was ransacked,' said Anne suddenly. 'That's serious.'

'But was it, though?' said Libby. 'He could just be very untidy. Remember that TV ad about the boy who was left home alone and his friend thought he'd been burgled?'

'But Ian must have had a look at it now,' said Patti, 'and he'd know the difference.'

Libby nodded gloomily and sighed into her drink. 'I sometimes think I've got some kind of reverse Midas touch. Whenever I go near anything or anybody ...' she trailed off.

Patti looked at her fondly. 'You go near people because they ask you to,' she said. 'I asked you for help when I first met you, didn't I?'

'It wasn't you actually,' said Libby. 'It was my dippy friend Alice.'

'So it was. But look how you helped in that affair.'

'I think I made it worse,' said Libby.

Anne laughed. 'She's determined to be the Harbinger of Doom, Pats, whatever you say.'

Libby grinned reluctantly. 'Sorry.'

The interior of the café was suddenly illuminated by blue flashing lights. Libby's heart thumped and she stood up unsteadily.

Patti surreptitiously crossed herself and went to the door. 'They've gone up the Manor drive,' she reported. 'And here comes Harry.'

Harry came into the restaurant looking white and sick.

'They found him,' he said, and sat down abruptly on the chair opposite the sofa.

'Have some wine,' said Libby, offering her own glass. Harry took it in a shaking hand and downed half of it. The three women looked at each other, not liking to ask the question.

'Where?' asked Libby eventually.

Harry let out a gusty sigh. 'On the stage.'

'The *stage*?' echoed three voices.

'It looked like an accident.' He topped up the glass and realised Libby hadn't got one. 'Get another bottle and glass, Lib.'

'I think I've had enough,' said Libby. 'Go on. The stage, you said?'

'He'd fallen off a ladder. The scaffolding was still assembled in the scenery dock, and he'd just detached the main ladder. Silly sod. If he'd used the scaffolding, he wouldn't have fallen.'

Anne held up a hand. 'Scuse me, but what scaffolding? Have you been painting the outside?'

'No, it's stage scaffolding,' said Libby. 'It has different platforms and is used for reaching the lighting barrels, painting – all sorts of things. It all comes apart and can be assembled differently – like Meccano.'

Anne looked puzzled, but Patti nodded.

'So he used a ladder and fell off it,' said Libby. 'Why?'

'Ian guessed he was looking at the Kabuki.'

'I explained that to you, didn't I?' Libby said to the other two, who nodded. 'So it has nothing to do with the ransacked room?'

'I don't know. As soon as they – Ben and Ian, that was – found him, Ian shooed us off. He'd already called for assistance to check the bedroom and Pete and I diverted them up to the theatre. We're to stay put for the time being.'

'Where's Peter now?' asked Patti.

'He went to tell them at the pub. They'll have to seal the room off, now. Poor old Seb will have to bunk down somewhere else.'

Peter pushed the door open.

'Ian had already sent the second police car to the pub, so they knew something was up.' He sat down heavily. 'None of them seemed to be able to take it in, though.'

'What about Max?' asked Libby.

'He was still sitting on the stairs. I didn't speak to him.'

'What do we do now?' asked Harry.

'Stay here, I suppose,' said Peter. 'You could go home, girls.'

For once not commenting on his use of 'girls', Libby nodded. 'You go, Patti, Anne. I'll stay here with Hal and Pete for a bit.'

Looking relieved, Patti and Anne left.

'Why do you think Ben's still up at the theatre?' Libby said, when Harry had closed the door behind them.

'He'll have to show them round, won't he,' said Peter. 'I hope they've let him go across and tell Hetty.'

'She's not going to be happy, is she?' said Harry.

'No.' Libby sighed. 'I mean, we've had murders connected with the theatre before, but never actually in it. I suppose he was sure it was murder?'

'Seemed to be, but I couldn't really see. He wouldn't let any of us go near the stage, not even Ben.'

Libby's phone began to warble inside the large bag which had replaced her basket.

'Ben,' said Libby, looking at the screen.

'Libby, it's me. Listen, could you come up to the Manor and sit with Hetty? She came out to find out what was going on, and although she didn't say much, you know her, I could see she was upset.'

'Of course,' said Libby. 'We were just talking about that. I'm on my way.'

At the same time as Ben said, 'Not on your own!' Peter and Harry said together, 'We'll come with you.'

'There,' said Libby. 'We'll all come.'

'Why did you say you'd come with me?' asked Libby, as Harry locked the front door of the café.

'Someone's just been killed in the theatre, Lib,' said Peter, taking her arm. 'Who knows where the killer is now?'

'Lurking in the bushes,' said Harry, taking the other arm. 'Waiting to pounce.'

'Don't be flippant,' said Peter. 'This is serious.'

'We're sure this is murder, then?' said Libby again.

'I've told you, we couldn't see, but Ian was certainly treating it as murder.'

Libby shivered. 'You know, I've never thought about it before, but it is a bit spooky walking up here in the dark.'

'You're hardly in the dark for long,' said Peter. 'Look, there's the theatre – all lit up.'

'And if you look back, you can see the lights from the high street,' said Harry.

Libby looked nervously towards the theatre. 'We don't go in there, do we?'

'No. Just into the house,' said Peter. 'Come on, here we are.'

They found Hetty sitting at the kitchen table with a mug of

tea.

'Right carry-on,' she muttered.

'Sorry, Hetty,' said Libby helplessly.

'Not your fault, gal.'

'Makes a change,' said Harry, *sotto voce*. Hetty glanced at him sharply.

'Want tea?' she asked. 'Or something stronger?'

'Tea would be fine,' said Libby. 'I'll do it, shall I?'

'You sit down,' said Hetty, getting to her feet, and suddenly Libby realised how much older she looked.

They sat down and Hetty moved the big kettle on to the Aga hotplate.

'What are they doing in there now?' she asked.

'Don't know.' Peter shook his head. 'I think Ben's having to stay there to show them how things work.'

Hetty shook her head and fetched three more mugs.

They sat in silence with their tea waiting and wondering what would happen. Eventually, Ben appeared, looking exhausted. Hetty immediately got up and fetched the whisky.

'What happened?' asked Libby, as he collapsed into a chair.

'They're taking the theatre apart, it seems to me.' He shook his head and accepted a whisky from his mother. 'Max won't be able to go on at this rate. Or if he does, we'll have to re-rig everything. He certainly can't rehearse in the theatre for at least the rest of this week.'

'So it is murder?'

'Oh, yes. Ian and the doctor – pathologist, whoever he was – were quite certain. He had fallen from the tower and then been hit over the head.' Ben looked sick. 'Quite distinctive, apparently.'

'So deliberately pushed from the tower?' asked Peter.

'I don't know.' Ben shook his head again. 'I suppose so.'

'Will they be there all night?' asked Harry.

'Probably. But Ian was going down to the pub to interview all the others. He said he'd let the dancers come back here when he'd finished with them, but I suspect it'll be a long night.'

'That's all right,' said Libby. 'I'll stay here to let them in.'

'Don't have to do that,' said Hetty. 'I don't lock the door, and I'll leave the hall light on. They'll come in when they're ready.'

'I'm not leaving you here on your own,' said Ben.

'You don't reckon any of them boys did it, do you?' said Hetty scornfully. 'Couldn't hurt a mouse, they couldn't.'

'They're very strong, Hetty,' said Libby.

'You do what you like then,' said Hetty. 'Help yourselves to whisky. I'm going to bed.'

The remaining four looked at each other when she'd gone.

'You two go,' said Ben. 'No sense in us all staying up. Lib and I will stay here until a few of them are back, then we'll go.'

'If you're sure,' said Peter.

'Come on,' said Harry. 'I've got to get up in the morning, even if you haven't, and I expect at some point someone will come to ask *us* questions, won't they?'

'Why us?' Peter looked surprised.

'To see if we heard any suspicious remarks when we were doing lunch.'

'I doubt it,' said Peter, 'but I suppose Ian might find it worthwhile getting our impressions.'

They said goodnight and left Libby and Ben sitting at the kitchen table.

It was another half an hour before they heard voices and Ian himself came into the kitchen. He looked surprised to see them.

'I thought you'd have gone home to bed!'

'We didn't want to leave Hetty in the house on her own,' said Ben. 'Under the circumstances.'

'No, of course.' He joined them at the table. 'I've brought most of the dancers back here and we'll finish questioning them in the morning. I've talked to Tobin, Long and Singleton, and again, they've been asked to be available in the morning.'

'What about the bedroom?' asked Libby.

'Nothing so far. Now I'm going to ask you to go home, and I shall want to talk to you tomorrow to get your impressions of everyone. Please, Libby, do *not* start asking any questions of these people. Your job is finished.'

# Chapter Twelve

'What do think we ought to do?' Libby said the following morning. 'Stay here, or go to the Manor? We won't be able to go to the theatre, will we?'

'I think we ought to go to the Manor,' said Ben. 'If all those boys have got to stay cooped up there Hetty's going to have to provide tea and coffee, so we ought to help.'

'Do you think Ian will let Harry take lunch up there?'

'I don't see why not. It depends if he's letting them go.'

'What, back to London? I shouldn't think so. They're all suspects, aren't they?'

'Yes, I suppose so. Come on then. We'll buy some extra biscuits on the way.'

Hetty had already wheeled the big urns into the sitting-room, where various young men lay draped disconsolately over the furniture. They greeted Ben and Libby with mildly hopeful expressions, then sank back into torpor. Libby emptied a packet of biscuits onto a plate and called out, 'Help yourselves', then rejoined Hetty in the kitchen.

'That Ian's been in,' said Hetty. 'He asked what we did about lunch and I told him Harry brought it. He said we could do the same today.'

'I'll call Harry then,' said Ben. 'Where's he interviewing people?'

'Theatre,' said Hetty. 'One by one.'

'How grim,' said Libby.

At just about twelve thirty, when Harry was due to appear with the lunch, Ian came into the kitchen.

'Can I talk to you two, now?' he said.

'Ben's in the office, shall we go in there?' asked Libby. 'And do you want coffee? You look shattered.'

He smiled grimly. 'I am rather, and yes, coffee would be great.'

'Go along then,' said Hetty gruffly. 'I'll bring it.'

'She's nice, your mother-in-law,' commented Ian as he followed Libby along the passage.

'Mother-in-law-elect,' said Libby. 'Not a real one.'

She let Ian have the most comfortable chair and perched herself on the old bentwood chair by the window. Ben's estate office hadn't changed at all since she'd known it, and probably not since his father took over.

'I just want to go over a few things you told me last night before we knew there was murder involved,' said Ian. 'Can you repeat the sequence of events from when Tobin first told you about the incidents in London?'

Libby patiently and obediently – she was getting used to police investigations – began the story from when Sir Andrew had turned up at the pub and asked for their help.

'Of course, he asked for Fran's help, too. I think Max was quite impressed by Fran.'

'And has Fran had any insights about the case?' asked Ian, smiling gratefully as Hetty brought in coffee on a tray.

'No – oh, except when she said that the incidents here were by a different person.'

'From the one in London?'

'Yes. It was just one of those things she knew, apparently. She has no idea why.'

'Is she coming over today?'

'I've told her about last night on the phone, but she didn't say she was coming. Why?'

'Because it might be interesting to see if she came up with the same theory about the murder.'

'If she thought the Kabuki incident was by someone different – surely it's the same person,' said Ben.

'We might be meant to think so,' said Ian. 'Anyway, go on, Libby.'

Libby continued her story up to and including the night out with Jonathan and Tom. 'And that's about it,' she concluded. 'And you know what we were doing last night.'

Ian's chin remained sunk on his chest. Libby looked uneasily at Ben.

'Looks as though you were right,' said Ben eventually.

Ian sat up. 'Yes, it does.' He stirred his coffee thoughtfully.

'What made you think it was serious?' asked Libby cautiously.

He looked across at her and smiled. 'I won't bite, Libby. I'm just rather annoyed that Tobin chose not to confide in the police. This could have been avoided, I'm sure.'

'How?'

'By finding out what Willis was hiding.' Ian stood up. 'I'd better go and have another word with young Sebastian Long.'

'Willis was hiding?' repeated Libby. 'Why would you think that?'

'There was an attempt made on him, even if it wasn't meant to kill. And his mutterings about further attempts to kill him sound very like a warning to me.'

'They do?' Libby looked astonished.

'If the attempt with the Kabuki curtain was intended to warn Willis, which it looks as if it was, then Willis's mutterings were intended to counter-threaten the perpetrator.'

'You mean, "try it again and I'll tell all"?' said Ben.

'Something like that.' Ian frowned. 'I'm not sure, of course, but we've got to find out.' He went to the door.

'Can the boys go out?' asked Libby. 'Or are they confined to barracks? They've got nothing to do, after all.'

'I don't want them going back to London, but as long as they stay in the area and let us know where they're going they can go out, yes.'

'Will you tell them?'

'I'll tell one of the officers on duty to let them know.' Ian gave them a quick smile and left.

'Why did you ask that?' said Ben, as they went back towards the kitchen.

'I thought some of them might want to go out,' said Libby. 'I could take a couple of them – oh, I don't know – to Canterbury?'

'Where's the bus Stan came down in? Couldn't they go out in that?'

'Oh, yes! It's parked round the back, isn't it?' Libby fished

93

out her phone. 'I'm just going to fill Fran in, then we'll go and ask them if they want to go anywhere.'

'Count me out,' said Ben. 'I'm going to have to sort out whether or not we open next week. I shall go and see if Max is free.'

Libby wandered out into the courtyard and watched white suited FOs plodding in and out of the theatre doors like heavy-footed ghosts. Fran answered the phone on the second ring, and Libby gave her a quick résumé of the morning's events.

'Ian wanted to know if you still thought the incidents in London and the attacks down here were made by different people?'

'I don't know that I've thought about it,' said Fran with caution. 'I would assume though, that the attack with the knife and the – ah – death of Stan were done by the same person, wouldn't you?'

'Ian meant, had you had any specific feelings about it.'

'I know what he meant,' said Fran irritably. 'How many times do I have to tell you I can't do this to order?'

'Wasn't me, it was him,' said Libby defensively. 'Anyway, I'm going to offer to take some of them out for a bit if they want. Ian says I can. Do you want to come?'

'Where, though? They aren't going to feel like a pleasure trip.'

'I don't know. I'll go and ask. I thought we could take their bus. You know, the one they came down in.'

'You ask them and let me know,' said Fran.

Feeling slightly deflated, Libby went back into the big sitting-room. Some of the dancers who were there looked up without much interest. Jonathan sat in a corner with a book and gave her a small smile.

'I wondered if anyone wanted to go out anywhere,' Libby said. 'You've got Ian's permission.'

'Who?'

'Oh, sorry, Detective Chief Inspector Connell. He's the policeman who was with us last night. A friend.'

'Oh. That's how he was there so quickly.' Jonathan was eyeing her suspiciously.

'Well, yes. He was having a drink with us in the pub, he usually does on Wednesdays. And Max told him about all the incidents, so ...'

'And were you and your friend Fran reporting everything we said to you the other evening?' Jonathan was now looking positively hostile.

'No!' Libby was shocked. 'Max wanted Fran and I to look into the incidents, I told you. And he *didn't* want the police to be involved. We can hardly be blamed for meeting a friend for a drink in *our* local, can we?'

'It just seems rather coincidental, that's all.' Jonathan was now looking sulky rather than hostile.

'I daresay it does if you've got either a suspicious mind or a guilty conscience.' Libby shrugged. 'I'll leave you to it.'

'Wait, Libby.' Jonathan stood up and put a hand on her arm. 'I'm sorry. It's such a surreal situation. None of us know what to think.'

'And I know even less than you do,' said Libby.

'I know. I'm sorry.' Jonathan looked down at his feet.

'So, do you think anyone wants to go out? I thought you might want to get away from the theatre for a bit. You could take the company bus, couldn't you?'

'I don't think any of us are insured to drive it. Just Stan.'

'Oh, dear. And you have to have a special licence for carrying passengers, don't you?'

Jonathan nodded. 'I really don't know what we're going to do without him.'

'I'd like to go out.'

Libby and Jonathan looked round to face a small, dark person with a rather intense expression.

'Have you met Paul, Libby?' said Jonathan.

'No, I haven't.' Libby held out her hand. Paul took it and held it limply for a moment.

'There's a grotto near here, isn't there?' he said.

'A grotto?' Libby thought back to the Victorian grotto she had seen a couple of years ago in the grounds of a local house. 'I know one, but it's in someone's garden.'

'No, this is like a prehistoric tomb. I saw it on television.

You must know it.'

'I don't know anything like that round here.' Libby frowned.

'I know what he means.' A blond youth came forward and also held out a hand. 'Hello, I'm Lee. We saw it on TV back in London and it struck a chord because we were coming here.'

'What was it, then?' asked Jonathan.

'It was one of these stones, you know, like Stonehenge, but there's just one of them.'

'Sounds like Grey Betty, that's just one stone,' said Libby.

'That's it, but they've found this mocked up tomb right near it,' said Paul. 'Somebody or other was saying it was a scandal and threatened the – what was it? – something of the site.'

'Integrity?' suggested Libby.

'Could be.' Paul nodded. 'I had a fancy to see it. Is it far?'

'Not really,' said Libby. 'Shall I see if I can find out anything about it?'

'I just thought it might be, you know, interesting,' said Paul with a shrug, but Libby thought his eyes looked very sharp. She turned and went back to the office.

'Can I borrow the computer?' she asked Ben. 'We've got a request for a little jaunt.'

After a bit of searching, she found an online news item which obviously referred to Grey Betty and its impostor neighbour.

'It's not open to the public, though,' she told Ben. 'It was found when the current owner of the property was doing some work.'

'I wonder why this Paul wants to look at it?' said Ben peering over her shoulder at the screen.

'No idea, but if a couple of them want to go, I'll take them in your car, if I may.'

Ben gave his consent and Libby went back to the sitting room.

'We can go and look at Grey Betty, if you like,' she announced to the room at large, 'but not the grotto, sadly.'

Paul shrugged. 'Better than nothing.'

Jonathan, Lee and two or three others protested at this somewhat churlish response, but Libby grinned.

'We'll wait until Harry's served lunch, shall we?' she said. 'He'll be up soon.'

Max, Damian, Ben and Sebastian joined them when Harry, accompanied by Peter, arrived with lunch, and the outing was discussed.

'Why does he want to go?' Max asked Libby quietly, watching Paul, who was enthusing about the grotto to a small group of dancers.

'I don't know, but I'm quite willing to take him and a couple of others, just to get their minds off this – thing.'

'It seems a bit ghoulish to me.' Max poured himself a mug of coffee.

'Ghoulish?' Libby was surprised. 'Why?'

'Aren't witches supposed to dance round standing stones?'

'Maybe,' said Libby unwillingly. 'I thought it was more Druids and people.'

Max sent her a shrewd look. 'And weird Morris dancing traditions?'

'Well – yes. I take it Andrew's been talking.'

'He's told me about some of your exploits, you know that. That's why I was hopeful … Tell me, do you think this could all have something to do with witchcraft? Real witches, I mean.'

'I honestly don't think so,' said Libby. 'For a start, there aren't any real witches. The ones Fran and I have come across have all been using so-called witchcraft and Devil worship as a cloak – or an excuse – for some very unpleasant goings on.'

'Like the cockerel?'

'That's just part of the trappings. No, sexual deviance and drugs, mainly. You know, like Aleister Crowley.'

'Oh, he was the writer who led some kind of quasi-religious movement, wasn't he?'

'That's him. Nasty.' Libby picked up her own mug. 'Anyway, it's all dangerous nonsense, and I'm pretty sure it hasn't got anything to do with Stan's murder.'

'Or all our incidents in London?' Max shook his head. 'I'm not sure.'

'Have you told Ian all this?'

'Your DCI? Well, I did just mention it. He didn't actually dismiss it.'

'In that case,' said Libby brightly, 'I'd better keep a close eye on young Paul while he's dancing round our standing stone, hadn't I?'

# Chapter Thirteen

In the end, Peter accompanied Libby, Jonathan, Alan, Lee, Paul and Will in Ben's latest Range Rover.

'How did you know the standing stone was near us?' asked Libby, as she negotiated the turn off the main road towards Steeple Mount.

'I recognised the name of the village,' said Will, 'although I realise now it isn't, is it?'

'No, our village is Steeple Martin, this one's Steeple Mount. There's also a Steeple Cross. We form the three points of a triangle.'

'Is there a story behind this Grey Betty?' asked Alan.

'I believe so,' said Libby, 'but I don't know the details.'

'Betty was supposedly a wife who misbehaved and got turned to stone,' said Peter. 'A bit like Lot's wife.'

'But it's older than that, obviously,' said Alan. 'That legend sounds a bit like our Pendle legends – sixteen hundreds.'

'Yes, but they're true,' said Libby.

'Real witches,' said Paul.

Glancing in the mirror, Libby saw Alan and Jonathan exchange glances across Paul, who sat between them.

'The stone itself – is it a dolmen?' asked Lee from one of the back seats, where he sat with Will.

'Part of one, possibly,' said Peter. 'I'd never heard of this fake tomb nearby, but that's what probably gave the estate owners the idea. More likely to be a menhir, I would have thought.'

Libby drew into the car park at the top of the village. 'We have to walk from here, I'm afraid. It's not far.'

'They won't care,' said Peter, as they followed the dancers out of the car park. 'They're all as fit as fiddles and tough as old boots.'

Indeed, they sped up the path towards the standing stone like mountain goats. Libby panted up behind Peter and stopped thankfully at the bench provided at the top.

'Where's Paul?' muttered Libby. 'Don't tell me we've lost him already.'

But Paul reappeared round the side of the stone waving excitedly.

'I've found the tomb!' he yelled.

'Oh, no,' said Libby under her breath.

The other dancers were clustered round him.

'… and the plaque says the stone is used for ancient rites every year,' he was saying as Libby and Peter joined the group.

'Yes, the local Morris sides celebrate May Day up here every year,' said Libby.

'But it must have its roots in older ceremonies,' said Paul.

'It might, but as far as I know the May Day celebrations here started in the nineteen fifties,' said Peter. 'Not very ancient.'

Paul looked disgruntled, but Alan laughed. 'Like our horrible ghoulish trade in the witches. All recent.'

'Our?' asked Peter.

'I believe Alan comes from the Pendle area,' said Libby. 'It was your idea, wasn't it? The ballet?'

Alan went bright red. The other dancers murmured encouragement and patted him on the shoulders and back.

'Well, I hope you get the credit for it,' said Peter.

'Oh, no, Damian and Max will get that,' said Alan.

'Why would Max get any credit for it?' asked Peter.

'He devised it,' said Alan, looking surprised.

'No more than the rest of us,' said Paul.

'Paul,' said Libby hastily, 'you said you'd found the grotto, or whatever it is.'

'Oh, yes.' Paul cheered up. 'Look, round here.'

He beckoned round to the other side of the stone. The ground fell away down a bank covered in vegetation. At the bottom, it had been cleared away to reveal what looked like the entrance to a Neolithic monument.

'It isn't even fenced off!' exclaimed Lee. 'I thought you said it wasn't open to the public, Libby?'

'It said it wasn't on the report I saw,' said Libby. 'It's on private ground.'

'I'm going down,' said Paul. 'Anyone else?'

'I'd rather you didn't,' said Libby.

Lee looked from Paul to Libby. 'I'll go down with him,' he said.

'So will I,' said Will.

Paul had already plunged down the bank. Will and Lee followed more slowly.

Jonathan sighed. 'Do you want me to go and haul them back up?'

'Leave them for a bit,' said Peter. 'There's no "Private" sign, is there? If they're challenged, they can say they didn't know.'

'Why was Paul so keen to come here?' asked Libby. 'He's a funny little person, isn't he?'

'He says he's interested in customs and things,' said Alan. 'He used to keep asking me things about the Pendle Witches. I kept telling him there were only modern customs and legends surrounding them, but he went on and on about Beltane and Samhain.'

'Sow-what?' said Jonathan.

'It's pronounced Sow-in but spelled S-a-m-h-a-i-n. Hallowe'en, as we know it,' said Libby. 'Sort of.'

Peter turned to Libby. 'Why has no one mentioned this before?'

'Wha –? Oh, I see what you mean.' Libby looked at Jonathan. 'Why didn't you tell us this?'

Jonathan looked puzzled. 'Why?'

'Fran and I took you out specifically to find out if there was anything in anyone's background that might give a clue to the incidents in London or down here.'

'But why would Paul's interest in that sort of thing have anything to do with it?'

Alan snorted. 'Oh, Jon! Can't you see? I admit I didn't think of it before, but it's obvious, isn't it?'

Jonathan's frown cleared. 'Oh! You mean the cockerel and all that stuff? The witches?'

'Well, it's a link, isn't it?' said Libby. 'Thank you for

101

picking it up, Pete.'

'Oh, you'd have got there sooner or later,' said Peter, looking thoughtfully down the slope to where the other three had disappeared into the undergrowth. 'Meanwhile, what do we do about it?'

'Tell Ian when we get back,' said Libby promptly.

'Do we have to?' Jonathan looked uncomfortable.

'Of course we do,' said Peter. 'This is a murder investigation, and as Libby will tell you, not telling the police something only makes you look guilty when they find out about it in the end.'

Jonathan looked at Libby. 'I suppose that's right?'

'Oh, yes. We've all been mixed up in enough cases to have seen it happen. And it only complicates matters.'

'Should we mention it to Paul?' asked Alan.

'Definitely not,' said Libby.

Peter wandered over to where a plaque told the brief story of 'Betty'. 'Ah,' he said. 'It says here she was a witch. That explains a lot.'

'Only Paul's interest,' said Libby. 'I'd better look her up when we get back. She's probably connected somehow to Cunning Mary and the Willoughby Oak.'

'Who?' said Jonathan and Alan together.

'A so-called witch from around the same time as the Pendle Witches, who was hanged from a tree locally called the Willoughby Oak. A nasty little group held meetings there supposedly in her honour. They ended up nearly killing someone.'

'Oh dear.' Jonathan looked nervously at Alan. 'Perhaps we shouldn't be doing this after all.'

'That is exactly what someone's been trying to do,' said Libby. 'Put you off. Shut down the production. Don't give in.'

'But we're probably going to have to,' said Alan. 'The police aren't going to let us carry on, are they?'

'Once they've finished with the theatre they might,' said Peter. 'It's Thursday today, and you were due to open when? Tuesday?'

'Wednesday,' said Libby. 'Nearly a week. They could well

102

be finished by then, and it isn't as if you've lost a dancer.'

'That sounds a bit heartless, you old trout,' said Peter, 'but I see what you mean.'

'Not sure I'd want to carry on,' said Jonathan.

'Oh, come on, Jon,' said Alan robustly. 'You know the old show biz tradition. Would Stan have wanted us to stop?'

'Yes, he probably would,' said Jonathan. 'He'd have wanted us all in sackcloth and ashes.'

Libby laughed. 'In that case, you don't want to give him the satisfaction. Come on, let's hike the others out of the mausoleum.'

Peter went down the slope and disappeared from view. They heard him calling, and eventually Will and Lee appeared out of the undergrowth looking dishevelled.

'Peter's had to go right inside that tomb or whatever it is to find Paul,' panted Will, as they climbed up beside the others.

'He *would* insist on going right inside,' said Lee. 'He was as excited as a schoolboy.'

Eventually, Peter emerged, propelling a sulky-looking Paul.

'Last time I take you anywhere,' he said as he pushed the dancer up the slope. 'He deserves a dressing-down from Max, if you ask me.'

'Why? What did he do?' asked Libby, as they began to make their way down the other side of the hill towards the car park.

'Tried to run away, then jumped out at me like some idiotic schoolboy.' Peter brushed down the sleeves of his jacket. 'It was bloody dusty in there.'

'I bet it isn't a mock-up,' said Paul suddenly. 'That's a story they've put out.'

'The archaeologists proved it,' said Lee. 'We saw it on that programme.'

'And what about the witches?' said Paul. 'They dance round that stone.'

Libby and Peter caught each other's eyes uneasily.

'So what if they do?' said Alan. 'They're just as much play-acting as we are, Paul.'

'No,' said Paul stubbornly. 'I don't believe they are.'

'Oh, come off it, Paul,' said Lee in a tired voice. 'Enough

already. There are no such things as witches and you know it.'

Paul simply shook his head and strode on ahead. The others followed anxiously.

Back in the vehicle, Paul said he wanted to do some shopping, and could they go to a supermarket on the way home.

'No,' said Libby. 'There's a perfectly good mini-supermarket in the village.'

'They won't have what I want,' said Paul.

'How do you know?' asked Alan. 'They've got most things. I've been in there.'

'They won't,' mumbled Paul, and sat back with his arms folded.

'Honestly, he's like a sulky child,' Libby muttered to Peter.

Peter cast her an amused look. 'And you never are?'

'How dare you!' Libby tried to toss her head and hit it on the grab handle. 'Ow.'

They arrived back at the Manor as it was getting dark and were met by Ian coming out of the theatre.

'Ah, just the people I wanted to see,' he said.

'Yes, that's mutual,' said Libby, grabbing Jonathan's reluctant arm. 'Let's go back inside.'

'What's this about, then?' asked Ian, once inside the foyer.

'Tell him, Jonathan,' ordered Libby, as Peter joined them, having ushered the other dancers into the Manor.

Jonathan recounted his story to Ian, prompted by Libby, who stood by triumphantly waiting for the reaction.

Ian sighed. 'Why has no one said anything about this before?'

Jonathan looked uncomfortably at Libby. 'We didn't think about it.'

'It was Pete who spotted it,' said Libby. 'The boy's obsessed with witchcraft and ritual.'

'Not that again,' groaned Ian.

'Do you think he might be obsessed enough to sabotage *Pendle*?' asked Peter.

'I've no idea, but not enough to kill Willis, I would have thought,' said Ian. 'Which one is Paul?'

'Small and dark. Looks a bit Celtic,' said Peter. 'Intense.'

'Oh, yes. I didn't interview him, but I didn't get the impression he was the best interviewee. Better get him in, then.'

'What did you want to see us, for?' asked Libby.

'I wanted to inform the dancers that I'm afraid we have to search their rooms,' said Ian, with an apologetic look at Jonathan. 'Sorry, but it is a murder investigation.'

'That's all right,' said Jonathan. 'Can't be helped.'

'Will they be able to go on next week?' asked Libby, as they went back outside.

'I should think so. Tobin asked me earlier. The problem is rehearsing. You can't have the theatre back yet.'

'I know,' Libby said to Peter as they made for the kitchen and Ian went to beard the dancers, including Paul, in the sitting-room, 'let's ask Beth.'

Bethany Cole was the vicar of the church which stood at the bottom of Maltby Close, almost opposite the Manor drive.

'Ask her what?' Ben stood at the sink filling the big kettle.

'If the boys can rehearse in the hall until they can get back in the theatre,' said Libby.

'Already done it.' Hetty's voice came gruffly from the larder. 'Flo's letting 'em have Carpenter's Hall.'

The original barn in Maltby Close had been a barn belonging to Flo's late husband, Frank Carpenter. It now provided a communal space for the residents of Maltby Close to hold gatherings, parties and concerts.

'Oh, well done, Flo,' said Libby. 'Did you tell her, Het?'

'Course I did. Nosy old besom was up here this afternoon as soon as she heard.'

'As long,' said Ben, 'as nobody decides to take a swipe at anybody in the churchyard after rehearsal, like they did last year.'

# Chapter Fourteen

Max, who had entered unheard while Ben was speaking, groaned. 'Oh, don't say that!'

Libby turned to him. 'Well in a way that was lucky for you. It brought you here.'

'And that was luck? With Stan getting killed?'

Ben laid a hand on Libby's arm as she opened her mouth. 'Don't say it, Lib.' He looked at Max. 'That was unnecessary.'

Max had the grace to look ashamed. 'Sorry. Uncalled for, I know.'

'Do you really think it was coming here that got him killed?' asked Peter in an interested voice, though his eyes were snapping furiously.

'No, of course not.' Max sighed and rubbed his face with a hand.

'Brought the killer with you.' Hetty's voice issued from the larder. Max looked startled.

'She's right,' said Libby reasonably. 'Sit down, Max.' Max sat. 'There's only one reason I can think of that would mean coming to Steeple Martin was a contributory factor in Stan's death.'

'What's that?' Ben was frowning.

'If the incidents in London were meant to stop the production and didn't.'

'But whoever it was wouldn't have gone from cockerels and rats to murder!' said Peter.

'No. That's why in a way I believe what Fran says.'

'What? That there are two different people at work?' said Max.

'Well, the rat looks like the London incidents, doesn't it? But the murder – it looks less thought-out.'

'That's true.' Ben nodded. 'Doesn't get anyone any further,

though.'

'So are you going to use the hall to rehearse?' asked Peter.

'Is it suitable?' Max turned to Libby, whose face darkened.

'If you're going to continue to be so ungrateful when everyone's bending over backwards for you, I think we might have to cancel next week's booking.'

After a short, shocked silence, Ben said, 'She's right, you know. We would be perfectly within our rights under the circumstances.'

Max put his head in his hands. 'I don't know what's come over me.'

Peter raised an eyebrow at Libby. 'Well?'

'If,' she said icily, 'you'll behave, I'll take you over to see the hall. I think perhaps I won't introduce you to the lady who organised this. She has a rather forthright manner.'

Ben suppressed a snort and Peter grinned widely.

Max looked up. 'Thank you,' he said quietly.

'Do I get the key from Flo?' Libby asked.

'Here.' Hetty retrieved a bunch of keys from her apron pocket. 'Amy says keep her informed.'

'Amy?' asked Ben.

'She's the Maltby Close warden, isn't she?' said Libby.

'I didn't know they had one,' said Peter.

'Flo says they don't need one, but several of them live alone, so it's good there's someone for them to turn to.' Libby stood up. 'Come on, Max.'

Max stood up and followed meekly to the door.

By now it was quite dark.

'You know Ian and his team are searching all the bedrooms?' said Libby as they walked down the drive.

'Yes, he told me. They've already done ours at the pub.' Max shoved his hands deep into his pockets. 'Look, Libby, I'm really sorry about putting my foot in it back there.'

Libby shrugged. 'It's shock. You wouldn't behave like that normally, I'm sure.'

'No, I don't think I would. I usually try desperately to keep the peace. I was always having to smooth things over for Stan.'

'He didn't strike me as being Mr Popular.'

'No, although they all appreciated his – what shall I say? – business skills. He was very good at seeing they were paid and organising digs, that sort of thing.'

'And was he a good stage manager?'

Max shrugged. 'A bit finicky. He was always cross if the dancers messed up his set.'

'Yes, I've known designers like that.' Libby said with a grin. 'He actually designed this set, didn't he?'

'Yes. It was experimental all the way, you see, so I couldn't afford to spend money on the set.'

'Very effective, though,' said Libby. 'We cross over here.'

They crossed over the high street and into Maltby Close. Libby indicated the larger house at the end of the row of what looked like smaller barn conversions, and were, in fact, the individual bungalows belonging to Flo and others of her age group.

They walked past these and on to the end. 'That's Amy's house, back there, if you should ever need to speak to her, or give the keys back,' said Libby. 'And this, at the other end, is Carpenter's Hall.'

She unlocked the big double doors, flicked up the lights and the room was revealed.

'Good floor,' said Max, bouncing lightly on the polished wood. Chairs were stacked up at either side of the room, and the shutters were down on a bar at the other end to the door.

'They have tea dances in here,' said Libby. 'Our friend Flo was a champion ballroom dancer in her youth and insisted they had a proper sprung floor.'

'She's lucky they could afford it,' said Max, prowling round the edges of the hall.

'She could,' said Libby. 'She named it Carpenter's Hall after her husband. This was converted from one of her husband's barns and she had the rest of the bungalows built to match.'

'I see. And she's the one who said we could borrow the hall?'

'Yes.'

'I must go and thank her.'

'Well, yes, but as I said, be very, very careful or she'll

blister your ears.'

Max grinned. 'I'll remember. Do we go now?'

'Have you finished looking round?'

'Yes. It's perfect. And we only have to cross the road. There's even a piano.'

'Why do you need a piano?'

'For Damian to play. Unless they've got a sound system.'

'Sure to have,' said Libby. 'Check with Flo.'

Lenny opened the door to Libby's tentative knock.

'Come to say thank you, Len,' she said. 'Is Flo here?'

'Here, gal.' Flo appeared with the inevitable cigarette and squinted up through the smoke at Max.

'I just wanted to say thank you very much, Mrs ...' he turned helplessly to Libby.

'Carpenter,' she said. 'Like Carpenter's Hall, remember?'

'Just call me Flo.' Flo turned to Libby. 'Good-lookin' fella, ain't he?'

'Spare his blushes, Flo!' laughed Libby. 'Seriously, it's very good of you. I was going to ask Beth if they could have the church hall, but this is much better.'

'And warmer,' said Lenny. 'And they got the littl'uns in the church hall of a morning.'

'The toddler group, of course,' said Libby. 'So this is better all round.'

'Thank you once again, Mrs – er – Flo,' said Max. 'And –'

'Lenny.' Lenny stuck out his hand. 'I'm Hetty's brother. Ben's uncle.'

'Lenny.' Max shook hands looking slightly bewildered.

'Come on, Max. I expect Flo was in the middle of cooking dinner,' said Libby. 'Bye, you two. See you at the weekend.'

'Is everybody here related?' asked Max, as they walked back towards the high street.

'A lot of them,' said Libby. 'It goes back to hop-picking in the war.'

'I'm sure I'll understand that statement eventually,' said Max, shaking his head.

'Don't worry about it,' said Libby. 'Know what? We forgot to ask about the sound system.'

'We can leave that for now,' said Max. 'Damian will probably enjoy playing his masterpiece again.'

'It's very atmospheric, isn't it? Did he really just work it up while you were workshopping the piece?'

'Yes, incredible, isn't it? He started by playing pieces of well-known works and then began improvising. We all preferred the stuff he was making up as he went along.'

'But then I suppose he had to score it for an orchestra? That's awfully clever.'

'Actually, it's only about ten musicians, but they make a good sound, don't they?'

'Tremendous,' said Libby. 'I do hope it gets to go on. It would be such a shame if it has to be stopped.'

'Yes,' said Max with a sigh. 'I'd feel bad for Alan, too. It was his idea, really.'

Libby gave him a quick, sharp look. 'Yes, the boys were talking about that on our way home this afternoon. Alan seemed to think only you and Damian would get the credit.'

'Did he?' Max turned a shocked face towards her. 'Oh, no, that's not right. It would be billed as "From an idea by Alan Neville, music by Damian Singleton, choreography, Max Tobin." That sounds right, doesn't it?'

'Yes, it does. Do tell him though. Not that he was complaining, he just seemed to take it for granted.'

'He would. He's one of the best, Alan. Most of them are great, but you get the odd wasp.'

'Like Phillip,' said Libby. 'He's amusing, though.'

'And a good teacher, surprisingly. Dan's perhaps a bit less committed than the others, but that's because he's got a new baby, and he's dependable, especially in the non-dancing roles.'

'Tom and Jonathan both seem like nice lads.'

'They are. The ones I don't know well are the auditionees.'

'Paul, Jeremy and Bernie. Paul came with us this afternoon.' Max looked at her. 'What did you think?'

'Bit – intense.'

'Febrile,' said Max.

'Yes,' said Libby, surprised. 'That's a good word. The others said he seemed very keen on folk customs. Did you find that?'

'He was very interested in the story of the witches. Of course, it was more or less all set when he joined, so he took no part in the formulation of the piece.' Max frowned. 'I think he might have been trouble if he'd been around from the beginning.'

'But you never suspected him of having anything to do with the incidents?'

'Oh, no.' Max shook his head. 'For a start, they began before he joined, and he seemed to be more for the witches than against them. Because that's what it seemed to be – someone against the witches. Don't you agree?'

They had reached the top of the drive by now.

'Do you want to tell them all about Carpenter's Hall?' said Libby. 'They'll all be lolling around the sitting-room, I expect.'

'Yes, I will, and tell them we've booked out the whole dining room at the pub tonight. Harry's got too many bookings to cope with us all. Will you join us?'

'I think they'd probably be glad to be rid of me for an evening,' said Libby with a grin, 'but I'll see what Ben says.'

As it happened, Hetty had cooked a roast chicken and asked Ben and Peter to stay for dinner.

'Harry's up to his ears,' said Peter, 'and doesn't want me underfoot, so I'm happy.'

'Me, too,' said Libby, collapsing into a kitchen chair. 'I feel as though I've been through a wringer.'

'Rehearsal rooms sorted?' asked Ben.

'Yes, all done. Have you had to let anyone know about next week?'

'No. As Ian says they can go on, there's no need. We'll need to work overtime to get everything up and running again when they let us in, but no one's going to be put out.'

'What about Stan's family? Has he got any?' asked Peter.

'No idea.' Ben shook his head. 'But they'll have been informed. Max and Sebastian will know the details.'

'Early dinner tonight,' said Hetty from the Aga. 'If you want a drink first, better get it now.'

'I'll dig out a bottle of red,' said Ben.

When drinks were poured and vegetables cooking, Libby said, 'I think we ought to talk to the other two who joined the company with Paul.'

'Why? You said Max told you that the trouble started before they joined.' Peter was leaning back in his chair, his legs crossed at the ankles, the persistent lock of hair falling over his forehead.

'Yes, but two things.' Libby leaned her chin on her hands. 'The onlooker sees more of the game, and second, one of them might have had a score to settle and taken inspiration from what had already happened.'

'That seems highly unlikely.'

'She's right about the onlooker seeing more of the game,' said Ben. 'They might have seen tensions that wouldn't have been obvious to regular members of the company.'

'I'm sure Ian or one of his minions will have talked to them already,' said Peter.

'Not in depth, though,' said Libby. 'Not as in having a chat.'

'And you can?'

'Yes.' Libby beamed. 'I shall offer my services as gofer tomorrow. Seb will be being Stan, so I shall be Seb. I know where things are, so I shall be useful.'

'Don't you go getting yourself into trouble, gal,' said Hetty, carrying a dish of succulent-looking glazed carrots to the table.

'Oh, Het! What trouble could I get into in Carpenter's Hall?' said Libby. 'I'll be fine.'

# Chapter Fifteen

Libby's offer of help was gratefully received by Max and Sebastian.

'Not that I'll need much help while we're in the hall over there,' confided Sebastian, 'as I won't have anything to do, really. Just push the odd prop about, but no Kabuki or anything.'

'What will you need me for, then?' asked Libby. They were in the theatre, Ian having allowed them to collect a few essential bits of equipment.

'Communications, mostly, I expect.' Sebastian piled a variety of items into her arms. 'We've no headsets over there, so I might need you to carry messages – mainly between me and Damian. God, I hope he doesn't muff the piano.'

'Why should he?' asked Libby, surprised. 'He wrote it.'

'But he hasn't played it for ages, has he? It's all been the recorded version.'

'Surely he wouldn't have forgotten it in just these few days. He's got the music scored, hasn't he?'

'I bloody well hope so,' said Sebastian, looking like a worried chipmunk, twitching whiskers and all.

'To be honest, Lib,' said Ian, emerging from the auditorium, 'I shall be glad to have them all out of the way for a bit. Good idea of yours.'

'Flo's actually,' said Libby. 'And they'll still be within easy reach of your handcuffs.'

Ian gave her a wry grin. 'As a matter of fact, I was tempted to get them out after I'd been through their rooms last night.'

'Goodness! What horrors did you find?'

'A fair amount of material that used to be described in the old days as being "within the meaning of the Act". Considered harmless now, of course.'

Ian's fastidious nostrils flared slightly. Libby was amused.

'Come on, now, Ian! You're a thoroughly modern, tolerant copper.'

'Oh, I know. And I fought along with the best of them for equal rights and against homophobia in the force. Some things still bother me, though.'

'Well, I shall keep all the little terrors out of your way unless you want them,' said Libby. 'Now I must go and let Sebastian into his new domain.'

It was a mild, damp, grey day, and as Libby and Sebastian trudged across the high street towards Maltby Close it began to rain.

'Now they'll all complain,' sighed Sebastian.

'Why? Because they'll get wet?'

Sebastian shrugged, as far as he could under his load of props. 'Oh, yes. They'll complain about anything.'

'They seem quite a nice bunch to me,' said Libby.

'Oh, they're all right, I suppose. Stan couldn't –' He broke off.

Libby looked at him. 'Couldn't what?'

What she could see of his face had gone pink. 'Nothing.'

'Couldn't stand them, were you going to say?'

'N-no, not exactly.'

Libby struggled to unlock the door of Carpenter's Hall without dropping her bundle. 'Here we are,' she said. 'Let's drop this lot on the stage and you'd better see what you need to do to get set up.'

Sebastian seemed to be relieved to be let off the hook, and scurried away to the other end of the hall. 'Couldn't stand them'? wondered Libby. Really? Not because some of them were gay, surely? Stan was gay himself. Then why? And not because they were what her mother used to call 'theatricals' – he was one, too.

The door banged shut behind her.

'Morning!' called Damian, sounding cheerful.

'Morning!' Libby called back. 'Piano's up here.'

'Oh, don't need that!' Damian came up beside her and took some of her pile of drapes. 'Where are these going?'

'On the stage, I think. Why don't you need the piano?'

'There's a sound system. I was a bit worried, to tell you the truth. I haven't got the whole score down here with me, as I've got the master recording, but your Ben asked someone or other if there was a sound system here, and there is. So all I've got to do is find it.' He grinned at her happily.

'I expect that was Amy,' said Libby. 'Shall I go and ask her where it is?'

'Oh, yes, that would be great. Is Seb here? I'll see if I can do anything to help.'

He seems extraordinarily chirpy, thought Libby, as she made her way along Maltby Close to Amy's house at the end. Considering there's been a murder.

Amy, a large, jolly person wearing a wonderful, old-fashioned crossover apron, said she would come along and point things out.

'There's the kitchen, m'duck,' she said. 'Kettle, urn and so on. Flo says you was to have whatever you wanted.'

She showed Damian where the sound system was and Sebastian where the limited range of lighting was.

'Not that you'll need that for your practising,' she said. 'But best to know where 'tis. All right now, Miss Libby? I'll be getting along then.' And she disappeared through the double doors.

'Is she for real?' asked Damian, wide-eyed.

'I thought they only existed in films,' said Sebastian, and they exchanged looks of youthful disbelief.

'Yeah – black and white Sunday afternoon ones,' said Damian, and they both dissolved into helpless giggles. It was Sebastian who caught sight of Libby's face, nudged Damian and disappeared smartly behind the curtains on the small stage. Damian retreated to the sound system with a weak smile and Libby sighed. Sometimes she didn't understand the younger generation.

One by one the dancers strolled in and pulled chairs from the stacks round the walls. They collapsed on them in their usual boneless way and muttered to one another. Sebastian returned from behind the curtains.

'The stage is far too small. It's just for a couple of musicians, not a pack of dancers.'

'Max didn't intend you to use the stage,' said Libby. 'This is a sprung dance floor.'

'Oh.' Sebastian looked doubtfully at the polished floor. 'I suppose it's no worse than our rehearsal rooms.'

'That is *not* very gracious, Sebastian.' Libby glared at him.

He went pink. 'Sorry. I don't think I'm reacting to anything normally.'

'Shock, I expect,' said Libby. 'I mean, even if you didn't like him, he was a big part of your life.'

Sebastian looked surprised. 'I didn't say I didn't like him.'

'Yes, you did.' Libby sat down on the edge of the stage. 'Has DCI Connell spoken to you about how Stan rescued you?'

'Rescued … Oh. Yes. Did you tell him about that?'

'I mentioned it. But I didn't know what it was all about, did I? So I couldn't tell him much.'

Sebastian shrugged. 'There wasn't much to tell.'

'But you said – implied – that he more or less had you in thrall. You were living with him.'

Sebastian was going pink again. 'Yes, well…'

'Seb, why are you embarrassed about it? Particularly in this world.'

Sebastian let out a long breath. 'Because you – *everyone* – assumes I'm gay. And I'm not. Stan was, but he hated it.'

Libby was wide-eyed. 'That's what you were going to say earlier. He couldn't stand them – the dancers. Weren't you?'

'Oh, hell.' Sebastian sank down beside her. 'Yes. He was weird, you know. He could be kind, but on his terms. When I was at college he was one of the guest lecturers. Just at that time I'd got myself into trouble because – well, it was drugs. And I couldn't pay. I was suspended from college and Stan found out. I still don't know how he did it, but the next thing I knew was the dealers had stopped chasing me and I moved into Stan's flat. For protection, he said. It's a lovely flat. I suppose I'll have to move now.'

'I suppose you will,' said Libby, amused. 'Are you clean now?'

'Oh, yes. I was never really hooked – I just got out of my depth. And thanks to Stan I got into theatre even without having my degree, so he did me an awful lot of good.'

'So you stayed because you were grateful? And he never made a pass at you.'

'Well – he did, but in a sort of agonised way, if you know what I mean. As far as I can tell he was brought up in an aggressively masculine household, and his male relatives were all as homophobic as anything. I think he was very ashamed of his sexuality.'

'Did he ever talk about his family? Did you meet any of them?'

Sebastian shook his head. 'Only mentioned them in passing. As far as I could tell he didn't see them.'

Libby thought about this. 'Did you know his father appears to have been a well-known criminal?'

'A what?' Sebastian's mouth dropped open.

'We think so. Chap called Wally Willis.'

'Bloody hell.' Sebastian passed a hand across his face.

'It fits, you know,' said Libby. 'He would have been intimidated by his father and his father's friends, so wouldn't dare come out.' Which was rather a leap, as none of them knew Stan and Wally Willis's relationship for sure.

Sebastian nodded. 'That needs some thinking about.' He slid off the stage, then turned back to Libby. 'Do you think that's how he stopped the dealers coming after me?'

'Could be,' said Libby, annoyed with herself for not spotting that. Sebastian nodded and walked off to greet Max, who had just arrived with Jonathan and Tom.

Max called them all to order and proposed warm-up in five minutes. They all unblushingly stripped off, and Libby, used to communal dressing rooms, found herself unable to keep her eyes off the splendid physiques displayed around her. She made her way round the edge of the room to Max's side.

'Anything in particular you want me to do?'

'If you could stay by Seb here and carry any message to Damian. If we need to stop or go back, it'll be easier if you nip round there than having to shout across the boys.'

'OK.' Libby sat down next to Sebastian, who looked at her sideways but didn't speak. Max ran a ten minute warm up, then called for beginners. Just like the real theatre, thought Libby, and immediately castigated herself.

She was only required to take messages to Damian three times, when Max stopped the dance and she had to tell Damian where to go back to. There was no more opportunity for conversation. After an hour, Max called a break and, remembering what Amy had said, Libby hurried into the kitchen and switched on the kettle. As it was, few of the dancers wanted tea or coffee as most had brought the ubiquitous bottle of water. One of those who did, however, was Dan Washburn, the blond giant dancing Roger Nowell.

'This is very kind of you,' he said, accepting a thick white mug. 'Must be a pretty grim time for you.'

Libby nearly said, 'We're used to it', but stopped herself just in time.

'Worse for you all, though. Looks as if Max is going ahead.'

'Yes.' Dan looked uncomfortable. 'Some of us think we shouldn't. We ought to pack it in and go home.'

'Do you? Oh, of course, you have a new baby, don't you?'

'Yes, but it's not that. It seems disrespectful, somehow. I mean, I didn't always get on with Stan – not many of us did – but he's dead, isn't he? And it seems it's something to do with the production, so how can we carry on?'

'I see what you mean,' said Libby, who honestly did. 'It just seems a shame to waste all the hard work.'

'Oh, well, we'd be dancing something even if it wasn't this,' said Dan. 'Even if it was only everyday practice.'

'Hard on Damian, though.'

'Why?' Dan looked surprised. 'He could re-name the work, couldn't he? In fact, we could turn the whole thing into something else. Something that wasn't to do with witches.'

'Do you think that's what the problem is, then?' asked Libby. 'Witches? Someone objects to the portrayal of witches?'

'After all that stuff in London ...' Dan trailed off. 'My wife's a Wiccan, you see.'

'Oh!' Now it was Libby's turn to be surprised. 'Does she

120

object?'

'She doesn't like it much. Thinks it glorifies Black Magic.'

'But –' Libby, about to say it was all hooey and always had been, stopped.

'Yes, I know,' said Dan with a rather sad smile. 'Silly, isn't it. But dead cockerels are pretty horrible, not silly. And murder is even worse.'

# Chapter Sixteen

After washing up the few mugs used by the company, Libby decided she'd done her bit and went home, texting Ben to tell him where she'd gone. Once home, she made herself a proper cup of tea, as she told Sidney, and phoned Fran.

'So there we are,' she concluded. 'Do you think I should report any of this to Ian, or will he accuse me of interfering?'

'He'll try,' said Fran, sounding amused, 'but you haven't been, have you? You've merely been playing your part as a sort of hostess and talking to the guests. In any case, I should tell Ian, especially about Dan's wife being a Wiccan.'

'Why especially that? She's hardly likely to have popped down here, parked the newborn infant and pushed Stan off a tower.'

'No, but it adds a new dimension to the story, doesn't it? And who knows that Dan doesn't agree with her?'

'Oh, I don't see that at all,' said Libby. 'He's the one who didn't want to come down here in the first place.'

'But that could be interpreted as trying to get the production stopped,' reasoned Fran. 'He might have thought the cockerel was the end of it, and when Max said they were coming down here to carry on, he tried to stop it by refusing to come.'

'But he didn't refuse, he came. And he's such a gentle giant.'

'"Murderers I have known,"' said Fran. 'Think about it.'

'I haven't liked most of them,' protested Libby.

'Just because you like Dan doesn't preclude him from being a murderer.'

Libby sighed. 'No, I know. So I tell Ian everything. I wish he had an email address. It would be much easier to send him an email than tell him, especially if I have to leave a voicemail.'

'You could text him.'

'It would take hours! I haven't got lightning thumbs like the kids have.'

'You could always go up to the theatre and tell him. He seems to have established a sort of incident room up there.'

'Has he?'

'He rang me from there a little while ago.'

'He what? Why didn't you tell me?' said Libby indignantly.

'I'm telling you now.' Fran was now definitely amused. 'He wanted, rather diffidently, to know if I'd had any what he called "thoughts" about Stan's death.'

'Oh. I bet he hated asking.'

'I think he did. But I told him I didn't know Stan or anyone else well enough.'

'That hasn't stopped you in the past.'

'I know, but I've told you before, I think that part of my brain, or whatever it is, has been dying off. Look how long it's been since I had any, well, feelings.'

'Three days ago,' said Libby promptly. 'When you told Jonathan, Tom and me that it was a different person who did all the stuff in London to the person who fixed up the Kabuki curtain.'

'Oh.' Fran was silent for a moment. 'But that was nothing, really.'

'It was quite significant. That's why Ian's asking you now.'

'I suppose so,' said Fran reluctantly. 'Anyway, I think you ought to tell him all about your little chats. Won't Harry be taking lunch up for the troops soon? You could go and snaffle a sandwich.'

'Max might have asked him to take the food to Carpenter's. Easier, really, it's just across the road.'

'True. Well, go up anyway. Hetty might give you lunch.'

'I'm not always thinking of my stomach, you know.'

'Not all the time, no.'

'Fran!'

Fran was laughing. 'Oh, go on with you! You know I'm teasing.'

'All right. I'll go up, but I was hoping to spend the rest of today in the conservatory.'

'Painting? Guy will be pleased!'

'Hmm,' said Libby uncrossing her fingers. 'I'll call you later and tell you what Ian says.'

After sending Ben another text saying she was now coming up to the theatre, she threw her latest cape round her shoulders, tossed her phone into her bag and left the cottage, tripping over Sidney on the way out.

The weather had been dry for the last couple of days, so the track from the top of Allhallow's Lane across the Manor farm fields wouldn't be too muddy, and Libby decided to go that way. It had the benefit of being away from the high street and Maltby Close, so neither the dancers nor Harry would see her if they did happen to be going to the Manor for lunch. Sidney, as usual, appeared from behind the row of cottages and trotted along beside her as far as the stile, then sat down for a wash.

She passed the row of rebuilt Hoppers' Huts and headed down towards the back of the theatre. As she got nearer, Ben appeared from the front.

'Thought you might come this way,' he said, 'so I came to meet you. Ian's in my office interrogating.'

'Interrogating who? The company are all in Carpenter's.'

Ben grinned. 'Flo and Lenny. He wanted to ask them about Stan's father.'

'Oh, he's definitely his father, then? Now, why would he want to do that? He's got all the resources of the Force to find out about Wally Willis. By the way, Seb didn't know about him.'

'I think he wanted to know what the public view of him was, and if they knew anything about his family.'

'Has he decided it's something to do with his father, then?' said Libby. 'Doesn't seem very likely.'

'He didn't actually confide in me, Lib.' Ben grinned at her and tucked her arm through his. 'Come on, let's go and see what Mum's got for lunch.'

'You shouldn't let her cook for you every day. You get fed at home.'

'I can't stop her. And Harry's taking lunch over to Carpenter's today, so there's no freebie food.'

'I came up to see Ian. I might miss him if we go into the kitchen.'

'Then go and knock on the door and tell him. He's not likely to be cross about being interrupted with Flo and Lenny.'

Libby followed her knock on the office door by sticking her head round it.

'When you've finished, could I have a word, Ian?'

He stood up. 'You can have one now. We'd finished, hadn't we, Flo? Lenny?'

'Yeah. Just 'avin' a chat, we was.' Flo creaked to her feet and she and Lenny went out into the passage. 'See you in the kitchen, gal.'

'What was it, Libby?' Ian sat down again. 'I hope Ben doesn't mind me appropriating his desk.'

''Course he doesn't.' Libby sat in the chair Flo had vacated. 'I just wanted to tell you a couple of things I picked up this morning.'

She repeated the story of Sebastian's drug problems, and Stan's unwillingness to come out, including her theory that he'd used his father's contacts to get the pressure off Sebastian.

'And finally,' she said, 'it turns out Dan Washburn's wife is a Wiccan and isn't overly keen on the ballet.'

Ian blinked. 'Is that relevant?'

'Well, she might not want it to go ahead. He might have tried to stop the performance by sabotage while they were still in London.'

'He could have simply pulled out, surely?' said Ian.

'Perhaps there were reasons why he couldn't do that. Money, for instance.'

'Perhaps, but I really think that's one of the slenderest motives you could come up with.'

'It is a bit contrived,' conceded Libby.

'However, there might be something in the drugs story.' Ian stared thoughtfully at the empty mug on the desk.

'Fran thought I should tell you.'

Ian lifted his head and smiled. He still fancies her, thought Libby. After all this time.

'Did she tell you I was trying to bully her into having one of

126

her moments?'

'Sort of.' Libby grinned back. 'She says she hardly ever gets them these days. Anyway, your bosses wouldn't like you consulting a witchy woman.'

'I may have been grumbled at in the past, but they leave me alone these days.'

'Now you've reached your exalted rank?'

'Something like that. Now I'm going down to Flo's hall to harry the dancers.'

'They'll be having their lunch.'

'Then I won't be disturbing them, will I?'

'Why don't you send an underling?'

'I shall be taking an underling with me, don't worry.' Ian stood up and came round the desk. Libby caught a whiff of tantalising male cologne and wondered again why he hadn't been snapped up long ago.

I suppose, she thought, following him out of the room, he works too hard to concentrate on relationships. Or maybe he was married in the past and won't risk it again?

'He was ready to risk a relationship with Fran though, wasn't he?' said Ben, when she put this to him.

'But he might only have seen that as a passing fancy,' said Libby. 'Except he still seems very fond of her.'

'He's very fond of you, too,' said Ben. 'That doesn't mean anything.'

'Soup?' asked Hetty.

Libby called Fran when she got back to Allhallow's Lane.

'He was interested about Stan and Seb and the drugs business,' she reported, 'but very dismissive about Dan's Wiccan wife.'

'Hmm.' Fran was quiet for a moment. 'It does seem unlikely.'

'But you said especially to tell him about that.'

'I know. It seemed important. But maybe I got it wrong.'

'Not exactly a moment, then?'

'No … but there was something.'

'Then you ought to tell Ian. He was saying today he was hoping for something from you, and you said you don't get

127

them any more.'

'They aren't as definite as they used to be. But yes, I'll tell him, although I shall feel a complete fool if there's nothing to it.'

'Suppose,' said Libby slowly, 'that there was something there, but not the obvious connection. Not Dan's wife, say.'

'But Wicca itself, perhaps? Yes, that's possible. But still unlikely. Wicca is supposed to be a very gentle, peaceful religion, isn't it?'

'I can't say I know much about it. They believe in the Earth Goddess, don't they?'

'I think there's a bit of confusion about Gods and Goddesses,' said Fran. 'I shall look into it. Anyway, I'll send Ian a quick text saying something ambivalent and leave it to him.'

'OK. I'm hoping to get away from here over the weekend. I had hoped perhaps the company would go back to London for the weekend, but Max wants to keep them working on the assumption that he will be allowed to open next week. And I've had enough of dancers.'

'Poor Hetty will have to stay there.'

'And Peter, too.' Libby sighed. 'Oh, well, I suppose I'll have to stay too, then.'

'You can come down here for the day, if you like. Or you and Ben could come down for supper tomorrow night and stay over.'

Libby brightened. 'Oh, yes! That's a great idea. I'll tell Ben.'

'I'd *ask* him, actually,' said Fran.

'I'm always diplomatic,' said Libby.

Fran's laugh could be heard in Canterbury.

# Chapter Seventeen

On Saturday, there was still a police presence at the theatre, but it was understood that Ian had taken himself and a colleague up to London. Max took the company over to Carpenter's Hall in the morning, Ben went off to the estate timber yard, Libby went shopping and Harry said he couldn't take lunch to the dancers as Saturday was his busiest lunchtime in the restaurant.

'You should have heard them,' Max told Libby later that afternoon when he called in to see her. 'I tried to tell them it had been a perk, and they were very lucky to have had it every day, but it was as though they'd been deprived of basic human rights.'

'What did you do?' Libby was amused.

'Seb and Damian went to the little shop and bought every sandwich they had.'

'Well, at least they're handmade,' said Libby.

Max smiled and fidgeted with his mug. Libby had supplied tea and was now waiting to supply sympathy, which she felt sure was going to be demanded.

'Have you learnt anything more from the boys?' he asked eventually.

'Your boys? No. Apart from the fact that it was drugs which got Seb into trouble when Stan rescued him.'

'Not entirely unexpected.' Max looked dissatisfied. 'At least Seb hasn't got a motive.'

'No.' Libby was surprised. 'Did you think he might have?'

'He was the closest to Stan. And I was sure he didn't really like him.'

'Difficult situation given they were living together.' Libby was unwilling to say anything else.

'Mmm.' Max took a sip of tea and put his mug down. 'Has your policeman said anything to you?'

129

'No. Well, he wouldn't. He's not allowed to discuss cases with members of the public.' Libby crossed her fingers.

'But you've helped him in the past.'

'That doesn't make any difference.'

'But you can make suggestions?'

Libby gave him a wary look. 'How do you mean?'

'If you hear something you can pass it on, can't you?'

'If I think it's relevant. Anybody can, and should. If you hear anything, you should tell the police.' Libby squinted at him. 'Have you heard something, then?'

'Not really.' Max was fidgeting again.

'Yes, you have. That was why you came, wasn't it?'

'You're too shrewd for your own good,' said Max with an attempt at a grin.

'Nosy, is what most people say. Shrewd is polite. Now, come on, out with it.'

Max sighed. 'It's not much, really. I just happened to overhear the two new boys –'

'Which two?'

'Jeremy and Bernie.' Max was surprised. 'Why?'

'Not Paul, then?'

'No-o. Why do you say that?'

'Just go on.'

'Well, it was about him, actually. You know they were all auditionees?'

'Yes.'

'They've stuck together to a degree because they're all new to the company.' Max stared into the fire.

'And?' prompted Libby.

'Jeremy and Bernie were talking about him.'

'I gathered that,' said Libby, after another moment's silence. 'What about him?'

'Apparently, he got thrown out of a panto chorus.'

'That's unusual, isn't it? What for?'

'That's the trouble, they didn't say. They both obviously knew all about it – whether they were in it as well, I don't know. But it sounded – I don't know – nasty.' Max looked up anxiously.

'I see what you mean.' Libby frowned at her mug. 'How can you find out what happened? Has he got a CV? Wouldn't it list all the productions he's been in?'

'Not always. We can check up on, say, the most recent, and anything we're familiar with, but it's only too easy for a dancer to leave something off. Something he's not proud of, or a flop.'

'And they get in on audition, anyway.'

'Yes. And those three were the best. He's a good dancer. Got a sort of inner energy. He can look really evil.'

'You said before that he might have been trouble if he'd been in on the beginning of the project.'

'Yes, and what I heard today seemed to confirm it. Sounds as if he's trouble in a company.'

'But was he around long enough to cause the problems in London?'

'Not the early ones.' Max made a face. 'But certainly the threats of burning and the cockerel.'

'I don't suppose Bernie and Jeremy would talk to me if I asked them about him, would they?'

'I don't see why not. You could try.'

'In an oblique fashion,' said Libby. 'Being tactful, you know.'

Max grinned. 'Aren't you always?'

'Ben and I are away tonight, but we'll be back tomorrow. I'll track you down then. Are you keeping them working tomorrow?'

'Probably, although I'll suggest they take some time off in the afternoon. They've worked really hard.'

'They certainly have, and they've all had a dreadful shock.' Libby stood up. 'I'll have to turn you out now, as I have to get ready to go out, but I'll see you tomorrow.'

Libby reported this conversation to Fran as they stood in the latter's kitchen broaching the first bottle of wine a couple of hours later.

'I would have thought it would be easy enough to do,' said Fran, decanting steamed broccoli into a dish. 'Just sit down with them and ask their advice on panto chorus.'

'All of them?'

131

'No, those two Max was talking about.'

'How do I separate them from the others?'

'I expect they tend to stick together. Isn't that what Max said?'

'I could try. But Paul might be sticking to them, too.'

'He doesn't seem to have done so yet, despite what Max told you. He went with you to Grey Betty, didn't he?'

'Yes.' Libby picked up the bowl of broccoli and the bottle of wine and carried them into the sitting-room.

'Now stop talking about murder and investigations while we eat,' said Guy, taking his place at the table. 'I don't want my salmon ruined.'

After dinner, the men cleared the table while Libby and Fran settled before the huge fireplace.

'Go on,' said Fran, as Guy hovered by the kitchen door. 'You know you're dying to go to the pub.'

'And you're dying to talk about murder,' said Ben with a grin. 'See you later.'

'Much more comfortable,' said Libby, with a sigh of relief as the front door closed.

'Poor men,' said Fran.

'Not a bit of it. It's a treat for them.' Libby reached for the current wine bottle. 'And we can speculate to our heart's content.'

'You mean you can.'

'All right, I can. But you can insert sensible caveats.'

'The most sensible of which would be stay out of it, but I don't see that being popular.'

'We were asked in,' said Libby. 'And Max came to me today. I'd feel I was letting him down if I backed away.'

'How many times have we had this sort of conversation,' sighed Fran. 'Pass the bottle.'

'So, go on. What should I say to Jeremy and Bernie?'

'What do they normally do at this time of year, which pantomimes have they done, is the discipline very different, how many of the company had they met before.'

Libby nodded. 'Makes sense. And just play it by ear after that?'

'You'll have to. They won't have read the script.'

'Why don't you come back with me?'

'Guy's closed tomorrow – it wouldn't be fair. I'll come up on Monday. And meanwhile, I've had another thought.'

'What?' Libby sat up straight.

'What about those other two who left. The original Demdike, was it?'

'Yes, and Chattox. I can't remember their names but I can find out.'

'They were frightened off, weren't they? Would they be angry that the production they helped to form was going on without them?'

Libby shrugged. 'They had the choice, didn't they? They can't really complain.'

'But perhaps they thought it should be cancelled and would be if they left. They might feel that they'd been forced out.'

'Maybe. I suppose I could ask a few more questions.'

'But don't get up Ian's nose. I'm sure he'll have asked about them, too.'

'He went to London today. Perhaps that's what he's doing.'

'There'll be a lot to do at the London end. That's where the whole thing started, after all, and where the company's based.'

They were quiet for a moment, both staring into the fire.

'Do you know, I'm actually surprised Ian's letting them open at all,' said Libby.

'So am I, but he didn't want to let them go back to London, did he? So it was an excuse to keep them here.'

'You mean he might pull it at the last minute?'

Fran nodded. 'Suppose he finds one of the dancers is guilty? He'd have to then.'

'Not if it was a minor character. They could probably still do it …'

'I don't mean from their point of view. I mean from his.'

'Oh.' Libby thought about it. 'I don't really see why.'

'Immaterial at the moment, anyway. We'll have to see what happens.'

'It's been kept very low-profile in the media. Once it gets out we'll have all sorts of journalists and photographers crowding up the drive.'

'Max isn't very famous,' said Fran. 'It shouldn't be too bad. Not as if they've got someone in the cast – do you say "cast" for ballets? – who's an international star.'

'No,' said Libby, thinking back to last Christmas's concert, which *had* featured an international star.

'Meanwhile, I suppose you just keep on keeping on, don't you?' said Fran. 'I hope you're getting paid for all this.'

'Oh, yes. Max, Ben and Hetty thrashed out a deal between them, and Harry struck his own about the lunches. Flo's donating use of Carpenter's for nothing.'

'Must be costing a lot.'

'Yes. I don't know how much, but think what he's got to lose if *Pendle* doesn't go ahead.'

'He won't make much out of a few days' run in Steeple Martin.'

'No, but if it goes well it's booked into a London theatre. You know that.'

'Oh, yes.' Fran smiled. 'I remember. "Off Broadway".'

'Yes.' Libby smiled back. 'I do hope everything's all right. I've got quite fond of them.'

'Even your little wasp?'

'Yes, even him. The only one I really can't take to is Paul.'

'The strange one who's into folklore and you want to talk to the others about?'

'Yes. Gives me the creeps.'

'Well, if he gets thrown out of pantos I'm not surprised.'

Libby shrugged. 'Oh, well. Maybe I'll find out tomorrow.'

'One thing I'm surprised about,' said Fran, looking curiously at her friend. 'Why aren't you more alarmed by all this? The rat, the attack with the Kabuki and now an actual murder. In your own theatre.'

Libby looked surprised. 'I don't know. It doesn't make sense, does it. I should be scared, shouldn't I?'

'Certainly nervous,' said Fran. 'But you seem remarkably calm.'

'Well, so are you.'

'But I'm not closely involved. Don't you worry that

134

whatever is going on, someone might try something with you? Or with Hetty? All the dancers are staying with her.'

'Oh, God,' groaned Libby, 'don't say that! Now I'll have to move into the Manor for the duration.'

Fran was amused. 'Talk it over with Ben. Perhaps he can camp out in his office.'

On Sunday morning, Ben and Libby took Fran and Guy out for breakfast at Mavis's Blue Anchor cafe at the end of Harbour Street.

'It always feels decadent, going out for breakfast,' said Libby. 'The younger generation seem to do it all the time.'

'If they bother to get up at all,' said Guy.

'I wonder if the dancers bother to get up on their days off?' said Fran. 'Sophie doesn't.' Guy's daughter Sophie lived above the gallery and shop.

'Are you actually closing today, then?' asked Ben.

'Yes. Once we're into November I'll have to open for at least half the day, but I thought I'd take this one and next off. So we're coming up to see the show next Saturday.'

'And stay overnight? Good idea,' said Libby. 'So we can return the compliment.'

'Meanwhile, we'd better get back and see if there are any developments,' said Ben. 'I know Max wanted the boys to have some time off today, and we don't want them plaguing the life out of Mum.'

'That's true,' said Libby. 'They do seem to be treating her like a universal Aunt.'

In fact, when they arrived back at number seventeen, it was to find a deputation of dancers on the doorstep.

'What's wrong?' Libby stumbled out of the Range Rover.

'We can't get into the theatre,' said Will Davies.

'You're not allowed into the theatre,' said Ben, following Libby.

'But Max is in there,' said Phillip.

'How do you know that?' asked Libby.

'He told us that was where he was going earlier. We thought he wanted us to go to the hall to rehearse, and he said not just yet, he had to go to the theatre.' Dan Washburn looked round at the others, who nodded in confirmation.

'And then he didn't come back, so we followed him,' said Phillip. 'And we couldn't get in.'

Ben got back into the Range Rover, followed by Libby.

'Don't worry,' he called out of the window. 'We'll go and see.'

'Oh, God,' muttered Libby. 'What's happened now?'

## Chapter Eighteen

'The most likely thing,' said Ben, as he bumped the Range Rover over the rutted track across the Manor land, 'is that he went in and got locked in because he didn't know about the self-locking mechanism on the main doors.'

'But I thought the police were there?' said Libby, hanging on to the grab bar.

'Obviously they aren't. Ian may have sent an all clear.'

They drew up outside the theatre and Ben unlocked the back door.

'Hello!' he called out, and switched the lights on in the scenery dock.

Libby went to switch on the worker lights and auditorium lights from the prompt corner. There was no sign of Max.

'Check the dressing rooms,' said Ben. 'I'll go up to the control box.'

Libby, dreading what she might find, went to check the dressing rooms. They were empty of everything but make up and costumes.

'Found him!' Ben's shout echoed through the building. Libby ran across the stage and up through the auditorium to the spiral staircase leading to the sound and lighting box. Arriving, breathless, at the top, she found Ben with a very sorry-looking Max, who was sitting in one of the swivel chairs with his head in his hands. Libby breathed a sigh of relief.

'What happened?'

'He said he came in here to find something and before he knew what was happening something hit him over the head and that was that. I've called Ian and an ambulance.'

'Don't want an ambulance,' mumbled Max.

'Look, mate,' said Ben, 'when the same thing happened to me a couple of years ago, I said I didn't either. But they made

137

me go, and I'm glad I did. Do you want anyone to go with you?'

'There's someone at the door,' said Libby. 'I'll go and open up.'

Outside she found a huddled group of dancers and a police patrol car. The dancers looked frightened, the policeman bored.

'DCI Connell reported an incident,' he said, shouldering through the dancers, who now looked affronted.

'Yes, come in officer.' Libby stood back for him to pass her. 'Up those stairs.' She turned to the dancers. 'Nothing to worry about. You go back to the Manor and we'll come and see you in a bit.'

'What about Max?' asked Jonathan.

'He's had an accident, but he'll be perfectly all right. They're going to take him to hospital just to be on the safe side.'

The dancers had gone back to looking frightened and muttered among themselves.

'Go on,' urged Libby. 'I'll tell you more when I can.'

They moved off towards the Manor and, after a moment, Libby followed.

'Hetty,' she said, dashing into the kitchen, 'the boys have all come back here – Max has had an accident. Can you rustle up some coffee for them?'

Hetty, with her usual admirable restraint, simply nodded. Libby dashed back out again. As she got to the theatre doors, she heard the ambulance coming up the drive, and waited for the paramedics. After showing them where to go, she sat down at one of the little tables in the foyer and waited for her heartbeat to slow down.

'He doesn't want anyone to go with him,' Ben said, coming down the staircase, 'But someone should. I'll go. Will you come and get us – or just me if they decide to keep him in?'

'Of course, but wouldn't it be better if I just followed the ambulance?'

'Think of the parking charges at the hospital,' said Ben with a grin. 'Besides, we don't want both of us to miss Hetty's Sunday lunch.'

'We'll just miss the wine,' said Libby. 'I'll go and tell her.'

At the door she met an irritated-looking Ian.

'What's the matter with this place? All these bangs on the head. Where is he?'

'Sound box. There's an officer with him.'

Ian didn't reply, merely took the spiral staircase two at a time to add to the crowd inside the box.

Ben reappeared.

'Ian says not to go with him. He's going to follow the ambulance, so he'll make sure everything's all right.'

'So has he said any more?'

'No. He can't even remember what he wanted, or why he went up to the sound box. I mean, there's nothing up there – not even the sound track. Damian's got that to use in the hall.'

'Perhaps he wanted to have a look at the lighting plot.'

'He wouldn't understand it even if he knew how our computer system worked,' said Ben. 'He's not exactly technically minded.'

'Do we know how he got in?'

'Oh, he has a key. It's more a question of how whoever hit him got in.'

'And were they allowed back in today?'

'Apparently, yes. One of the officers gave Max the all clear when they left yesterday evening.'

'But only Max had a key?'

'Yes. He asked Hetty this morning if she knew when we would be back, and of course she didn't know, so we assume he decided to come over on his own. Look, they're coming down.'

The paramedics were gingerly bringing Max down the spiral stairs on what looked like a folding chair, followed by Ian and the uniformed patrol officer.

'I think they'll keep him in,' said Ian, stopping by their table. 'He's a bit dazed and doesn't seem to know what happened. He's lucky it wasn't worse.'

'Do you know what hit him?' asked Libby. 'It couldn't have been an accident?'

'No. There's nothing up there that could have done it, and nothing with any traces of blood. We'll know more when a

139

doctor's seen him. Meanwhile, I'll get the team back in.' He sighed. 'What a disaster. Why didn't he wait for you to come back?'

'No idea. Whatever it was it must have been urgent.'

'If nothing else, it proves that our killer's still here and is part of the company,' said Ian. 'Now, I'm sending this officer to hold the fort until my team gets back here. He has to keep an eye on our lovely boys. Are they all at the Manor?'

'All the dancers. I don't know about Damian and Sebastian,' said Libby.

'I'll call in there on the way past and send them up here.'

'Do you trust them to come up on their own?' asked Ben.

Ian tutted. 'I'll bring them,' he said shortly. 'Will you go and join the others?'

Ben's eyebrows rose. 'Are we suspects? We've only just got back from Nethergate.'

Ian grinned. 'No, I want to know what you can pick up from the gossip.'

The dancers in the large sitting-room were surprisingly quiet. The uniformed officer stood self-consciously by the door.

'DCI Connell has given us permission to tell you what has happened,' announced Libby. The officer looked startled. 'And to ask you to remain here. He will be sending his team back to check over the theatre and ask if you know anything about what happened this morning. He is bringing Damian and Sebastian up here to join us.'

'What *did* happen?' came a chorus.

Libby moved to the big urn to pour herself a cup of coffee. 'Apparently, Max let himself into the theatre and went to the sound box. Then someone hit him on the head. He doesn't know what happened, or even why he went over there.'

'But he'll be all right?' said Paul.

'The paramedics seem to think so, but DCI Connell thinks the hospital will keep him overnight.'

Damian and Sebastian burst through the door, both looking pale.

The dancers all turned to them.

'What are we going to do?' said Tom.

'Don't ask me,' said Sebastian. 'I was only Stan's assistant.'

'And I'm only the bloody rehearsal pianist,' said Damian, and sat down suddenly on the floor.

'You all right, mate?' Young Lee went down on his haunches next to him.

'Oh, God, I don't know,' said Damian. 'No, I'm not. This is all so awful.'

'Come on,' said Libby, 'let's all make ourselves comfortable. Can I get you coffee, Damian?'

Eventually, she got them all settled on the large sofas and armchairs under the dubiously watchful eye of the officer. Ben grinned at him and left for the kitchen.

'So tell me what happened this morning,' said Libby, looking round at the serious faces. 'Did Max come up here first thing?'

'He was just finishing breakfast in the pub when I came down,' said Damian, who seemed to have taken hold of himself.

'And he was just going out of the door when I arrived,' said Sebastian.

'Did he say why he was going to the Manor?'

'He said he was going to the theatre,' said Damian.

'One of the policemen had come over to the hall yesterday afternoon to tell us the theatre was clear,' said Will. 'It was when Max had gone over to see you.'

'Did he say anything to any of you?' Libby asked the dancers.

'We were all in here having breakfast. He looked in and asked if we'd seen you and Ben because he wanted to go to the theatre,' said Dan. 'We said we hadn't, and he went off to the kitchen to ask Hetty.'

'So everyone knew where he was going,' said Libby, frowning.

'But we were all here!' Paul's voice was high. 'It couldn't have been one of us. None of us could have been hiding in the theatre.'

There were murmurs of agreement from all corners of the room.

'And Ben and I weren't even here,' said Libby. 'Weird, isn't it?'

'But what are we to do?' repeated Tom. 'They'll close the theatre down again, and we were supposed to open on Wednesday.'

'If Stan was here,' began someone, and then stopped.

'Once the police have talked to you,' said Libby, 'I should go and find yourselves some lunch at the pub – Harry's always extra busy on Sundays – and either go over to the hall on your own, or come back here. You might know a bit more by tomorrow. Are you ready to go, do you think?'

'Oh, yes.' Jonathan looked round at his colleagues for agreement. 'As long as we keep going on Monday and Tuesday, I think we could go up on Wednesday, even if Max isn't there. What do you think, Damian?'

'I suppose so. I don't really know. I don't have to play, do I?'

'No, but you know what it should look like,' said Libby.

'Yes.' Damian shrugged.

'Very different from the cheerful person of Friday morning,' Libby told Ben when she went into the kitchen. 'The police have arrived. There are scenes of crime in the theatre and a couple of plain clothes bods questioning the dancers. But I don't see how it could have been any of them. As young Paul said, they were all together. None of them could have been hiding in the theatre.'

'I do wonder what Max wanted in the lighting box,' said Ben. 'There's nothing up there.'

'Perhaps he was going to leave a note or something. For Peter, perhaps. He doesn't know where Pete and Harry live, so he'd have had to leave it there, because the caff isn't open yet.'

'Was he intending to rehearse there today, I wonder?' said Ben. 'He didn't say anything to the dancers?'

'No. The police told him they could use the theatre when they finished rehearsing yesterday. None of them said what they did or said last night.'

'And he didn't tell them this morning?'

'No. Just came in to ask if anyone had seen us.'

'That's right,' said Hetty. 'D'yer want dinner at lunchtime or

142

dinnertime today?'

Ben and Libby both laughed. 'Bringing us down to earth as usual, Mum,' said Ben. 'What's more convenient for you?'

'I'm a bit behind with the extra coffee, so six o'clock do yer?'

They agreed, just as a knock sounded at the front door.

'I'll go,' said Ben, levering himself away from the sink where he was leaning.

'It'll be more police,' Libby said to Hetty.

But it wasn't.

'I'm so sorry to bother you,' said the tall young man in the beautifully cut suit. 'I'm looking for Max Tobin.'

# Chapter Nineteen

'You'd better come in,' said Ben. 'At least, as long as you aren't a journalist.'

The young man looked shocked. 'No, of course I'm not.'

'Hey, look – it's Owen!' called a voice from the large sitting-room.

The young man turned round to greet the crowd of dancers who piled out into the corridor.

Ben, joined by Libby, stood and watched as greetings were exchanged. Eventually, he butted in.

'Perhaps you'd better come with me and I'll explain what's been happening.'

'Happening? Oh – I know about the murder …'

The dancers had fallen silent.

'Yes, go with Ben,' said Tom, giving the young man a little push. 'He'll tell you.'

Libby led the way into the kitchen and offered coffee or tea. The young man declined both.

'So you're Owen, a friend of Max's, I take it?' said Ben.

'Max's partner,' said Owen. 'Owen Talbot. I run the school.'

'Ah,' said Libby. 'Good to meet you, Owen. This is Ben Wilde, my partner, his mother Hetty Wilde, and I'm Libby Sarjeant. We run this place between us.'

'Yes, Max said.' Owen smiled. 'He was very impressed. He does know I'm coming today, but he wasn't at the hotel, and I didn't know where this rehearsal room you've been using is.'

Libby and Ben looked at each other, Ben gave a slight nod and Libby launched into an explanation of the morning's events, while Owen became paler and paler.

'You sure you don't want coffee?' said Hetty gruffly, when Libby ground to a halt.

'Perhaps I will, now,' said Owen. 'Then I must go to the

hospital.'

'Of course you must, but we ought to check that he's still there. For all we know they might have taken one look at him and decided to send him home,' said Libby.

'I suggest we call DCI Connell first and ask him,' said Ben. 'He went to the hospital with Max, you see.'

'You do it, Ben,' said Libby. 'Ian will only get cross with me.' She turned to see a bewildered expression on Owen's face. 'The DCI is a friend of ours. It can get awkward. So tell me, are you just down here for a visit?'

'Yes. We've given the students the week off and they're all coming down to see the piece on Thursday. Max seemed pleased last night that it was going to be able to go ahead even after all the trouble.'

'You spoke to him last night? Did he say anything to you? Out of the ordinary, I mean? Only no one seems to know why he went over to the theatre this morning, or more specifically into the sound box, not even Max himself.'

'He doesn't? He could speak, then?'

'Oh, yes. Grumbled about having to go in an ambulance.'

'That sounds like Max.' Owen managed a slight smile. 'But no, he didn't. I just confirmed that I'd be down today and he said he'd give the boys an afternoon off.'

'Nothing else at all?'

'No – just trivial, ordinary, everyday stuff. I said should I bring his mail down, that sort of thing.'

'Does he get much mail?' asked Libby. 'Only I don't any more. It's all email and texting.'

Owen smiled. 'Ours, too, but we do get proper post. Student applications, that sort of thing. The occasional letter. We got one this week, as it happens, from a friend of ours in Italy.'

'That'll cheer him up, won't it?' said Libby. 'Anyway, here's Ben. What did Ian say?'

'He says go by all means, he'll meet you in the A and E department. He thinks Max will be discharged after some X-rays, and asked if you would bring him back here?'

'Not home to London?'

'He said here. That may be Max's choice.'

146

Owen finished his coffee and stood up. 'Thank you for the coffee and for filling me in.' He sighed a little. 'I expect I shall see you soon.'

'He was nice,' said Libby, when Owen had been seen off in his racy black saloon.

'I wonder why Max has never mentioned him?' said Ben.

'No reason to, I suppose. I wanted to ask him loads of questions about the incidents in London.'

'Libby!' warned Ben. 'Don't start prying. And why would he know any more than any of the others?'

'Well, you never know. What about other students? The ones who aren't in the company? Was there any jealousy?'

'I expect Ian will ask all those questions, so I shouldn't worry about it, if I were you.' Ben turned to his mother. 'Is there anything we can do for you, Mum?'

'No, you get off. Tell Peter and Harry to come to dinner, too.'

Libby went into the large sitting-room, where she found three police officers talking to the dancers.

'Sorry to interrupt,' she said, 'but just to say Ben and I are off now, and Max told Owen that you were having the afternoon off, so we'll see you all tomorrow.'

At the bottom of the Manor Drive they turned right and knocked on Peter and Harry's cottage door.

'Hello! To what do I owe this honour?' Peter, in jeans and a dilapidated sweatshirt, opened the door.

'We bring news,' said Libby, 'and to invite you and Hal to Hetty's for dinner at six.'

'Well, come in, then, and I shall offer you a libation.'

Provided with beer for Ben and red wine for Libby, between them they told Peter this morning's news.

'Good Lord,' said Peter. 'How spectacular. I suppose the young man couldn't be bluffing and came down hours earlier to hit Max over the head?'

'He couldn't have got into the theatre,' said Ben. 'That's the stumbling block.'

'What about the back door. That's the way you got in.'

'Because I've got a full set of keys. So have you. But

147

nobody else has. So even if someone had stolen Max's own keys – which they hadn't, because he opened the theatre himself – they wouldn't have the keys to the back door. And all the doors are alarmed, anyway.'

'We don't always set the alarm, though,' said Libby. 'We're rather lax about it, but there isn't much to steal.'

'There's a hell of a lot of very expensive equipment in the FX box,' said Peter.

'I suppose so,' conceded Libby, 'but think how long it would take to get it all out. And Hetty would be sure to hear.'

'I don't suppose burglars would know or care about Hetty,' said Ben.

'Anyway, it means Owen Talbot couldn't possibly have been the one who bopped Max on the head,' said Libby. 'In fact, at the moment it looks as though nobody could have.'

'If only we knew what he was looking for,' said Ben.

'I expect he feels the same,' said Peter. 'Now do you want another drink, or are you going to save yourselves for tonight?'

Declining, Ben and Libby strolled back up the Manor drive and round to the back of the theatre, where Libby remembered just in time that they'd left the Range Rover. When they got back to Allhallow's Lane, Ben opened a tin of soup for lunch while Libby phoned Fran to keep her up to date.

'So that's that, so far,' she finished. 'It's obviously all tied in, but how and why, goodness alone knows.'

'Doesn't it seem all a bit cack-handed to you?' asked Fran.

'Cack-handed? How do you mean?'

'Amateurish.'

'I expect most murders are amateurish unless they're gangland killings,' said Libby. 'You don't train to become a murderer.'

'No, but spur of the moment. Opportunistic.'

'My argument still applies.'

'All right.' Fran laughed. 'But it seems as though Stan's murder and the attack on Max were both a reaction to something. Not planned like the rigging of the rat. Or the Kabuki curtain.'

'That's true,' said Libby thoughtfully. 'Like a small boy

'lashing out, sort of thing.'

'Exactly,' said Fran. 'Not that the idea would gain any weight with Ian.'

'It sounds exactly like Paul, though,' said Libby.

'The folklore enthusiast? How did he seem this morning?'

'Much the same as the others. It was he who pointed out that none of them could have hit Max as they were all together in the Manor.'

'Not all,' said Fran.

'Eh?'

'Surely Sebastian and Damian were still at the pub?'

'Oh, golly! So they were! They both even told us about seeing Max as they were having breakfast. Ian had to collect them to bring them up to the Manor.'

'So there you are. Two people who weren't in the Manor.'

'Yes, but they were together having breakfast at the pub. And there's still the problem of how whoever it was got in. We've gone over the key problem and no one could have got in unless they'd pinched Max's keys and had copies made.'

'Or Ben's, or Peter's.'

'They couldn't have got hold of those. Anyway, my soup's ready, so I'm going now. As soon as I get any more news I'll let you know.'

Sunday afternoon passed pleasantly and at a quarter to six they walked back to the Manor anticipating Hetty's traditional Sunday roast.

'Lamb!' said Libby coming through the door.

'With garlic and rosemary,' said Peter, from his seat at the kitchen table.

'Fetch the wine, Ben,' said Hetty. 'Sit down, gal. Nothing to do.'

'Have you heard anything from the boys, Het?' Libby asked.

Hetty shook her head. 'They all trooped off to the pub when the coppers went. I heard some of 'em come back during the afternoon.'

Ben reappeared with two dusty bottles.

'A crowd of them went past the caff,' said Harry, 'and a couple of them looked in to see if I had any room, but I didn't. I hope they all got served at the pub.'

'So we don't know if the hospital discharged Max,' said Ben.

'And Ian hasn't told us a thing,' said Libby.

Everyone laughed.

After a convivial dinner, Libby looked into the large sitting-room and found a few of the dancers there watching television.

'No news?' she asked. They all shook their heads, and Libby retreated.

'We could call in at the pub on the way home,' said Libby, as she and Ben loaded the dishwasher after Hetty had retired to her own little sitting-room.

'We all could,' said Harry from the sink, where Hetty had generously allowed him to scrub some of her pots, a job she normally preferred to do herself.

'Get a move on, then,' said Peter, 'or they'll have all gone home to bed.'

After excusing themselves to Hetty, they made their way down to the drive to the pub, where, along with Damian and Sebastian, Owen was sitting with Jonathan, Tom and Phillip.

'What happened?' Libby asked Owen. 'Did they let him out?'

Owen pushed back his chair and stood up. 'Oh, yes, I should have told you. He's upstairs in bed, with strict instructions to stay there until the doctor sees him in the morning. He wanted to thank you.'

'What for?' said Ben.

'Finding him, I think,' said Owen. 'Let me get you a drink.'

'Ours are on the way,' said Ben, nodding towards the bar, where Harry and Peter stood in conversation with the barmaid.

'So what did DCI Connell want to know?' Libby asked. 'And what could Max tell him?'

'Nothing.' Owen shrugged. 'He really doesn't know why he was there and doesn't remember anything about being attacked.'

'Did he have anything with him?' asked Ben. 'That might give us a clue.'

'Again, nothing. Normal wallet, car keys and hotel key. Oh,

and theatre keys.'

'Oh, dear.' Libby shook her head. 'And I suppose we don't know if the police found anything at the theatre.'

'I only spoke to the inspector before I saw Max,' said Owen. 'He seemed rather irritated, I thought. Perfectly polite, of course.'

'Yes, he's got a lot to be irritated about,' said Libby. 'We'll let you get on with your drink. Maybe see you tomorrow.'

She and Ben joined Peter and Harry at their normal table by the fireplace in the other bar.

'Nothing,' she told the other two. 'A complete mystery. Max has no memory of the event.'

'Did I, when I got hit on the head?' asked Harry.

'Yes, I think so,' said Ben, 'and I know I did when I was.'

'So did I, when I was,' said Libby. 'Although mine wasn't very hard, was it. Wow. Think of that. All three of us having been hit on the head.'

'In the course of *your* enquiries,' said Ben, pointedly.

'Oh, well,' said Libby comfortably. 'Perhaps he'll have remembered by the morning. And who knows what might happen then?'

# Chapter Twenty

When a uniformed officer turned up on the doorstep of number seventeen Allhallow's Lane on Monday morning, it was to inform Libby that she could open up the theatre.

'Really made my heart sink,' she told Ben. 'I wondered what on earth had happened now.'

'Good news, though,' said Ben. 'We'd better tell Max and see what he wants to do.'

'If Owen lets us get near him.' Libby stirred her tea. 'Should we call in or just phone the pub?'

'Phone the pub,' said Ben. 'I'll do it.'

Owen, who said Max seemed a lot better this morning, said he would ring them back when they'd talked it over. When he did, it was to say that Max would like the dancers to rehearse on-stage and he, Owen, would run the rehearsal.

'I know more or less everything about the piece,' he said, 'and there isn't anyone else, is there? With Stan gone.'

'I suppose he's right, really,' said Libby, as she and Ben walked up the drive to the theatre. 'Sebastian couldn't do it, he hasn't a background in dance and they wouldn't take any notice of him.'

'Damian probably could,' said Ben. 'He knows the music, after all.'

'You get the feeling that the dancers … well, I don't know – but they almost seem to hold him in contempt.'

'Do they?' Ben looked surprised.

'Just a feeling I got.' Libby stopped in front of the Manor. 'I'll go and tell the boys the good news, if they haven't already heard, while you open the theatre.'

The dancers had already heard. Owen had called many of them and asked them to pass the news on to the others, so Libby found them all ready for action in the large sitting-room, with their sports bags and bottles of water.

'Good to be back to normal,' said Tom, grinning at her.

'Hardly that,' said Libby. 'Are you all happy to be working with Owen?'

'Course!' Tom looked surprised. 'He runs the school. Max and he set up the business together.'

'And Sebastian will be all right with the backstage stuff, will he?'

'There's not much to do,' said Tom. 'Except that bloody curtain.'

'Yes. Will you continue to use that?'

'I don't know. Nobody's keen.' Tom shouldered his bag and saluted with his water bottle. 'See you later.'

After Libby had been into the kitchen to inform Hetty, unnecessarily, of the state of play, she called Harry, who agreed with much sighing and posturing to resume provision of lunches despite Monday being his day off. Then she went across to the theatre to inform the company that they wouldn't starve today.

'Very difficult,' murmured Owen, after she'd delivered her announcement. They were watching the dancers warming up, and Libby was quite frankly astounded at the positions achieved.

'It's like watching human snakes,' she said.

Owen smiled. 'I suppose it is, a bit. But what I was going to tell you was – they don't want to use the curtain.'

'Tom mentioned it to me back at the Manor,' said Libby, 'and I should think Sebastian least of all. Who can blame them?'

'What do you think we should do?' Owen turned a worried face towards her.

'Me? Good Lord, I've no idea. Why don't you rehearse without it today and then talk to Max later? I assume you're going to do a straight run, or whatever you call it in dance.'

Owen smiled again. 'Yes, we are, to get it back into their heads and for me to see it.' He stepped forward and clapped his hands, bringing the movement on-stage to a halt. 'OK, beginners. Straight through from the top.' He turned to look up at the FX box. 'You ready, Damian?'

There was a moment of silence, then Damian's head appeared in the window.

'Er – I don't quite know what's wrong, but the equipment seems to be stuck.'

Everyone stood perfectly still until Ben appeared at the side of the stage.

'Don't worry,' he called, calmness itself in jeans and a sweatshirt. 'I'll come up.'

Now a buzz of conversation broke out on the stage and Owen turned to Libby.

'That was where Max was found, wasn't it?'

'Yes,' said Libby brightly. 'I expect we'll find that the SOCOs messed up the settings or something.'

'SOCOs?'

'Scenes of Crime Officers. The people you see in the white spacesuits.'

'Oh.' Owen looked up to the box, where the top of Ben's head could now be seen. 'What do we do if it won't work?'

'I don't know,' said Libby. 'We can't borrow sound equipment from anywhere else – it isn't portable.'

Peter appeared at her side. 'We can, you know. It won't be as good, but if someone has a good-quality player, or a computer that still takes CDs, we can plug that in.'

'I have,' said Libby. 'But wouldn't it be better to upload it and play it direct from the computer? Or the tablet. There's a tablet up there, isn't there?'

'Yes,' said Peter. 'I shall go up and join the rescue party.'

'Thanks,' said Owen and turned back to the stage. 'Take ten, but don't go far.'

Ben disappeared from the box and Libby went into the foyer to catch him as he came down.

'I've got the CD,' he said. 'I'm just going to upload it and send it to the tablet as an MP3. That will go through the speakers.'

'I thought that all out by myself!' said Libby. 'I am so impressed. What had happened?'

'I'll tell you later. Got to get this done.' And Ben vanished out of the main doors.

Peter peered down from the top of the spiral staircase. 'Looks like another attempt at sabotage.'

'Oh, no! How did the police miss it?' Libby sat down at one of the little tables with a thump.

'I doubt they were looking for damage to electrical equipment, and it didn't show.'

'Max must have disturbed them.'

'Them?'

'Whoever it is,' said Libby. 'He, she or it. I wonder why he doesn't remember?'

Owen came out of the auditorium doors. 'I've just called Max to tell him what's happened. I asked him if he thought anyone was in the box when he arrived, and he said no. He can remember that much – going up the stairs and into the empty box.'

'They must have hidden when they heard him coming,' said Libby.

'We still don't know how they got in, though,' said Peter, slowly descending the staircase.

Damian appeared next, looking pale and distracted.

'I don't know what we're going to do,' he said. 'How can we go on?'

'Brace up, lad,' said Owen in a bad northern accent. Libby smiled at his brave attempt at encouragement.

'It'll be fine, Damian,' said Libby. 'Ben and Peter will sort it out, you see if they don't.'

'However,' said Peter, 'you must report it to the police, Lib.'

'Oh, God. If I do that they'll close us down again.'

Owen and Damian looked at each other.

'Do we have to?' asked Owen. 'After all, it hasn't harmed anyone.'

'But it has,' said Damian. 'It harmed Max.'

'That's true,' said Peter. 'You haven't got a choice, Lib.'

Ben emerged triumphant through the theatre doors. 'Sorted. Let's go and check it out,' he said.

Libby put a hand on his arm. 'Ben, Peter says we must report it to Ian.'

He looked surprised. 'Of course. I've already done it.'

'Oh.' The other four looked at one another.

'And how did he take it?' asked Libby. 'Does he want us to shut up shop again?'

'He didn't say so,' said Ben. 'He said his people had done a thorough job up here yesterday but they could hardly have taken apart the equipment. He seemed to think it gave the perpetrator a motive.'

'That's what we thought,' said Libby. 'So we can go ahead?'

'Yes, once I can get upstairs.' Ben glanced at Damian sitting despondently on the bottom step. 'Come on, Mozart. Let's get going.'

Peter grinned and followed them up, and Owen and Libby returned to the auditorium. Within a very few minutes the opening chords of Damian's score echoed through the space and galvanised the dancers into movement. Owen went up to the stage to speak to Sebastian, and as the lighting changed *Pendle* began to come to life.

There was a noticeable hesitation as the moment for the reveal of the Kabuki curtain came closer, but they carried on and looked relieved when nothing happened at the appointed time. The dancing seemed to take on a new energy after that, Libby thought, watching entranced.

They broke for lunch when Harry appeared demanding to know where they all were. Owen was smiling, and all the dancers were buoyant. Libby left them to it and went to help Hetty with the tea and coffee urns.

'You must be relieved,' she said to Damian, when she went back to the large sitting-room.

'Of course,' he said wanly.

'You don't look it.'

'Well ...' He frowned down at his plate. 'To tell you the truth I'm beginning to think we ought to call it off.'

'Oh! Why? Everyone's worked so hard. *You've* worked hard. It's your first proper score, isn't it?'

'But look at the misery it's caused. All the stuff in London and now Stan murdered and Max attacked. I tell you, it's jinxed.'

He looked so unhappy Libby was compelled to put an arm

157

round his shoulders and give him a quick hug.

'Don't say that too loudly – you know how superstitious theatricals are. Actors, dancers, musicians – well, *you* obviously are.'

He gave her another weak smile. 'Poor old Stan was, too.'

'Stan?' Libby's voice rose. 'He was the last one to be superstitious I would have thought. He seemed so down to earth.'

'Hard as nails, I bet you thought? Well, he was, in a lot of ways. But show him a black cat or a magpie and he spat venom.'

'Did he? Then he must have been particularly upset by all that mischief in London.'

Damian's face was a picture. 'Oh, he was.'

'Oh?' prompted Libby, when he didn't say any more.

'He thought the show should come off,' said Damian eventually with a sigh.

'But he carried on working on it, didn't he?'

'He's a salaried employee, isn't he? Or was,' Damian corrected himself.

'I suppose so,' said Libby. 'I'd better leave you to get on with your lunch.'

She wandered over to where Ben was deep in conversation with Peter. Harry was again at the centre of an admiring group of dancers.

'Did we know Stan thought the show should come off before they came down here?' Libby butted in to the conversation.

Ben's brow wrinkled.

'Did we? Can't remember.'

'I think it was mentioned,' said Peter. 'I'm sure you said something about it.'

Owen appeared behind Peter's back.

'Libby, Max has asked if you could possibly go down and see him this afternoon.'

'Yes, of course. Any particular reason?'

'He said he wanted to talk everything through. I think he's worried.'

# Chapter Twenty-one

Max was sitting in an armchair in front of the window overlooking the high street. His head was bandaged and he looked pale – and unshaven. Quite unlike the Max Libby was used to.

'Don't get up,' she said, going over and dropping a kiss on the unbandaged part of his head. 'Are you sure you're up to this?'

'Of course I am.' He put out a hand and Libby took it. 'I'm so grateful to you for everything, Libby. Especially for finding me.'

'Don't be silly.' Libby squeezed his hand and let it go. 'And it was Ben who actually found you.'

'I know.' Max sighed. 'We've been nothing but a nuisance to you ever since we arrived, have we?'

'Nonsense. You've added a bit of excitement to our lives.'

'I thought you had more than enough of that, according to Andrew.'

'Occasionally.' Libby grinned. 'No one would believe us if we were in a book.'

'Anyway, it can't be pleasant actually having murder on the premises. But what I wanted to say was, do you think I should pull it now?'

'Pull it?' Libby stared in astonishment. 'Of course not. If the police have given you permission to carry on, why should you? Everyone's put so much into the show.'

'But think what's happened. All the incidents in London, then the rat, the knife in the curtain and – Stan.'

'And you. And the sound equipment,' added Libby. 'But you're still OK, more or less, and Ben and Peter have sorted the sound.'

'I know, Owen told me. But don't you see, all this is

designed to stop the show. And I think that's what we should do.'

'Then whoever it is has won,' said Libby. 'And we might never know who killed Stan and attacked you.'

'I'm not sure I care any more. I just don't want anybody else put at risk. Tell me, what are the boys saying? Owen didn't really get anything from them yesterday.'

'Well,' said Libby carefully, 'they all seemed very pleased this morning. It went terribly well.'

'Even the curtain?'

'We – I mean they – didn't use it.'

Max nodded. 'What I meant was, have any of them said they thought we shouldn't go on?'

Libby sent him an assessing look. 'Dan didn't think you should when I spoke to him the other day. Or at least, he said his wife didn't. Did you know she was Wiccan?'

'No!' Max looked taken aback. 'I wonder why he didn't say?'

'Now, why do you think? However, he's staying. He didn't even go back to London for the night on Saturday. As for the others, I don't know. Damian, perhaps. He seems very thrown by it all.'

'Scared, do you think?'

'Definitely. Given half a chance he'd be hot-footing it back to London with his tail between his legs.'

'Are none of the others scared?'

'I think so, but they aren't actually saying so.' Libby looked down at her hands. 'And you still can't remember what happened yesterday?'

'No.'

'How about we go through the events leading up to it and see if anything strikes you?'

Max frowned. 'From when?'

'Why don't we start from the day before? Your phone call with Owen, for instance.'

'I don't see what that's got to do with anything.'

'You were going to the theatre for something. Therefore, something must have triggered that. The only thing different

160

from your routine down here was the phone call. So what did you talk about?'

'God, I don't know.' Max shifted in his chair impatiently. 'Just, you know, how are you? Any problems, that sort of thing.'

'Owen asked if he should bring your mail down.'

'There was no need. It was mostly business stuff that could wait.'

'And a letter from a friend in Italy.'

'Oh, Sergio, yes. But that was just a letter from a friend – addressed to both of us.'

'Nice to get an actual letter,' said Libby. 'I was saying to Owen, I hardly get any these days. It's all social media or email.'

'Yes.' Max smiled. 'Sergio's a bit old-fashioned. He lives in the wilds with no mobile reception and no Wi-Fi, so all his communications are by letter.'

'How does he manage?' asked Libby. 'Doesn't he need a computer for work?'

'No. When he needs to he goes to Perugia.'

'Where's Perugia?' asked Libby.

'Capital of Umbria. Lovely place.'

'Oh, Anne and Patti – remember them? – they went to Umbria a couple of years ago on a painting holiday. They said it was beautiful. Anyway, that doesn't get us any further, does it?'

'No. And that was it, really. We talked about Owen coming down here, getting the dog looked after and shutting the school for the week. That was it.'

'Nothing there, then. And nothing happened on Saturday evening?'

'No. I went to bed quite early.' He frowned. 'There was something …'

'Something happened?'

'No, something I thought of. And I thought about it in the morning. But I don't know what it was.'

'You went off to the theatre early. Seb and Damian said you'd finished breakfast by the time they came down.'

'Yes.' Max was still frowning. 'I was in a hurry.'

'Well it's a start,' said Libby. 'If you've remembered you thought of something and you were in a hurry, you might remember what the thing was. Or is.'

'I suppose I might.' Max sighed and leant his head back against the chair. 'But I'm still not sure we shouldn't pull it.'

'How about if I go back and ask Owen to take a straw poll? And if we check with the police? If they all said to go ahead with it, would you feel happier?'

'I might,' said Max with a tired smile. 'It's worth a try.'

Libby stood up. 'I'll get back, then. Is there anything you want before I go?'

Max started to shake his head and winced. 'Must remember not to do that. No thanks, Libby. I can ring room service if I want anything.'

'Oh, do they have room service? I didn't think they did.'

'I think it's just for me, under the circumstances,' said Max with another faint grin. 'I suspect your policeman sorted it out.'

'He's good at that,' said Libby. 'Right, I'm off. I'll let you know what I find out.'

She walked back to the theatre thinking hard. Max was no help at all, and might well decide to pull the production whatever the general consensus of opinion was. She could understand that, of course; when you took all the incidents, threats and attacks together it could seem madness to continue and simpler all round to pack up and return to London. After Fran's query on Saturday night, she was actually beginning to feel slightly scared herself.

When she arrived back at the theatre she saw Ian's car parked outside.

'Hello,' she said, finding him in the foyer about to go up the spiral staircase. 'They're mid-rehearsal, you know.'

'I need to have a look at this ruined equipment.' He paused, looking down at her with irritation stamped clearly on his features.

'Can't it wait until they break? And I don't think it's completely ruined, actually. Ben will know.'

'Where's he?'

'Backstage, I expect.' Libby looked at her watch. 'I don't

162

expect they'll be very long. They were only doing Act Two this afternoon.'

Ian came back down the stairs. 'What's happening, then?'

Libby looked at him thoughtfully. 'Well, Max is in two minds about going ahead. He wants to know who in the company would prefer to stop. I said I'd find out and ask you – or the police, anyway – what they thought.'

'I've told him he can go ahead,' said Ian, looking even more irritated. 'What more does he want?'

'You don't think that could be tempting fate?'

A gleam came into Ian's eyes.

'Ah!' said Libby. 'That's what you want to happen! But suppose someone else is hurt?'

'We're taking precautions,' said Ian obliquely. 'And I could address the whole company about not taking risks.'

'When they finish here,' said Libby, 'I'm going to ask Owen to canvass the company about their thoughts. You could do it then.'

Ian uttered a grunt which could be interpreted as agreement and followed her into the auditorium.

As Libby had thought, the company had just arrived at the final tableau. She went up to Owen and told him what Max had said and indicated Ian, standing frowning at the back. Owen nodded, clapped his hands and went up to the stage.

'Listen, everyone. Max is concerned that there may be some among you who feel that under the circumstances this production ought to be pulled. I have to tell you, we have the permission of the police to go ahead, and DCI Connell is here to have a few words, too. So what do you all think?'

The dancers all looked at one another. No one said anything. Then Damian called down from the FX box.

'I think we ought to pull it. There have been too many incidents.'

A ripple of murmurings went through the company.

'It went so well today, though,' said Tom. 'Owen was pleased, weren't you?'

'I was,' said Owen. 'Shall we ask DCI Connell what he thinks?'

Libby watched as Ian came to the front and stood looking up at the dancers.

'If you carry on,' he said, 'it will be sensible to take precautions. Don't go anywhere alone, check dressing rooms and bedrooms carefully and Ben, I'm sure, will be checking backstage with Sebastian to make sure everything is safe there. There will be a police presence here all the time until you leave, but you might not know it.'

'You mean there's someone here already?' asked Dan.

Ian smiled grimly. 'It seemed sensible after Max was allowed home yesterday.'

'How come the equipment got damaged then?' asked someone.

'That was done when Max was attacked. We should have had someone here then. We know better now.'

'There's been a lot of hard work put into this production,' said Owen, 'and to put it crudely, a lot of money spent. If the majority want to pull it, fair enough, but as long as the police think there's minimal risk, I think we should go ahead.'

'A patrol car will be driving by at intervals throughout the night,' said Ian, 'and further security measures will be taken.'

'But we know someone can get into the theatre,' said Jonathan. 'Someone got in to rig the rat and the Kabuki and someone got in to attack Stan and Max. So there's someone here who has a set of keys. How can we stop them coming in at night again?'

'I don't think that's the problem,' said Ian.

Ben appeared diffidently on the side of the stage. 'We are taking extra security measures,' he said, 'but as Ian says, we don't think that's the problem.'

There were more mutterings. Even Libby was puzzled.

'You are due to open on Wednesday, I believe,' said Ian. 'You haven't much time to decide. I leave it to you. Now I'm going up to take a look at the sound equipment. If anyone has any private concerns, they can come and see me up there.' He disappeared through the auditorium doors.

The dancers went into a huddle on the stage, where Sebastian joined them. Ben came down and joined Libby.

164

'What extra security measures?' she whispered. 'And why don't you think it's a problem?'

'Hasn't it occurred to you that the burglar alarms have never gone off? I know we sometimes forget to set them, we've already talked about this, but not once has an alarm gone off. Ian's pretty sure, and so am I now, that whoever is doing this is not getting in on their own.'

'What?' gasped Libby. 'You mean there's an accomplice?'

'No. Think about it. Max came in and went up to the sound box. There was no one there as far as he can remember. But what would be easier than to slip in behind him unseen and follow him up there?'

'He'd have to be awfully quiet,' said Libby dubiously.

'Dancers are light on their feet,' said Ben. 'And as for the rat and the knife, the theatre was open from first thing that morning. Anyone could have gone in before the rehearsal started.'

'What about Stan?'

'Same as Max. Someone knew where he was going and what he was doing and followed him in.'

'Oh, Lord,' said Libby. 'This is getting worse and worse.'

## Chapter Twenty-two

Libby waited until Owen came down from the stage.

'They want to go on,' he said. 'Well, perhaps "want" is too strong a word, but they feel it would be a waste to cancel now, and they're all going to take extra safety precautions.'

'Will you tell Max?' asked Libby.

'Yes.' Owen sighed. 'This whole thing has turned into a bit of a fiasco, hasn't it?'

'It has a bit. But *Pendle*'s a good piece, it deserves to be seen.'

'Thanks. I had nothing to do with it, of course, except to encourage from the sidelines.'

'But you trained some of the dancers, didn't you?'

'Jonathan, yes, some time ago. And young Lee.'

'Jonathan was expressing doubt about the production going on,' said Libby. 'How is he now?'

'Resigned, I think would describe it best,' said Owen, with a short laugh.

Libby smiled. 'They'll all be fine once you open.'

'If nothing else happens,' said Owen. With these valedictory words he went back to the stage and Libby left the auditorium.

Ben was in the foyer talking to Ian.

'Are they going on?' he asked.

'Looks like it,' said Libby. 'Are you sure you're not using them as bait, Ian?'

Ian looked amused. 'Now would I do that? Anyway, we have other lines of enquiry.'

'You have? Apart from the company?'

'As you know, we have to look at the victim. And in this case he had a life apart from the Tobin Dance Theatre. We have to investigate that other life.'

'But …' began Libby.

'Libby, it's police business,' said Ben. 'Leave it to Ian. He knows what he's doing.'

Ian grinned. 'Sometimes. Now I'm going to carry on sleuthing.' He pushed open the auditorium doors and disappeared.

'Bother. I wanted to ask him what he found out upstairs.' Libby turned a disgruntled face to her beloved.

'I doubt if he would have told you.'

'Perhaps not. But what I was going to say to him was, it's all very well Stan having another life, but how would that life connect with this one? It would have to be someone in the company, wouldn't it?'

'You mean if his murder was connected to another part of his life, someone would have had to infiltrate the company? That's a thought.' Ben did, indeed, look thoughtful.

'And,' said Libby, warming to this theme, 'Stan was keeping the secret but felt threatened. That explains what he meant when he said "they" were going to get him next time.'

'If we've thought of it, you can bet Ian has, too.'

'Of course he has, that's why he told us about the other life.' Libby cast a speculative glance at the auditorium doors. 'I bet he's in there now grilling poor Seb.'

Ben laughed. 'Poor Seb! I'm going to go and see if there's any clearing up to do. I'll see you at home.'

Libby, pausing at the Manor to say goodbye to Hetty, set off home. On the way, she called Fran.

'You're walking!' Fran accused.

'Yes, but I couldn't wait until I got home. Ian's looking into Stan's "other life" as he called it.'

'What does that mean?'

'Life outside the Tobin Dance Theatre. And it occurred to me, we've never looked him up, have we? Or his granddad or father, or whoever he was. Wally Willis. I know Ian's asked Flo and Lenny what they remember about him.'

'Didn't you say at some point it couldn't be anything to do with him?'

'Did I?' Libby gave Nella at the Farm Shop a desultory

wave. 'But we did wonder if it was through his family connections he called the drugs mob off Seb, didn't we?'

'You did, I believe. So you want me to look him up before you get home and relay you the results?'

'Well, I can do it myself when I get home ...'

'But I can cut out the leg work. OK, I'll start now. Speak later.'

Fran rang off, and Libby tucked the phone into the pocket of her cape. Modern technology was a wonderful thing.

As she turned the corner into Allhallow's Lane, Bethany Cole, the vicar, was just coming out of her front gate.

'Hello, Lib. I hear you've got yourself another murder?'

'Oh, don't!' groaned Libby. 'I was saying only the other day, I'm a positive jinx, aren't I?'

Beth laughed. 'Course not! People come to you – it's not as if you go looking for them! I must say I'm looking forward to this production. I'm a huge fan of the male *Swan Lake*.'

'So am I, but this isn't anywhere near as glamorous. They're rather gruesome, the witches. Patti and Anne are coming on Wednesday.'

'I'll see if they've got any tickets left for Wednesday, then. When's the box office open?'

'Online, all the time. Otherwise leave a message on the answerphone. I'll look for you on Wednesday, then. Regards to John.'

'Of course. Oh, by the way, have they had any protests from religious groups?'

Libby stopped and turned round. 'I'm not sure,' she said warily. 'Why?'

'There are a few hard-line Christian groups who are still inflamed by the thought of witchcraft.'

Libby frowned. 'I know there were ...'

Bethany flicked her long, fair plait. 'Oh, there still are. Mostly the rather strict sects, you know?'

'The sort that still think the theatre's a creation of the devil?' said Libby with a grin.

'That's them. I only ask because a few years ago I was involved with a production of *The Crucible* –'

169

'That's the Salem witches, isn't it?'

'Yes, and we were targeted by one of these groups. Very unpleasant.'

'You were?' Libby's interest quickened. 'When you say targeted, how do you mean?'

'Oh, anonymous letters, graffiti, that sort of thing.'

'Nothing worse?'

'I don't think so. Why?'

'The dance company were targeted like that in London. Could I tell our tame policeman about your experience?'

Beth shrugged. 'If you like, if you think it might be relevant. But it can't have anything to do with the murder, can it?'

'I don't know, but the sequence of events began with that sort of targeting, so it's worth telling him. Thanks, Beth.'

Libby arrived at number seventeen, opened the door, tripped down the step and pulled out her phone.

'Is Ian still there, Ben?'

'I'll have a look.' She heard him move, then a shout. 'Yes. Why?'

Libby repeated Beth's tale. 'I just thought he ought to know.'

'I'll tell him. He might call in on her when he leaves here.'

'She was just going out when I saw her.'

'He can try the church, then. Thanks, Lib.'

Libby discarded cape, bag and phone and went to put the kettle on. By the time it boiled, she'd booted up the laptop and rung Fran again.

'There are quite a lot of links, and a lot of them are completely irrelevant, but I've emailed you those I think are useful. There's one story in particular you'll be interested in.'

'There is? What?'

'Have a look. You'll see. I'm going now, I've got Chrissie arriving any minute.'

'Lucky you. How's Cassandra?'

'Don't you mean Montana?'

'I meant the cat, not the daughter.' Chrissie and her husband Bruce had chosen what their elders thought a very silly name for their only child, and a more sensible one for their cat.

'Very well, thank you. And I still get told off for calling the child Monty.'

Libby giggled. 'I'm not surprised. Not known for their sense of humour, your daughter and son-in-law. Go on, then, off you go.'

Libby poured her tea and opened Fran's email. There was a link to an obviously professional CV, with photographs of productions, a link to Stan's former drama school, where he was listed as a visiting lecturer, a few links to productions, one to the Tobin Dance Theatre and none linking Stan to Wally Willis. However, Fran had obviously done a search on this name, too, and here there were more interesting stories.

Fran had put three stars by one link. When Libby opened it, she saw why.

'Willis accused of taking part in Satanic sex orgy,' read the headline.

'Golly,' said Libby to Sidney, who had come to sit next to the laptop. The article went on to describe, in guarded 1970s terms, that the 'orgy', held in the crypt of a disused church, involved both blood-letting and the involvement of children.

The accusations were revealed as part of Wally Willis's trial for implication in a dozen murders.

'He really was a bad boy,' Libby told Sidney. 'I got it the wrong way round when I was talking to Seb, didn't I? Stan wasn't frightened of what his father would say about him being gay, he was frightened of turning out like his father.'

A knock on the door startled Sidney, who shot into the kitchen.

'Ian!' Libby stood aside to let him in. 'What can I do for you?'

'Tell me what your vicar said to you. She's not in.'

Libby repeated what Bethany had told her.

'And there's another thing on similar lines,' she said. 'I expect you know this already, but Stan's father was involved in so-called Satanic orgies. Well, one, anyway.'

Ian sighed. 'Yes, we know. It was a nasty little ring of people who were quite high-profile.'

'High-profile criminals?'

'And others. You've read about the Krays, haven't you? And their social circle?'

'Yes, but it wasn't them, was it? It would have come out by now.'

Ian looked pointedly at Libby's mug. 'Any more in the pot?'

Libby grinned. 'Am I the only person you know who still makes tea in a pot?'

'No, you're not, surprisingly.'

Libby looked at him sharply. 'Who?'

'Oh, just a couple of people I know. My mother included. Tea?' Ian looked hopeful.

Frustrated, Libby went into the kitchen and topped up the teapot. 'Right,' she said. 'Carry on about the orgies.'

'It was – well, I suppose you'd have called it an organised gang – of criminals who had links to both politicians and show-business personalities. They were often photographed at restaurants with them and emerging from nightclubs. All of them looking for the next high.' Ian's mouth turned down at the corners. 'Very unsavoury.'

Libby handed him a mug. 'And I suppose some of the cases have come to light in recent times?'

Ian nodded and followed her into the sitting-room. 'There were a couple of young women and young men who tried to report it in the seventies, but they weren't believed. What I find incomprehensible is that these orgies were brought into evidence in Willis's trial, yet no further action was taken regarding the children.'

'Different times,' said Libby, shooing Sidney off the sofa. 'But does it have anything to do with Stan's murder?'

'You're bound to have thoughts about it,' said Ian, with a grin. 'So let's have them.'

Libby repeated her theory about Stan's fear of becoming like his father. 'I think he must have equated his sexuality with his father's – er – proclivities. This is why he was denying his sexuality. Maybe.'

'Could be. It could also be why he was against *Pendle* itself.'

## Chapter Twenty-three

Libby gaped. 'He *what*?'

'Oh, yes. I thought you would have worked that out.' Ian gave her a tired smile.

'Seb and Damian said he wasn't all for it, but not that he was actually *against* it. So ...' Libby's mind was grappling with this new idea. 'That turns everything on its head, doesn't it?'

'It certainly puts a new slant on things.' Ian sipped his tea. 'And your vicar's story of hard-line religious cults adds another dimension. Although we did have a profiler suggest something similar.'

'You've had a profiler on the case?' Libby was surprised.

'Yes. I'm not much in favour of them as a rule, but there were aspects of psychological disturbance, certainly regarding the incidents in London.'

'Oh, yes, I suppose there were.' Libby was thoughtful for a moment. 'So does it look as if Stan was killed *because* of his objection to *Pendle*?'

'Possibly.'

'And not to stop *Pendle*?'

'Again, possibly.'

'You're not going to tell me.'

Ian laughed. 'I've already let out far more than I should. You talk it over with Fran and see where you get to. Only whatever you do, don't go barging off on some hare-brained wild goose chase.'

'As if we would,' said Libby. 'Oh, I know what I was going to ask you – did you find out about Paul's background?'

Ian's expression became guarded. 'In what way?'

'Well, I told you he was thrown out of a cast, didn't I?'

'I think it was mentioned.'

'And he was very keen on seeing the shrine and Grey

Betty?'

'I don't see how that's relevant.'

'Neither do I, at the moment, but I want to know why he was slung out of a panto cast.'

'Haven't you ever wanted to get rid of somebody in your cast?' Ian eyed her over the rim of his mug.

'Often,' said Libby. 'So have you found anything out?'

'Not about that, no.'

'So you have found something out?'

'We're looking into the background of everybody connected with the production, from Max Tobin downwards,' said Ian, and Libby sighed in frustration. He stood up and handed her his empty mug. 'I must go now.' He touched her cheek with a long finger. 'You're often a great help, Lib, both of you, but I can't tell you everything. You know that.'

Libby sighed again and stood up. 'I know. I'm grateful for any crumbs.'

As soon as Ian had gone, she called Fran.

'I can't talk now,' said her friend, as Libby heard a child's wail in the background.

'Oh, sorry, I forgot you said Chrissie was coming. Can you call me back when she's gone?'

Fran sighed. 'I suppose so. Is it urgent?'

'Well, no, I suppose not, but there's news. From Ian.'

'OK. I'll call you later.'

Balked, Libby took a turn round the sitting-room, then went to peer into the fridge to see if there was anything for supper. When she'd decided on jacket potatoes with whatever she could rustle up to go with them, she returned to the computer and began to search for hard-line religious cults. She was still wading through the multiplicity of sites when Ben arrived looking harassed. Libby immediately got up and went for the whisky bottle.

'What's happened now?'

'Damian's thrown a wobbly and said they can't use his music.'

Libby stopped mid-pour. 'Oh, no!'

'Oh, yes.' Ben sank down on the sofa. 'And he did it loudly.

So, of course, the whole boiling got into a shouting match. It was just as well Ian had gone. Did he come here?'

'Yes, on his way somewhere else. Beth wasn't in, but I told you that. So what was the upshot?'

'Owen carted Damian off to the pub to talk him out of it and Sebastian and I were left to try and calm the dancers down. With what success I don't know. But I made them all go back to the Manor and not to disturb Hetty on any account.'

'Would they?'

'They were all looking for someone's shoulder to cry on, and as you've said, Hetty is a bit like a favourite aunt, despite the fact that she hardly says a word.'

'Oh, dear. Do you think I'd better go up in case she needs support?'

'*I* need support, you daft bat.' Ben caught her arm and dragged her down beside him. 'I don't know what I did to deserve a bunch of hysterical dancers on my case all day.'

'They aren't usually hysterical,' said Libby cautiously.

'Well, they were this afternoon.'

'Did you get any idea of who was in favour of going on and who wasn't?'

'Owen asked them that earlier, didn't he? And the general consensus was that they all wanted to carry on. If you remember, at the time, it was only Damian who seemed ambivalent.' Ben sipped his whisky.

'Well, I hope Owen doesn't drag him up to see Max. Poor old Max couldn't cope.'

'What did Ian say?' Ben stretched out his legs.

Libby told him.

Ben whistled. 'That puts a different complexion on things, doesn't it?'

'That's what I said. It looks as though someone is trying to make sure *Pendle* goes *on*, rather than the other way round.'

'And Stan was trying to stop it?'

'Ian didn't exactly say that, he just said Stan was against *Pendle*. Do you suppose he thinks Stan was behind the incidents in London?'

'Perhaps he does. Perhaps he was. What does Fran think?'

Libby stood up. 'I haven't told her yet. She has Chrissie and Montana visiting.' She pulled a face.

'Rather her than us,' said Ben. 'Where's my dinner, woman?'

Fran called later in the evening sounding exhausted.

'They've only just gone,' she complained. 'I had to give them dinner.'

'Isn't it a bit late for Montana to be up?' said Libby.

'I said that at six o'clock. Chrissie then brightly informed me that she thought they were staying for dinner. I then asked what Bruce was doing for dinner. He, apparently, was at some flash business dinner. And Montana wouldn't eat the lasagne.'

'I hope you didn't go and find her something else?'

'No.' Libby guessed Fran was grinning. 'I told her there wasn't anything else. Chrissie kept suggesting things until Guy lost his temper.'

'Oh, good for him! What did he say?'

'If we'd have known they were coming we would have prepared something suitable, but as we didn't they'd have to lump it. Or words to that effect.'

'Did Chrissie take umbrage?'

'A bit, though she couldn't argue. But it was all a bit exhausting. So, come on, tell me this news.'

Libby filled her in on everything she and Ben had learnt during the afternoon.

'I think the most surprising is Damian refusing to let them use his music,' said Fran.

'He really doesn't think they should go on. I'd say he was scared,' said Libby. 'And in a way, it does seem disrespectful.'

'Surely they've got a master tape or whatever it's called? They could still use it?'

'Then he'd probably sue them. Actually it's now programmed into the theatre's sound system, so as soon as that's fixed they could use it, even if he withheld the master CD. It is odd, though, because he was so thrilled to hear it through the system when he first arrived. He couldn't stop listening to it.'

'He's probably got the horrors about the whole thing now,

though,' said Fran. 'Do you think Owen will talk him out of withholding permission?'

'Max will, if Owen takes Damian up to see him. Poor Max. He was in two minds about going on today, too.'

'Now, about Stan. You read that link I sent you?'

'Yes, I told you, and Ian knew all about it. I want to know how he worked out that Stan was against the production. He said he thought I would have worked it out, and told me to talk to you about it.'

'So there are clues, then. What did Sebastian tell you?'

'Nothing except how he and Stan met and how Stan was practically psychotic about his own sexuality. Which must be related to what his father did ... here, you don't think his father could still be alive, do you?'

'How old would he be?' asked Fran. 'Those news items were dated in the sixties and early seventies. He could be as young as seventy, so it's definitely possible.'

'A bit old to have a son of Stan's age, surely?'

'Not a bit of it. Some of Sophie's friends have parents older than us.'

'Anyway,' said Libby, 'alive or not, he was obviously not exclusively gay if he had Stan.'

'No, just a thrill-seeker,' said Fran. 'and Ian was right, I think, when he said there were signs of psychological disturbance in the incidents in London. And Stan was in the perfect position to create those. For instance, he wouldn't have been rehearsing with the dancers, so he was free to get to all the lockers.'

'Oh, yes, I hadn't thought of that. I'm still not sure I get Stan's motive for not liking the show, though.'

'Surely something to do with the Dennis Wheatley-style set-up his dad was involved with.'

'That was devil worship, though, wasn't it?'

'That's what the witches were accused of – being in league with the devil.' Fran sighed. 'It's all pretty sordid.'

'I started looking for hard-line cults online earlier after what Beth told me,' said Libby. 'The trouble is I didn't know what search terms to use. I got lots of results about the Plymouth

177

Brethren and other groups of Brethren, but I was looking for something like those little chapels, you know?'

'Chapel of Zion? You know, the little tin chapel on the road into Nethergate.'

'Oh, I'd forgotten that. Yes, I suppose I mean that sort of thing. I don't know what they all believe in, but I was assuming they'd be terribly strict and not approve of witches or actors.'

'It was people like that who Beth was talking about? Who targeted *The Crucible*?'

'Yes. She didn't say which group it was, but it sounds awfully similar, doesn't it?'

'In which case,' said Fran, 'it was nothing to do with Stan.'

'Unless ...' Libby paused. 'Suppose Stan had joined a group like that as a response to what his father had done?'

'It seems a bit extreme,' said Fran doubtfully. 'I can understand him denying his sexuality, but to actually go as far as joining some extreme sect, or cult?'

'I was thinking more of a hard-line Calvinistic group. Strict Baptists or something.'

'None of the recognised branches of the church would stand for illegal goings-on like that, though,' said Fran. 'No, if anything, it would be a sect, or a cult. Something secret.'

'Where they keep their daughters at home and never let them out, and marry them to their brothers – that sort of thing?'

Fran laughed. 'I doubt if they're as extreme as that. But I know that there are organisations now set up to help people break free of those sorts of cults. They practice mind control, and they're terribly successful.'

'Somehow that doesn't sound right,' said Libby. 'I can envisage a Prophet of Doom-like preacher bringing down wrath on his congregation about the wickedness of witches, or men prancing about as women, but not the cult aspect.'

'Well, it doesn't apply if Stan was the one behind the incidents in London, does it?' said Fran. 'That sort of strict religious group doesn't come into it at all.'

## Chapter Twenty-four

Libby woke in the morning to the sound of the landline ringing. Ungluing her eyelids, she struggled to sit up and realised it had stopped. She also realised she was alone, and then heard Ben coming up the stairs.

'That was Hetty. Someone tried to get into the theatre again.'

'What? When?'

'Sometime during the night, obviously. No one heard anything, but when Sebastian went to open up with Max's keys he found signs of forcing on the doors.'

'Why didn't the alarm go off?'

Ben passed a weary hand over his face. 'No idea. Perhaps it doesn't go off unless you actually get the door open. I'll check with the alarm company.'

Libby swung her legs out of bed. 'So they're obviously going on with the show?'

'Yes, they must be. I could wish they'd let us know.' Ben turned to go back downstairs. 'I've made tea.'

Sitting over tea and toast at the kitchen table, Libby said, 'For the first time, I can honestly say I wish they'd never come here. Max said they'd been nothing but trouble, and he was right.'

'More trouble for Stan,' said Ben.

'And that wouldn't have happened if they hadn't come here,' said Libby.

'If someone was trying to stop the production they would have carried on trying to do that wherever they were. They might have gone straight into their London theatre and it would all have happened there.'

Libby nodded gloomily. 'I just hope nothing else happens. I feel like running away until it's all over.'

'I thought you were keen to solve the mystery?'

'I was keen to *have* it solved. After the conversation with Fran last night I don't feel as though we've got anywhere near. And it's all more unsavoury than we first thought.'

'I thought,' said Ben, buttering more toast, 'you'd discarded the idea of the hellfire chapel and the hatred of witches?'

'I don't know,' said Libby. 'If Stan was behind the incidents, I can't see where they'd come in. I think it was just Beth's suggestion that put that into my head.'

'What about young Paul?'

'What about him?'

'I thought you said he seemed interested in Grey Betty and the mock shrine?'

'What would that have to do with hellfire chapels?'

'They would be against pagan beliefs, too. Could it be that he's secretly a member?'

'Oh, Ben – that's worse than even I could come up with.' Libby laughed. 'What a leap into the unknown.'

Ben grinned. 'Just following your lead, my love!'

When Libby arrived at the Manor, she was met by an irritated Ian and several bored looking uniformed officers.

'This is getting ridiculous,' he said. 'What on earth's going on, Libby?'

'Why ask me? I would far rather be shot of the whole thing, now.'

'One thing's for sure,' said Ian, eyeing a boiler-suited figure subjecting the theatre doors to a detailed examination, 'this is no professional.'

'Professional criminal, you mean?'

'Certainly nothing to do with Willis's father.'

'Do you mean to say he's still alive?' Libby was surprised.

'Oh, yes. Alive and voluble. You would have thought the police were behind everything.'

'He's not in prison, then?'

'No.' Ian grinned. 'Allegedly been "going straight" for years now. And denied any knowledge of the – ah – *rescue* of young Sebastian.'

'Was he telling the truth?'

'I doubt it. I think he was genuinely upset, and Stan's mother – who is a lot younger than her husband – was devastated.'

'Oh, dear.' Libby's hand went to her mouth. 'That's so horrible. Poor woman. Whatever Stan did to get himself murdered ...'

'He didn't deserve it, and neither does she,' said Ian. 'Just another of the unpleasant facts about murder.'

'A warning to everyone who treats it like an intellectual puzzle,' said Libby, looking up at him warily.

'It is indeed.' He patted her shoulder. 'Go and see to the living, woman. Your young Paul is kicking up a fuss this morning.'

'Oh, God, if it isn't one it's another. Has Damian calmed down?'

'I haven't seen him. Was he being troublesome?'

'Threatening to refuse to let them use his music, yesterday.'

'Was he, now?' Ian looked thoughtful.

'Has that got some significance?'

'No idea.' He gave her a tired smile. 'I must go and see what the troops have discovered. Oh, and you can use the theatre, but go in through the back door.'

'Thanks. By the way, you said Paul was kicking up a fuss. Did you find out anything about him?'

'I told you, we've looked into everyone's background.' He turned away. 'See you later.'

Libby glared after him in frustration.

'I thought you said you wanted to opt out now,' said Ben, coming up behind her. 'Not carry on poking into things.'

'Did you hear any of what Ian said?'

'Only his Parthian shot.'

Libby repeated what Ian had told her. 'So we might as well let them know they can go in.'

They went together into the Manor and into the sitting-room, where they found the entire company looking tense and nervous.

'You can use the theatre,' said Ben. 'I'll show you into the back door.'

'Thanks, Ben.' Max, head bandaged, stood up. Owen hovered next to him.

'Should you be here, Max?' asked Libby.

'Couldn't stop him,' said Owen with a rueful smile.

Libby looked round for Damian and spotted him tucked away by the coffee urns looking gloomy.

'I told him we'd use it whether he said we could or not,' said Owen, seeing the direction of her gaze. 'In the end he accepted it.'

'Why does he think you should stop now?' asked Ben.

'Because he's afraid of more things happening. And, of course, with the attempt on the theatre last night, he thinks he's proved his point,' said Max. 'But no damage was done, except to your front doors – which we'll pay for, of course – and your friend Peter managed to get your sound system working again, so with or without Damian, we can go ahead. And I'm going to use the Kabuki. Will you check it, Ben?'

'Doesn't Seb want to do it?' said Ben.

'I think he'd rather not,' said Owen.

'Right. Let's get going. Full dress rehearsal today, isn't it? If you have dress rehearsals in dance theatre.'

'We do.' Owen smiled. 'We'll do a straight run, then if there are any tech problems, we'll go back. We haven't really got time to do a full tech run *and* a dress.'

Ben led everyone out of the Manor and round to the back of the theatre. Everyone except Damian, who glared defiantly at Libby as she approached him.

'Be it on their own heads,' he said. 'Even last night there was another attempt on the theatre. Someone wants to stop us, so why don't we stop?'

'Because they'd win. You don't give in to blackmail, Damian.'

'I do,' said Damian, deflating.

'Don't you want to see your lovely music played to an audience?'

'They won't be taking any notice of it, they'll be watching the dancers.'

'You're determined to see the black side, aren't you?'

182

He looked up in surprise. 'Is there another side?'

Libby sighed. 'OK, OK.' She sat down beside him. 'So who do you think has been doing all this?'

He looked at her sideways. 'Me?'

'Yes. You must have had an idea. The onlooker seeing more of the game sort of thing.'

'Oh. Yes, I see.' He rested his chin on one hand and with the other brushed the heavy hair away from his eyes. 'Well, I really don't know. The only one who seemed a bit – well – dubious about the whole thing was Stan himself. And none of us knew why.'

Libby, who thought she did, nodded. 'So do you think Stan was killed to make sure the production went ahead?'

Damian widened his eyes at her. 'But that doesn't make sense. It would go ahead with Stan or without him.'

'Unless someone thought Stan could stop it, somehow.'

'How do you mean?'

'Suppose it was Stan who was behind the incidents?'

'*Stan*? Are you mad?'

Libby shrugged. 'Just a thought.'

'However much Stan disapproved of a production – or anything to do with the stage – he would never do anything to jeopardise it. He was a bit of a fanatic.'

'Perfectionist?'

Damian nodded. 'I would say so. You saw how he used to dress. Looked like a shop window dummy.'

Libby had to agree. 'What about the dancers? Were there any he didn't like?'

'I don't think he liked any of them,' said Damian, with his first smile. 'He admired Max – and Owen to an extent – but the rest he tolerated.'

'And the new boys? The auditionees?'

'I'm not sure he took any notice of them at all. I didn't see any sign of it, anyway.'

'What about you? What do you think of them? Do they fit in?'

'They're OK. That Paul is a bit strange. He's as nervous about the production as I am.'

183

'Thinks it ought to stop?'

Damian frowned. 'Actually, I'm not sure. He was going on about it this morning, but I couldn't make out what he was upset about.'

'Apparently,' said Libby, deciding to take a chance, 'there was a rumour going round that he was chucked out of a panto cast. Did you hear that?'

'No!' Damian looked surprised. 'I wonder what he did? Not very usual, is it?'

'Upstaging the star?'

Damian laughed, and Libby felt pleased with herself for getting him to relax. 'Could be. Some of the Dames! I could tell you some stories!'

'I know,' said Libby. 'I've worked with some.'

'You? Oh, of course, you put on a panto here, don't you?'

'Yes, but I meant in my younger days when I was a full-time pro.'

'Oh, were you?' Now Damian looked interested. 'Did you work with any of the greats?'

Libby treated him to a couple of anecdotes, then stood up.

'Well, I'd better go and help Hetty in the kitchen. I'll see you later.'

'I might as well go over,' said Damian, also standing up. 'Thanks for the chat, Libby. I feel a bit better now.'

She beamed at him and went off to the kitchen, where she found Hetty sitting at the table reading a newspaper.

'Want a cup of tea, gal?'

'No, thanks, Het. I've just been cheering up a member of the company. Have they been a nuisance this morning?'

'No. Very quiet, except some bloke roaring about retribution or something.'

'Small and dark, was he?'

Hetty nodded. 'Know him?'

'Paul something. Looks vaguely Welsh. He was the one who wanted to go and see the mocked up shrine by Grey Betty.'

'Ah. Welsh chapel – that'd be it.'

'Really? How do you know?'

'We had a couple of 'em in London, and we even had one

here. Not that they was Welsh, o'course. They were strict.'

'There was one here? Good lord!'

'Up along New Barton Lane, it was. Near New Farm bungalows. Tin shack. You could buy 'em from catalogues.'

'You could?' Libby was incredulous.

Hetty grinned at her. 'Instant buildings!'

'Good – er – heavens. Who built it?'

''Oppers, mainly. Some of 'em was religious, see, but not Church of England. So they built their own. Didn't mix with the rest of us. We 'ad the Sally Army up on the common on Sundays, they all went off to their chapel.'

'The things I didn't know about Steeple Martin,' marvelled Libby. 'And this Paul reminded you of the people who went there?'

'Put me in mind of some of 'em. Surprised he's in this 'ere ballet if he is. They was always against theatre, and witches. Cor, you should have heard 'em about witches.'

# Chapter Twenty-five

'But,' Libby said later on the phone to Fran, 'that was mere speculation.'

'It makes a change from your speculations,' said Fran.

'Well, I thought it did. It was Ben and Hetty speculating.'

'But you'd already wondered about him because he seemed keen on the fake shrine or whatever it was and the standing stone.'

'I know, but it was because he seemed keen on – oh, I don't know – pagan stuff. This is speculating that he's completely on the other side.'

'Either way,' said Fran, 'I can't see that he has anything to do with either the incidents or the murder. He's a red herring.'

'I suppose so.' Libby sighed. 'I do rather feel as though I want them all to go home now. It's not very pleasant having our theatre damaged.'

'No – or to be the site of a murder. Do you think you'll be all right about it when they've gone? You won't feel a bit, I don't know, odd, about going on-stage?'

'Good Lord, no!' said Libby, surprised. 'I'm not that sensitive. Anyway, I can't afford to be. Panto rehearsals start next week.'

'I think I would be. I'm glad I'm not doing panto.'

'Yes, but you're – well, you know. You're supposed to be sensitive. Come to think of it, if you went on-stage you could probably –'

'Stop right there,' said Fran. 'We agreed that I'm going off the boil, so I'm certainly not going to do that. Ian will get to the bottom of it. Probably already has.'

'Well, he hadn't earlier. He's pretty cheesed off about it, actually. There seems to be no rhyme or reason to any of it.'

'Except that there must be somewhere. Although it does

seem a bit odd. Was Stan killed because of his objection to *Pendle*? That can't be true, because he couldn't have stopped it and showed no sign of doing so. If he was behind the London incidents, was he killed in revenge for those? Seems equally unlikely.'

'And what did whoever-it-was want in the theatre last night? And why attack Max?' Libby shook her head at the phone. 'It doesn't make any sense at all, does it?'

'It doesn't seem to. But there has to be cause and effect somewhere. I expect the boring part of police work will solve it.'

'What I'm surprised about is that it hasn't been all over the media,' said Libby.

'It was a small item in the local paper,' said Fran. 'Just "Man dies in accident at theatre". That was all.'

'In Jane's paper?'

Jane Baker was assistant editor on the Nethergate Mercury, which existed largely online in this digital age.

'Yes, but it didn't have her by-line. I'm surprised she hasn't been in touch.'

So am I, thought Libby as, right on cue, the landline rang.

'Libby? Campbell McLean here.'

'I might have guessed,' said Libby.

'Yes, you might.' Campbell McLean was a pleasant young man who just happened to be Kent and Coast Television's chief reporter. 'Especially as I understand this "accident" took place nearly a week ago.'

'Dear me. Didn't the police put it out?'

'All anyone's been able to get out of the police is that it was an accident. But my sources tell me it isn't that simple.'

'And who are your sources?'

'You don't get me there, Libby!' Campbell laughed. 'Come on, what happened?'

'Someone had an accident.' Libby was furiously trying to find Ian's number in her mobile with one hand.

'Who?'

'Look, Campbell, if the police have given out no details, there probably isn't a story, and I'm certainly not to going to say anything, am I?'

'So something did happen?'

'I've told you, I'm not saying anything. Ask the police if you want to know.'

Campbell sighed. 'Does Fran know?'

'Know what?'

'Oh, Libby! Give me a break.'

'I don't know what you've heard, but I doubt very much if any of it is true,' said Libby, crossing her fingers. 'And now, I have to go. I have food to prepare.'

'All right, but I'll be back.'

'Don't be melodramatic,' said Libby, and ended the call. She found Ian's number and rang it.

'Yes,' barked Ian. 'I'm busy, Libby.'

'I know, but I've just had Kent and Coast on the phone.'

'That idiot McLean, I suppose. What did you tell him?'

'Nothing. I didn't even admit there'd been an "accident" as he put it. Apparently that was in the *Mercury*.'

'Good, keep it that way. We've tried for a blackout on it, but these days it's difficult. I'm surprised there's been no social media storm. The dancers are always on their phones.'

'I think Max asked them not to. Probably under threat of banishment. Anyway, I've told you now, so if anyone else approaches me, I'll carry on playing dumb.'

Ian laughed. 'Difficult for you! I must go.'

Within minutes, the phone rang again.

'I've just had Campbell McLean on,' said Fran.

'Yes, he phoned me.'

'Why didn't you warn me?'

'Because I phoned Ian to warn him. You didn't say anything, did you?'

'No.' Fran laughed. 'He tried to trick me by saying he'd spoken to you and all he wanted was confirmation. So I guessed you hadn't said anything. If you had, he wouldn't have bothered with me, he'd have filed his report straight away.'

'Thank goodness. The dancers have been incredibly good and not splashed it all over social media, so it's been kept quiet so far, but I doubt if that will last.'

Libby went back to the Manor to see if she could cadge some of Harry's lunch, and found everyone in a buoyant mood.

'It went so well, Libby,' said Max, who was positively glowing. 'Everything worked perfectly.'

Libby kept the old adage of 'good dress rehearsal, bad first night' to herself. Perhaps it didn't apply to dance, anyway. 'Even the curtain?'

'Yes. Ben and Seb had checked it earlier, so we used it. Seb did wear gauntlets, though!'

'Oh, good.' Libby smiled weakly. 'And how's Damian now?'

'He's cheered up,' said Owen. 'At least, I think he has.'

Libby helped herself to a taco and wandered into the kitchen, where she found Hetty and Ben drinking soup.

'Went well, I understand.'

'It did,' said Ben. 'What have you been doing?'

'Putting off the media.' Libby pulled a face. 'Bloody Campbell McLean. Called me, then when I wouldn't tell him anything, he called Fran. I've warned Ian.'

'He and the SOCOs have cleared off now, and told me I can repair the door. The damage was so slight it looks as if whoever did it was rather half-hearted about it, or changed their mind as soon as they'd begun.'

'That's a relief. Max is pleased that the boys haven't let anything out on social media.'

'He warned them about that in London,' said Ben, 'and told them again after the rat and the Kabuki accident. And after Stan they were all scared into submission. I think at that time they all thought it could be them next.'

'Poor buggers,' said Hetty.

'Well, with any luck we can keep it out of the headlines, at least until the weekend,' said Ben. 'When they get back to London they can deal with it from their own headquarters.'

'Yes, but who will?' said Libby. 'Stan would have done all that.'

'There must be someone else in the office.' Ben frowned.

'It doesn't sound as though there is.' Libby tore off a piece of Hetty's kitchen roll, wiped her fingers and returned to the sitting-room. Harry waved from a huddle of dancers.

'Hello, petal. Have you eaten?'

'Had a taco. Have they told you the latest?'

'About the desperate criminal who tried to break in? Yes. And Pete's filled me in on everything else.'

'All a bit of a pain, really. Are you going to do this all week?'

Harry gave her a crooked smile. 'Can't let the little guys down, can I? Except for Saturday. But I've said we'll do a buffet for after the show.'

'That's kind of you, Hal.'

He shrugged. 'They've all been through it, haven't they? And Max is paying me.'

'Not enough, I bet. And it's all the effort you have to go to.'

'Oh, get away with you. No trouble.' He gave her a hug. 'Besides, we've got our theatre's reputation to keep up, haven't we?'

She strolled over to rejoin Max and Owen.

'By the way, Max, have you been able to remember why it was that you went to the theatre the other day?'

Max lost his smile. 'No, I haven't. The doctor isn't sure that I ever will.'

'That's odd, isn't it. You can remember going in there, but not why.'

Max began to look restless. 'Look, Libby, I really don't think it's important. Nothing's been stolen –'

'But our equipment was damaged,' Libby cut him short and Max's colour rose.

Owen frowned at her.

'Libby –' he began.

'Now don't you tell me to leave him alone, Owen. We – the family – have bent over backwards to help. First of all to see if Fran and I could pick anything up about this silly business of the incidents in London. We went to a lot of trouble to get the Manor ready for the dancers, and Hetty's been a brick about supplying breakfast and quantities of free tea and coffee, Harry's gone above and beyond the call of duty providing lunches and even Mrs Carpenter offered you free use of a rehearsal space.'

'I didn't –'

'No, Max, I know you didn't ask us to do all of that, if that is what you were going to say, but it was done. And we've had the police all over the place, and now damage to the front door as well as to the sound equipment. So please don't say something isn't important and worse, that nothing was stolen. Yes, it was. A life.'

She stopped, annoyed with herself that she'd lost her temper and suddenly aware that the entire room had gone quiet and was listening. Ben had appeared in the doorway and was looking surprised, while Harry was leaning against the wall next to him, arms folded and with a smile on his face. She took a deep breath.

'So, yes. It is important. Someone has to get to the bottom of all this to stop these things happening.'

Max and Owen looked at one another.

'Hear, hear!' called a voice from the back of the room, and Tom was seen to be applauding over his head. Surprisingly, the rest of the dancers all joined in. Even Damian and Sebastian were smiling.

Max sat down suddenly and smiled ruefully.

'I'm sorry,' he said. 'I should have realised.' He looked round his company. 'Does anyone want to stop? Should we pull out?'

The dancers looked at each other and murmured.

'No,' said Tom, finally. 'If we can keep the theatre safe – and ourselves, of course – I think we should go on. We've come this far. But to be fair, I think it should be up to Libby and Ben. As Libby says, they've had to put up with a lot.'

All eyes turned to Libby, who was looking at Ben. He came over to stand beside her.

'I happen to agree with every word Libby said – although that's pretty rare,' he added, raising a laugh. 'But you've all worked hard and it seems a shame to waste all that. Besides the money it's cost to hire us for two weeks.' He got another laugh.

'Thank you, Ben.' Max looked at his feet. 'I did say to Libby the other day I thought perhaps we should pull out, but I never really wanted to.' He looked up at his company.

'I don't know who or what is behind all this, but I want you all to promise to watch out for each other and the theatre for the next few days. Once we get to Saturday, we're safe.'

# Chapter Twenty-six

Tuesday afternoon passed quietly. The dancers rehearsed, Ben stood by to assist Sebastian should it be needed, Peter attended to the lights and Libby shut herself in her conservatory to paint.

'When you think about it,' Libby said to Ben that night over chilli con carne, 'it must have cost Max a fortune, this exercise. Meals every night, either in the pub or at Hal's, for everyone, all the accommodation …'

'I expect it's going through the company books,' said Ben. 'He's hardly using his own money.'

'I wonder if he's had to pay Damian for the music?'

'That's a point. Although Damian's a salaried employee, as far as I can tell, so perhaps it comes under his terms of work.'

'Seems a bit harsh, if so. And Max did say the programme will say that's it's Damian's score and from an idea by Alan.'

'I expect they're just pleased to be acknowledged,' said Ben. 'And the company did workshop it, so it's a joint enterprise.'

'Which makes it even more surprising that one of them is trying to sabotage it.'

'Sure it's one of them, are you?'

'Who else could it be? Only they're not regarding one another with suspicion, are they? You'd expect them to be avoiding each other.'

'I don't suppose they can believe that any of them could do it. You said that when you and Fran took Tom and Jonathan out they couldn't think of anyone capable of harming the company.'

'Except the ones they didn't know.'

'The auditionees? But they all seem completely harmless.'

'Except Paul.'

'Oh, don't start on him again!' said Ben. 'Poor bloke! He's come in for more speculation than anyone else. Even from my mother.'

The subject was dropped in favour of discussion of what to watch on television for their last night off until Sunday. Although Libby was not involved in the production, she would be attending to bar and front of house duties for the week.

On Wednesday morning, Libby awoke with a feeling of anticipation, slightly tempered by apprehension. All through early morning tea and breakfast she was subconsciously waiting for the phone to ring with news of some fresh disaster. By the time Ben left to go and attend to neglected duties in the estate office, she was hopping about like a cat on hot bricks.

Finally, abandoning the painting she had been attempting the day before, she packed up her things and set off to the Manor. She waved at Beth Cole putting a poster up on the village notice board, Ali at the eight-till-late putting out trays of bread on his counter, Nella at the farm shop putting out her trays of fresh vegetables and Harry having a morning coffee at the big table in the window of The Pink Geranium. Her village, she thought. How comforting it was, and how glad she would be when they went back to normal.

Normality was something that looked unlikely as she approached the Manor and saw, parked carelessly on the forecourt, a large and ostentatious black car.

Cautiously, she approached the door and listened.

'I'm sorry,' she heard Ben say, 'I'm afraid I can't let you into the theatre just at this moment. I can get a message over there, and perhaps Max can come over as soon as he's free –'

''E'll bloody come over when I says so,' came back a guttural voice, 'and so you tell 'im.'

Libby stepped into the hall and was confronted by a broad, black, barathea back, topped by a huge head of white hair.

'Libby,' said Ben, 'this is Stan's father.'

Wally Willis turned round and Libby saw that he was leaning on two sticks.

''Oo are you then?' he said.

Libby smiled as pleasantly as she was able. 'Libby Sarjeant,' she said. 'Pleased to meet you, Mr Willis.'

He narrowed tiny, dark eyes at her. 'You summat to do with

this set-up?'

'Part-owner and my partner, Mr Willis,' said Ben smoothly, coming to Libby's side. 'Would you like to come into my office?'

Wally Willis grunted, and Ben held out an arm to usher him forwards. Over his shoulder he mouthed, 'Phone Ian' at Libby, then asked aloud, 'Would you like coffee?'

'Tea,' said Willis, and stumped into the office. Ben winked at Libby, who went to the kitchen.

'Still 'ere, is 'e?' said Hetty. 'I've boiled the kettle.'

'Oh, good,' said Libby. 'He wants tea. I'll take it in, but Ben's asked me to phone Ian first.' She made a face. 'He's revolting, isn't he? I don't want to touch him.'

However, Ian's personal phone went straight to voicemail, and his work one Libby was nervous about using. In the end she sent texts to both numbers, then called Fran very briefly to let her know what was going on.

Wally Willis was sitting, legs akimbo and hands on knees, in the big chair opposite Ben, who sat looking calm and superior (she thought) on the other side of the desk.

'Tea,' said Libby, putting the tray down on the desk. 'Mr Willis?'

He looked suspiciously at the tray, his eyes widening slightly at the sight of the china teapot.

'Ur,' he said.

Libby poured tea into two cups and politely asked if he took sugar and milk.

'Milk.'

She poured a little milk into both cups and passed one each to Ben and Willis.

'Will you excuse me,' she said. 'I'm expecting a phone call,' and nodded slightly at Ben's raised eyebrows.

'Phone rang,' said Hetty as she returned to the kitchen. She snatched it up and checked. Ian.

'Hello,' she said. 'Sorry, I was giving Wally Willis tea.'

Ian spluttered. 'Tea?'

'He didn't want coffee.' Libby grinned at Hetty.

'What's he doing there?'

'I think he wants to see Max, but he started off by trying to get Ben to let him in to the theatre.'

'Is Max in the theatre?'

'I assume so, I only arrived just before I called you and Willis was already here.'

'Damn. Look, don't let him get away. I'm coming over.'

'Where are you?'

'Does that matter?'

'Yes. I wanted to know how long you might be.'

'Oh, I see. I'm in the office. I'll be about twenty minutes.'

Libby ended the call.

'Did you see Willis first?' she asked Hetty.

'We come out into the hall together when we 'eard the door,' said Hetty. 'Doesn't look as if 'e could knock the skin off a rice puddin' now, does 'e?'

'He still looks dangerous to me, though,' said Libby. 'And nothing like his son. Flo said he was small and neat, like Stan. He's certainly put on weight.'

'That was the little feller with the glasses, wasn't it?'

'Yes. I'm just wondering if I should nip over to the theatre and let them know he's here.'

'I shouldn't, gal. Worry 'em before they need to be.'

'I suppose you're right. Shall I go and see if Ben needs rescuing?'

Hetty snorted. 'You can try!'

'… and 'e's responsible whether 'e likes it or not,' Willis was saying as Libby re-entered the office. 'Employment law, innit?'

'I don't think it works quite like that in a case of murder,' said Ben, 'unless, of course, the employer is the murderer.'

'I reckon 'e is,' said Willis. 'Morally.'

Libby saw Ben's mouth twitch, and had to bite her own lip. Ben caught her eye and she nodded. Willis swung round in the chair as far as he was able.

Before he could speak, Libby said sweetly, 'Did your wife not come down with you, Mr Willis? I suppose she's devastated.'

His face darkened. 'You leave 'er out of it.'

'Oh,' said Libby. 'Right.'

He turned back to Ben. 'You gonna get that Tobing or whatever 'e's called out 'ere, then?'

'Not just yet, Mr Willis. If you'll just be patient a little longer.'

'Then I'll go meself.' Willis grabbed his two sticks propped up by the chair and struggled upright. Neither Ben nor Libby made a move to help him, but Libby went to the door and stood in front of it. Willis turned to face her breathing heavily. 'Get out of my way.'

'Mr Willis, we'll tell Mr Tobin you're here shortly, if you'll just wait for a minute or two.'

'I said get out of my way!' roared Willis.

The door opened behind Libby.

'Don't you shout like that in my house,' said Hetty, coming round to stand by Libby, arms crossed in front of her apron. 'Sound like a bloody docker, you do.'

Taken aback, Willis wobbled on his sticks, and Ben quickly rounded the desk to support him.

'Get off,' he muttered, but Ben held on.

'I think 'e ought ter go,' said Hetty. 'Don't want the likes of 'im in my 'ouse.'

Amused, Libby said, 'Shall we put him out, Hetty?'

'I'm not goin' bloody anywhere,' said Willis, eyeing Hetty warily.

'Then it'll 'ave to be the police,' said Hetty, unmoved. 'Ben, call –'

'All right, all right.' Willis struggled back to his chair. 'Bloody women.'

Ben stifled a snort and Hetty winked at Libby. Just as she did so, they heard the unmistakable sound of tyres on gravel.

'That'll be Ian,' said Libby, and went to let him in.

'You've just missed Hetty getting the better of him,' she whispered, as she led him and a wide-eyed detective constable to the office.

'I wish I'd seen that,' he whispered back and entered the office behind her.

'Hello, Hetty, Ben,' he said. 'This is DC Irons. Who's this?'

199

'Mr Wally Willis,' said Ben. 'Stan Willis's father.'

'Oh, yes.' Ian didn't hold out a hand. Neither did Wally Willis. 'I believe one of my officers went to see you in London last week?'

Willis nodded, looking even more wary now.

'Is there anything we can do for you now you're here?' continued Ian.

'Let me into that theatre.' It came out as a growl.

Ian glanced at Ben, who shook his head.

'Not just at the moment, sir.' Ian moved round to the side of Ben's desk, forcing Willis to turn and face him. 'Who did you want to see?'

'That bloody Tobing!'

'Mr Max Tobin, would that be, sir?' Ian said mildly. Libby had to turn away and discovered Hetty had, too. While they both struggled to contain their mirth, Ian was going on.

'I'm afraid he can't tell you any more about your son's death than I can. What did you want to know?'

''Is fuckin' fault, innit?' The roar was back.

'No, sir, Mr Tobin had nothing to do with the death. In fact, he was attacked himself.'

Willis goggled and suddenly sat down again.

Hetty cleared her throat and went to pick up the tea tray. She glanced at Ian, who nodded and smiled, and left the room.

'Now, Mr Willis,' said Ian. 'As you're here, perhaps you wouldn't mind answering a few questions. DC Irons will just take a few notes.

'Already talked to your lot.'

'I know, sir, but there are a few things I'd like to clarify.'

''Oo are you?'

'Detective Chief Inspector Connell, I'm senior investigating officer on the enquiry into Mr Willis junior's death.'

Willis grunted.

'Ben, Libby, I'm sorry to turn you out, but ...' Ian smiled deprecatingly.

'OK, we're going,' said Ben with an answering grin. 'Come on, Lib.'

As they left, they heard Willis ask, 'Friends o' yours, are

they? That's 'andy, innit?'

'What a horrible man,' said Libby as they entered the kitchen.

'Lots like 'im in the East End,' said Hetty. 'Ought to ask Flo up to have a look at him.'

'As a curiosity?' suggested Ben. 'Are you making Ian tea?'

'Yes. Mugs this time. 'Ere, Lib, you can take 'em in.'

'I'll bring the sugar in case DC Irons wants it,' said Ben, artlessly.

Ben knocked on the door and opened it for Libby, who went in and put the two mugs down on the desk. Ben offered the sugar to DC Irons, who shook his head, looking embarrassed, and he and Libby regretfully left the room.

As they did so, the front door opened and Sebastian almost fell through it.

'Is it Stan's father? Is he here?'

'Yes, he is. I thought you said you didn't know him?' Libby frowned at him.

'I don't – but he'll know me, won't he? Oh, God, don't tell him I'm here!'

# Chapter Twenty-seven

Ben steered Sebastian into the sitting-room.

'Now, what do you mean by that? And if you didn't want him to know you were here, why did you come over?'

'Because he's bound to come to the theatre and I wouldn't be able to get away from him!' Sebastian sank on to one of the sofas, head in hands.

'Why are you scared, Seb?' Libby sat down beside him.

'After you told me Stan's father was a criminal it was obvious how I'd been let off the whole drugs thing. The more I thought about it the more likely it seemed. And Stan used to threaten me. I wondered what he could do to me, but I didn't dare try to find out.'

'And how did you know he was here?' asked Ben.

'Max recognised the car. He'd gone up to the box and noticed it when he was coming down. We've finished over there, and he was going to give his pep talk.'

'OK,' said Ben. 'Go into the kitchen. Where are you sleeping now, by the way?'

'Oh, they've let me back into the room in the hotel. They've taken all Stan's stuff away.'

'Right, well, go into the kitchen, as Ben says, and we'll let you know when it's safe to come out,' said Libby.

She showed a quivering Sebastian into the kitchen with a 'Look after him, Hetty!' and returned to Ben.

'Did he seem unduly scared to you?' asked Ben.

'Hmmm.' Libby looked thoughtful. 'He did rather. Why, do you suppose? He professed to know nothing about Stan's father or how the drugs barons or whoever they were let up on him. Do you think he was lying? I thought he was telling the truth at the time.'

'He's had time to think about it since then. He might even

have had a look on the internet. Probably scared him stiff reading about what Willis got up to back in the sixties and seventies.'

'Perhaps that's it. I wonder if Ian will let him see Max?'

As if in answer to her query, Ian appeared at the sitting-room door.

'I'm sorry to be a nuisance,' he began, and Libby raised her eyebrows, 'but would one of you mind fetching Tobin over here?'

'I'll go,' said Ben.

'Sebastian's hiding in the kitchen,' said Libby. 'He doesn't want to meet Stan's father.'

'Now why would that be?' Ian frowned.

'Go and ask him?' Libby suggested.

'Not until I've supervised the meeting between Willis and Tobin. He might be an old man, but he could do some damage with those sticks.'

'Do you think he still has the power to cause any real grief?' asked Libby.

'Associates, you mean? There's certainly some influence there, especially if Seb is right and Stan got the hounds called off. When was that?'

'I don't know. Couple of years, maybe?'

Ben arrived, with Max in tow looking worried.

'What does he want?' he asked Ian.

'Satisfaction,' said Ian with a grin. 'But I felt it was only fair to let him see you.'

'Under supervision,' put in Libby.

'Exactly,' agreed Ian. 'Ready?'

'Aren't you two coming?' Max looked at Libby and Ben.

'No. Not our business,' said Ben. 'We'll wait here.'

'Shall we go and relieve Hetty in the kitchen?' suggested Libby.

'You go. I'll stay here and wait for Max,' said Ben, so Libby went back to the kitchen, where she found Sebastian sitting at the table gloomily contemplating a mug of tea.

'You seem to have done nothing but make tea this afternoon, Het,' she said to Hetty, who stood leaning against the Aga, arms

204

folded, watching Sebastian.

'You want some?' asked Hetty.

'No, thanks. I've just come to cheer Seb up.'

Sebastian looked up. 'Has he gone?'

'No. He's in there talking to Max, now.'

'To Max? What for?'

'It was Max he came to see. I think he holds him responsible for Stan's death.'

Seb's eyes widened. 'He thinks *Max* killed Stan?'

'No, I don't think that, I think he thinks that because it happened while Stan was in Max's company he bears the responsibility.'

'That's mad.' But Seb wasn't quite as firm about it as he could have been, thought Libby.

'You've got a doubt, there, haven't you?' she said.

'Well, I just thought – unless it was actually being in the company …'

'Something to do with the company? Or the piece itself?'

'Well, yes.' Seb looked up at Libby. 'After all, Stan didn't like *Pendle*. He didn't think we should be doing it.'

'And you never knew why that was?' said Libby.

'No-o. But then, I never knew what was behind half of Stan's moods. He was a very difficult person, you know.'

'I gathered that,' said Libby. 'I wish there was someone else we could talk to about him. And don't suggest his father.'

'You know, I'm surprised he's here.' Seb looked back at his mug. 'They didn't see much of one another.'

'I thought you didn't know anything about his father?' Libby narrowed her eyes at him.

'I didn't!' said Seb quickly. 'No, what I meant was, over the time I was living and working with him, he never once went to see his father.'

'How do you know?'

'He never went out,' said Seb simply. 'Only to work, occasionally to the theatre or another ballet company, and I always went with him.'

'I see.' Libby tapped a finger on the table. 'But there are other forms of communication. Perhaps they were in touch by email, or on social media? Although I can't see Willis senior as a user of either.'

'I'm sure they weren't.' Seb shook his head.

'But you do think now that it was the father's criminal connections that got you off the hook?'

'Well, you pointed it out.' Seb wasn't looking at her.

Ben put his head round the door.

'He's going.'

'Willis?'

'Yes. With a very bad grace.'

Libby got up and went out into the hall. Wally Willis was manoeuvring out of the front door, still talking.

'Some bugger's goin' to pay for this. And where's that little shit Sebastopol or whatever 'e calls 'imself? Causing my son all that trouble.'

'What trouble was that, Mr Willis?' asked Ian, still smooth.

But Wally Willis declined to answer, merely grunting again and stumping to his car, which Libby suddenly realised had a driver, who at Willis's approach jumped out of the driving seat and went to open the rear door for his passenger.

'Real "Mr Big" stuff,' murmured Libby.

'He'd like to think so,' said Ian, turning back to the office. Ben and Libby watched the big car turn and go down the drive until they were certain their unwelcome guest had gone. Then they followed Ian into the office. Max was sitting in a chair by the window looking forlorn.

'What did he say?' asked Libby.

'Very little to any purpose,' said Ian. 'Bluster, mostly. I think we'd spiked his guns. If he could have gone straight into the theatre and cornered Mr Tobin there – well, I think there might have been some damage.'

Max sighed. 'But he's right in a way, isn't he?'

'Right? How?' said Ben.

'He got murdered because he was employed by me. He was here because of me. It has to be something to do with *Pendle*.'

Ian regarded him thoughtfully. 'Do you have any idea what he meant by Sebastian Long causing Stan Willis trouble?'

Max lifted his head. 'Did he say that? I've no idea, I'm

206

sorry. I know he got Seb out of a spot of bother, but it didn't seem to cause him any trouble. The first I knew about it was when he turned up with Seb in tow and said he'd be working with him now.'

'So did he ask you to pay him?' said Libby.

'No, but I did. Actually, Seb has turned out to be incredibly helpful, although I wouldn't say his heart was in it.'

'I think he's hiding something,' said Libby.

'Everyone's hiding something,' said Ian. 'Comes with the territory.'

'Yes, but when I first talked to Seb about Stan's father being a criminal – of course, I didn't know he was still alive, then – he didn't seem to know anything about it, yet now he's obviously scared.'

'Which argues that he's found something out,' said Ben. 'But how? The police took all Stan's belongings.'

Ian looked at Max. 'Still not remembered what you went to the theatre for, Mr Tobin?'

'No. Oh – you think I might have gone to look for something to do with Stan?' He paused. 'And – what? Seb came and bashed me on the head and took it?'

Ian shrugged. 'Let's have Mr Long in and ask him.'

'Oh, I say!' said Max, turning a pleasant shade of pink.

But Libby was already at the kitchen door.

'Come along, Seb,' she called. 'Come and join the party.'

Seb shuffled along the corridor towards the office and sidled into the room behind her.

'Did you follow Mr Tobin into the theatre on Sunday morning?' Ian asked without preamble.

Seb's mouth dropped open. 'No, I did not!' he stuttered. 'I was having breakfast – Damian can tell you!'

'I thought you only came down as he was going out of the front door?' said Libby. 'And Damian was only there a minute or two before you.'

'Yes, but then I went and sat at Damian's table. I didn't follow him. You can ask Damian.'

Ian nodded and turned back to Max. 'Is that right, Mr Tobin?'

'As far as I know,' said Max, frowning. 'I remember leaving the pub.'

'Would you mind leaving me and Mr Long alone for a minute or two?' Ian said. 'Sorry to turn you out again, Ben.'

'That's all right,' said Ben, looking mystified.

'Come on, Max,' said Libby, looking annoyed.

'Coming,' said Max, looking intrigued.

They all stood outside the office staring at each other.

'What's that about?' whispered Max.

'I expect he wants to ask Seb what he's hiding, and if he's found anything out over the last few days. There's got to be something,' said Libby. 'And how did you recognise the car? Seb said you did.'

'He came to pick Stan up one day. Stan saw the car and said "That's all I need, my bloody father." Or something like that.'

'Seb said they never saw one another. Why didn't he see the car?'

Max shrugged. 'I think it was before Seb joined us.'

'So perhaps when Stan was asking for his help,' Libby said to Ben.

'I'd better go back and make sure they're packing up.' Max sighed and went out.

'I'll go over and help,' said Ben. 'What are you going to do?'

'I have no idea. Shall I wait here for you?'

'If you like. Ian might confide in you when he finishes with Seb.'

'Some hopes.' Libby gave him a peck on the cheek and went to join Hetty in the kitchen. A few moments later Ian came in.
'Sorry about that, Lib,' he said with a grin. 'I know you were dying to stay.'

'Well, I was. I thought you were going to ask Seb what he'd learnt in the last few days. Did you?'

'I did. From what you said, it seems he now knows more than he did when Stan died. But he wouldn't tell me.'

'Do you think it's important?'

'I think it might be what got Max banged over the head. But to be honest, I can't see that Wally Willis has got anything to do with it. I certainly don't think he had his son killed.'

'Had him killed?'

'Well I doubt if he could have managed it himself, don't you? He can hardly move. No, I think we'll have to keep on poking around in the backgrounds of all these dancers.'

'Have you asked at their home addresses? All that sort of thing?' said Libby.

'We've made enquiries where we thought we needed to,' said Ian repressively. 'We're good at that.'

'Sorry,' said Libby, feeling a blush creep up her neck. 'I'll shut up now.'

## Chapter Twenty-eight

'I was thinking,' said Libby. 'I could perhaps pop up to London to see Andrew.'

Ben looked at her, surprised. 'What for? He'll be down on Saturday.'

'I thought I might be able to find out more about some of the dancers.'

'Libby! Stop poking your nose in – and anyway, what would Andrew know about Max's dancers?'

'He might be able to introduce me to the school.'

'They've got the week off, remember? And besides, the students are coming down tomorrow.'

'Thursday,' said Libby and sighed. 'So there's no point in going to London?'

'No, of course not. And Ian will have looked into anything he thinks necessary. He's been up to London himself, hasn't he?'

'Yes,' said Libby, 'but he wouldn't say why.'

Ben laughed. 'Oh, Libby, you're priceless!'

'But not in a good way,' said Libby, with another sigh. 'If only …'

'If only what?'

'Well, I want to be rid of the whole shebang, but while they're still here, and things like Wally Willis arriving keep happening, we can't. And that means I want to know what happened.'

'That's convoluted, but I think I know what you mean.' Ben patted her shoulder. 'Never mind, tonight they start their run and things will be different. Have you got enough people for front of house?'

'Fran's coming up and Bob the butcher said he'll come in. I've got to be on the bar. That should be enough.'

'And will keep your mind off murder,' said Ben comfortably.

Libby, left alone, looked in at the rehearsal and finally went to see if she could help Harry with the dancers' lunch.

Donna, Harry's right-hand woman, back part-time now her toddler was at nursery, waved her into the kitchen.

'No wonder you can leave the caff at lunchtimes with Donna here,' said Libby.

'I'm just hoping she won't nip off and have another baby,' said Harry, slicing lettuce at eye-watering speed. 'Here – wash your hands and you can carry on with this.'

'I shall be slow,' said Libby, taking off her cape and going to one of the sinks.

'I don't care. I just need help. Have you found out anything new?'

Libby told him about the visit of Wally Willis.

'But Ian doesn't think he's got anything to do with the murder, and actually, I agree. He did seem properly upset about it – in a funny way.'

'Complete red herring, then?'

'Yes.' Libby frowned. 'Although I can't help thinking that there's something about him …'

'How do you mean? Look, don't stop chopping while you think. I thought birds were supposed to be good at multi-tasking?'

'Birds, Harry Price? Bit outdated, isn't it? And yes, of course we're good at it. But what puzzles me about Stan and Wally Willis is that young Sebastian thought Stan had nothing to do with his father. Yet we're certain that it was Wally who got the drugs barons off Seb's back.'

'Drugs barons? Blimey, gel, that's going it a bit, isn't it?'

'Well, you know, the people who were hounding Seb for money. I told you all about that, didn't I?'

'Tell me again.'

Libby repeated the whole story.

'Sounds a very odd set-up altogether, if you ask me,' said Harry. 'All this denial stuff. Doesn't ring true.'

'I agree, but Seb assures me *he* isn't gay, and says he didn't have that sort of relationship with Stan.'

Harry started packing his baskets with food. 'Shove that lettuce in here,' he said handing over a large plastic container. 'What I think is that Stan and his father did see one another, whatever young Seb thought – and he could be lying. At least, I bet they were in touch by text or email or something.'

'I asked him that. He said not.' Libby was washing her hands again.

'And Seb didn't like Stan. I bet he's hiding something.'

'Who, Seb?'

'Course. Sure to be.'

'I don't know,' said Libby doubtfully. 'And as for Stan being against the whole production –'

'You didn't tell me that,' said Harry, draping Libby's cape over her shoulders. 'Come on, you can carry that basket.'

'I can't remember what you know and what you don't know,' said Libby, following him out of the restaurant and smiling at Donna.

'Let's go over it on the way up the drive,' said Harry. 'And I will treat you to one of my witty insights into the problem.'

Libby, interrupting herself frequently, went back over the whole story.

'The trouble is,' she said at the end, 'what we knew at the beginning – or even the middle – is different to what we know now.'

'That, petal, is self-evident. Just think: if you knew everything as soon as a crime was committed, you'd pick up the criminal with one hand and open the prison door with the other. Simple.'

'Hmm,' said Libby. 'The problem is people concealing things because they think it will make them or someone else look bad.'

'It often does,' said Harry. 'Come on, let's go and feed the hungry horde.'

Libby recognised the state of nervous tension and excitement emanating from the dancers and felt a sympathetic frisson in her own abdomen. Some of them were too wound up to eat, others ate more than usual. Max watched over them with worried benevolence.

'They'll rest this afternoon,' Owen told her as she helped him to coffee. 'Except they won't, of course.'

'Is there anyone special coming tonight, do you know?'

'Not as far as I know,' said Owen. 'The school's coming down tomorrow and various influential people are coming Friday and Saturday, but Max wanted them to get used to an audience before putting them under extra pressure. I don't think any of their friends and relations are coming. It's a bit far out for them.'

'Real life in the sticks,' said Libby, with a grin.

Owen looked embarrassed.

'It's all right, we are off the beaten track as far as London goes, although we have commuters who drive to the station in Canterbury for the train every day. But it's a long way to come for a performance. And I expect all the aforesaid friends and relations will go to performances when you transfer to London.'

'*If* we transfer to London,' said Owen gloomily.

Libby left them to it and went home. Unable to settle, she soon went out again and went to visit Flo and Lenny to tell them about Wally Willis.

'Oh, yeah, I remember that,' said Flo, when Libby told her about the orgies mentioned at the trial. 'I reckon it was all 'ushed up. You didn't 'ear so much about kiddy-fiddling in them days.'

Libby made a face. 'What a horrible expression.'

Flo shrugged. ''Orrible business. I mainly remember the murders 'e was supposed to be mixed up in. And there was that burning. Remember, Len?'

'Burning?' Libby's ears pricked up.

Flo frowned. 'Some bloke – can't remember 'oo but 'e was famous – was set fire to on some 'eath or other just outside London.'

'Supposed to be like some old, mad monks or something,' put in Lenny.

'Medmenham!' breathed Libby.

'Med what?' asked Lenny and Flo together.

'Medmenham. The Mad Monks of Medmenham. They were what came to be known as the Hellfire Club back in the eighteenth century. They were aristocrats who met secretly and indulged in all sorts of weird practices.'

'Practices?' repeated Flo.

'Well they drank a lot, and had a lot of women.'

'That don't mean much,' said Lenny.

'No, but there was a lot more besides,' said Libby. 'Devil-worship and Black Masses, that sort of thing.'

'Oh, not that again!' said Flo. 'You bin messing around with "that sort of thing" before. Not nice.'

'I agree it isn't nice. But I thought of this connection before, and now it's beginning to make sense.'

'Bugger me, gal, if you don't take the biscuit.' Flo shook her head. 'Drink yer tea.'

As soon as she decently could, Libby left Flo and Lenny and on her way home rang Fran.

'Well, I do see there is a connection with the threats of burning, but is it enough of a connection? It only connects with the incidents in London, not with Stan's murder.'

'Should I mention it to Ian?'

'I don't think so,' said Fran. 'He'll know about this burning in Willis's past already and he'll have looked into it if he thinks it's necessary.'

'I suppose so,' said Libby. 'I'm going to look it up when I get home anyway.'

Back at number seventeen and awash with Flo's strong tea, she opened the laptop and began a search through Wally Willis's past villainy. To her surprise, although she found several references and contemporaneous reports, Willis was barely mentioned in connection with the outrage, most journalists preferring to concentrate on the similarity to Francis Dashwood's infamous club she had mentioned to Flo and Lenny. Rumours had apparently been circulating about a rejuvenated Hellfire Club, which chimed with what Libby already knew about Willis and his associates, but now, the burning of a member of the minor aristocracy on a deserted heath not far from the Abbey itself made the connection with

Dashwood's Mad Monks a media dream, although with no social media, internet or mobile phone networks back then the coverage was limited to radio, newspapers and some television news.

'I think,' said Libby to Ben when he came in later, 'that it possibly *was* Stan who was behind the incidents in London, and he was so horrified by what his father had been part of that he saw the whole *Pendle* thing as an abomination. You can see how you could align the celebration in dance of the Pendle Witches with the celebration of wickedness in the Hellfire Clubs, can't you?'

'It's a stretch, but I suppose so,' said Ben. 'Is there anything to eat?'

'Oh, bother, I forgot,' said Libby, trying to look contrite. 'There's some frozen bolognese in the freezer ...'

Ben sighed. 'OK. I'll dig it out.'

'And I'll put the kettle on,' said Libby brightly. 'So, to carry on –'

Ben rolled his eyes.

'Anyway,' Libby said to Fran when she arrived to help at the theatre, 'if it was Stan, he would be very bothered by all this, and the threat of burning he would see as perfect justice.'

'It's a stretch.' Fran echoed Ben. 'But I suppose I can see a tenuous connection. Now what am I supposed to be doing?'

Libby stationed Bob the butcher by the main doors to take tickets and Fran by the auditorium doors to show people where to go. If anyone needed to buy tickets, she would sell them from the bar.

Before they opened the doors to the public, she did the rounds of the departments. Peter and Damian were in their eyrie, Damian looking nervous and Peter looking relaxed. Ben and Sebastian were backstage already looking bored. The dancers were in the dressing rooms in various attitudes of preparation and Max was trying not to fuss over them. Owen appeared from the other side of the stage.

'All serene?' he asked. 'I've just had a look at the Kabuki and everything seems fine. Not that I can climb up and look.'

'No, I'd rather you didn't,' said Libby. 'Are you coming front of house? I need to open the doors to the ravening public.'

'Yes, I'll keep an eye on the house for Max. He won't come out yet.'

'There's already a small queue out there,' said Bob, as Libby approached with the keys.

'Good,' said Libby. 'They deserve an audience, now.'

She took up her place behind the bar and began taking orders for interval drinks while keeping an eye on the steady trickle of people arriving. Owen hovered between Bob and Fran and, about five minutes before curtain up, Libby saw him greet a tall young man whom Libby immediately identified as another *danseur*. Owen noticed Libby observing them, and taking the young man by the arm, led him over to the bar.

'Libby,' he said, 'meet our original Demdike, Paddy Milburn.'

# Chapter Twenty-nine

Libby looked up at the young man standing before her.

'Hello, Paddy.' She smiled and held out her hand, which he took with a diffident smile of his own.

'Hello.' His voice had a faint Irish accent. 'I'm sorry now I didn't stay with the company. This all looks lovely.'

'Thank you,' said Libby. 'Perhaps I'll see you later. I think it's time to take your seats.'

Owen and Paddy moved towards the auditorium doors and Libby came out from behind the bar counter.

'Who was that?' asked Fran as she closed the doors.

'The original Demdike. The one who left after all the threats.'

'Really?' Fran's eyebrows rose. 'He doesn't look like someone who's easily intimidated.'

'No.' Libby was thoughtful. 'But we don't know exactly what the threats were.'

'Will told us it was burning. "What they do to witches", wasn't it?'

'Yes, but he said he hadn't seen Paddy's or Gerry's, so we don't know exactly. Perhaps it was worse than that.'

'And in your head you've linked it all up with Wally Willis and the Medmenham Monks, haven't you?'

Libby stared defiantly at her friend. 'Even you have to admit it's a coincidence.'

'OK, it's a coincidence, but absolutely nothing to do with Stan's death.'

'I'm sure there's a link,' said Libby. 'And I wonder why Paddy's come down to watch? Surely he'd have waited to see it in London – if he wanted to see it at all, which I'm surprised at.'

'He was involved from the start, why wouldn't he want to

see how it turned out?' said Fran. 'Don't start making mysteries where there are none, Lib.'

'Hmm.' Libby wandered back to the bar. 'I suppose I can't leave the bar and go and watch, can I?'

'Not unless either Bob or I stay here,' said Fran. 'And you've seen it already. Let Bob go in and watch if he wants to.'

Libby turned to where Bob was still standing at the front doors. 'Do you want to go in and watch, Bob?' she called.

'Thanks,' Bob called back. 'Can I slip in at the back?'

Libby and Fran began to lay out the pre-ordered interval drinks.

'I wonder where all these people have come from?' said Fran, idly polishing a glass. 'I didn't recognise many of your usual crowd.'

'I don't know. The online bookings are done through an agency website, we just get told a list of names and the tickets are printed automatically. A couple of phone bookings came through, and they're transferred to Ben's office phone, but no one we recognised. I know it was advertised on dance websites and in dance magazines so I suppose that's where a lot of them came from.'

'One woman said she was from one of the local dance schools. I suppose he researched them and sent them details.' Fran replaced the glass.

'Easy to do on social media,' said Libby. 'I'm glad he's got a good house. They've all worked so hard, and it's been so traumatic over the last couple of weeks.'

'Well, if the motive behind it all was to stop the production, it didn't work.'

'And if it was to make sure it went ahead, it did work. Either way, it's over now. We just hope tonight goes smoothly and they get their transfer.'

A burst of clapping heralded the interval and an excited, chattering crowd poured into the foyer. Libby and Fran were kept busy serving those who had not pre-ordered drinks and fielding questions to which they didn't know the answers. Libby noticed Paddy talking to Damian and hoped he'd come to the bar. She wanted to know what he thought, and if he still wished he'd stayed with the company.

'Going well.' Owen appeared at the bar looking triumphant. 'They seem to love it.'

'It certainly sounds like it,' said Libby. 'Drink?'

'Not yet. I'll celebrate later with Max.' He moved away, and Libby again looked for Paddy, only to find he'd disappeared.

The bar gradually cleared and Fran and Libby began to load the glass washer.

'I wanted to ask Paddy what he thought,' said Libby. 'Did you see him?'

'Only in the distance, talking to Damian.'

'Yes, sympathising, probably.'

'How so?'

'Well, Paddy backed out, and Damian nearly did, didn't he? Although he must be pleased with the response it's getting.' Libby began wiping down the counter with industrial cleaner.

There was a spontaneous burst of applause from the auditorium.

'I bet that's the Kabuki,' said Libby, looking up at the FX box. Peter looked down and gave her a thumbs up.

The second half was shorter than the first, and it was only just after ten o'clock when prolonged cheering and clapping broke out. Libby and Fran opened the auditorium doors and stood at the back watching as the young men discarded their characters and took their bows as themselves.

Max came out, took a bow and led the applause for Damian, while the audience craned round to see him, and finally, the company left the stage.

In the foyer, he was surrounded by people congratulating him, while he modestly disclaimed responsibility, introducing the dancers, as one by one they emerged from the dressing rooms. Eventually, only the company were left.

Owen had disappeared, and now returned holding aloft four bottles of champagne. 'Hetty kept them cold for me,' he announced, 'so it didn't spoil the surprise for Libby!'

Libby and Fran hurriedly began setting out wineglasses. 'No flutes, I'm afraid, Owen,' said Libby.

Max raised his glass as soon as it was filled. 'Here's to you all, for making Pendle such a success.' He turned to Libby. 'Including our wonderful hosts!'

As the hubbub died down, Libby asked what Paddy had thought of it. 'I didn't see him after the show to ask,' she said.

'Neither did I,' said Max. 'Owen?'

'No, I didn't either. I wonder why? As he took all the trouble to drive down here.'

'I wanted to know what he thought of the music.' Damian appeared behind Owen.

'Didn't you ask him in the interval?' said Libby. 'I saw you were talking to him.'

'Yes, but he'd heard it in rehearsal. I didn't ask him what he thought of the orchestration. He's a musician as well as a dancer, you know. Classical violin.' Damian looked worried. 'Do you think he hated it and left early?'

'Surely if he'd hated it, he would have told you in the interval,' said Max. 'Don't look so worried, Damian. I'm sorry I didn't get a chance to speak to him, though.'

'He said he wished he'd stayed with the company when he arrived, didn't he Owen?' said Libby.

'He did. He didn't know much of the detail of our saga down here, because, amazingly, the boys have kept quiet.'

'He knew about Stan, though,' said Damian. 'He was asking me about that. I said none of us knew what had happened.'

'Good. Best to keep quiet,' said Max. 'Now, we must let Ben and Libby lock up. Come on, everybody, drink up.'

Half an hour later, they had seen Fran off in her car, and Ben, Libby and Peter walked down the drive.

'Come and have a drink in the caff,' said Peter. 'Hal will want to know all about it.'

Harry had anticipated their arrival by placing various alcoholic beverages on the big, pine table in the right-hand window. Libby slumped into the sofa in the left-hand one.

'Everything worked perfectly,' Peter announced. 'Even the dancers.'

He and Ben gave their opinion of the evening's performance, Kabuki curtain and all.

'The audience gasped and clapped,' said Ben. 'Very

gratifying.'

'And the music?' asked Harry.

'Well, they all cheered when Max waved up at the box,' said Peter, 'although they could have been cheering me, of course.'

'And one of the original dancers came down,' said Libby. 'And vanished before we could ask him what he thought.'

'That's a bit odd, isn't it?' Harry topped up his glass.

'I thought so. He drove all the way down here, Owen said. And didn't stay.'

'You would have thought he'd want to talk to the other dancers,' said Ben.

Peter frowned. 'My journalist's nose is twitching.'

'Why?' asked Libby.

'It seems more than odd. Almost as if he was spying.'

'Spying?' the other three echoed.

'What for? Who for?' said Harry. 'Someone Max has pissed off?'

'I don't know. It's probably nothing. But apart from Owen and Damian he didn't speak to anybody and sloped off before he could see anyone afterwards. Either he hated the whole thing, or ...'

'But I don't see what he could say to anyone that would – I don't know – reflect badly on the company. They virtually made the whole thing up from a standing start and Max himself has funded this production.' Libby scowled into her glass. 'There's nothing wrong with any of it.'

'On the face of it, no,' said Peter, 'But we have had one murder and one serious attack. Perhaps he was down here to find out about that.'

'To damage the company? But it wouldn't! Not now. It's opened. If anything, if the news got out now it would be good publicity.'

'Libby!' Ben protested.

'I'm not saying it's not bad taste, but you've got to admit that the ghoulish public would be very interested.'

'She's right,' said Harry. 'It pains me to say so, but she is.'

'Or,' said Peter, 'could he have had something to do with the incidents in London – even down here – and have come to see

223

what the result was?' He looked at Libby and grinned. 'And now I sound like you.'

'But he was the one who received the worst of the threats,' said Ben.

'Camouflage,' said Peter and Libby together.

'It's possible, isn't it?' said Libby. 'Unlikely, but possible.'

'You've spent the last week and a half theorising about what could have happened, what's behind everything and whodunit, and every theory has been more unlikely than the last,' said Harry. 'And if I were you, I'd shut up now, because there's a policeman coming to get you.'

'I wondered where you were,' said Ian putting his head round the door. 'I saw some of the troops go into the pub. They all seemed cheerful.'

'Sorry, we should have remembered it was Wednesday,' said Libby.

'Come in, Ian.' Harry stood up. 'Coffee?'

'As yours is far better than the pub's, yes please.' Ian came inside, pulled up a chair and sat down. 'So how did it go? Anne and Patti said to tell you they've got tickets for tomorrow.'

'Oh, yes,' said Ben. 'I forgot to tell you.'

'It went very well,' said Libby. 'Pete and Ben can tell you more. Fran and I spent the evening in the foyer and doing the bar.'

Harry reappeared with the coffee pot and Ben and Peter launched into a description of the evening's performance.

'And no incidents?' asked Ian. 'Did you use the curtain?'

'Yes, and it got a round of applause,' said Ben. 'No incidents, and a very happy company.'

'Well, I hope that's the way it stays,' said Ian. 'I'm only sorry we haven't managed to find out more about the murder and the attack on Max.'

'Actually –' began Libby.

'Libby, shut up!' said three voices.

Ian looked amused. 'What? Let her speak so she can shoot herself in the foot.'

The other men laughed and Libby looked affronted.

'I was only going to say that one of the dancers who left

224

because of the threats in London turned up, and disappeared again before he could speak to anyone.'

Ian's smile disappeared, too.

'Who was that?'

'Paddy something,' said Libby, looking startled. 'Millward? Milburn – that's it.'

'And has anybody tried to get in touch with him to ask why?'

'No!' Libby was surprised. 'We discussed it after the show. I suppose one of them should have done.'

'It might have looked like asking for praise,' said Ben.

Ian shook his head. 'In view of what's been happening around this company over the last couple of months, I think it's more like asking if he's safe!'

# Chapter Thirty

Everyone looked at Libby, who sighed.

'OK. Who do I ask?'

'Max, obviously,' said Ben.

She found the number in her phone and pressed call. It was answered almost immediately.

'Libby? What's up?'

'Well, nothing really, but – er –' Libby cleared her throat and looked frantically at Ian, who reached over and took the phone.

'Max? This is DCI Connell. I wonder if you could do me a favour? Yes – thank you. Could you ring …'

'Paddy,' whispered Libby.

'Paddy. I believe he came down this evening? Yes, that's what Libby told me. We're just a little concerned that he hasn't been seen since the interval – exactly, we thought the same. Could you do that and ring me back? Yes, this number's fine. Thank you.'

He handed the phone back to Libby, who handed it back.

'It's you he's going to be ringing – golly, that was quick.'

'Yes?' said Ian. His face was serious. 'I see. Yes, I'll get back to you. Have you got a home address for him?'

Ian ended the call and once more handed the phone back to Libby.

'The phone's switched off and the address is in London.' He stood up. 'I may be being alarmist, but I think we need to look into this.'

'Shall I come and open the theatre?' asked Ben. 'Although there was no one left there when we locked up. I'd done the rounds.'

'Yes, but don't forget other people have got keys,' said

Libby. 'Someone got in and got to Stan and Max.'

Ian, his own phone to his ear, nodded at Ben and then started speaking in low tones.

'Oh, dear.' Libby looked at Peter and Harry. 'Looks like Ian thinks your journalist's nose was right.'

'I just hope it's not a re-run of last Wednesday,' said Peter.

'A week ago! So much has happened.' Libby shook her head. 'What shall we do?'

Ian ended his call. 'You can go home. I've got officers on the way who will go with Ben to the theatre, and I'm going back to the pub to talk to Damian, as he seems to be the only one this Paddy spoke to.'

'Apart from Owen,' said Libby. 'But that was only as he was coming in.'

'Then I'll speak to him, too.'

'Can't I come with you?'

Ian's exasperation showed plainly in his face. 'No, Libby. Just leave it. Ben, will you wait here for the officers?'

Ben nodded.

'Stay here with us if you don't want to go home, petal,' said Harry. 'I know you won't settle.'

Libby gave him a grateful smile and Ian left the restaurant.

'We seem to have started another hare,' said Peter.

'It's my fault,' said Libby. 'I shouldn't have mentioned it.'

'But supposing something has happened to Paddy?' said Ben. 'Better to find out quickly. And Peter had picked up on it, too. Not just you.'

They sat making desultory conversation for another twenty minutes, before the door was pushed open and a uniformed officer peered in.

'Mr Wilde?'

'Yes.' Ben stood up and joined him. 'I'll see you lot in a bit.'

Libby shivered. 'I hope they don't find anything.'

'So do I,' said Peter. 'I'm not very happy with our theatre being used as the scene of the crime.'

The door opened again and Max came in, followed by Owen.

'May we come in?' asked Max.

'You are in,' said Harry, standing up.

'Sorry,' said Owen, 'we'll go.'

'Don't be daft,' said Harry. 'Come in and sit down. Coffee? Or something stronger?'

Max more or less collapsed into the chair vacated by Harry.

'I'm on whisky,' said Libby helpfully.

Max smiled at her gratefully and Peter got up to fetch glasses.

'Now,' said Harry, pouring whisky with a generous hand. 'What's happened?'

'Your inspector came to ask about Paddy,' said Owen.

'Yes, we know. We told him,' said Libby.

'His phone's switched off,' said Max in a tired voice. 'And no one had a home number for him, but several people had Gerry's number.'

'Who's Gerry?' asked Harry.

'The other dancer who left in London,' said Owen. 'He and Paddy were both threatened with burning. So Jonathan called him. And he said Paddy has no landline.' He shrugged. 'Which isn't unusual. Most young people don't, these days.'

'Most of the boys didn't realise he'd been in the audience and were quite upset because he hadn't stayed to speak to everyone,' said Max. 'And that was what was bothering your inspector.'

'Well, it bothered us, a bit, didn't it?' said Libby. 'As Owen said, he drove all the way down here, and when I met him before the show he seemed to be really looking forward to it.'

'What did Damian say?' asked Harry.

'Not a lot. Just what he said to us in the theatre,' said Owen. 'He's worried in case Paddy didn't like the music.'

'But Paddy would have been dancing to it in London, wouldn't he?' asked Peter. 'He'd have said then, surely.'

'But it's changed quite a bit,' said Max. 'I think I told you, we were all improvising at first, it was only towards the end that the music and the choreography firmed up.'

'Oh, I see! I was puzzled about that,' said Libby. 'But why would he worry about Paddy not liking the music?'

'Paddy is a classically trained violinist as well as a dancer. He's great friends with our friend Sergio. In fact, he was supposed to be coming down here with Sergio on Saturday, but couldn't make it.'

'Which makes it all the more odd that he didn't stay to speak to you all,' said Libby.

'Is Sergio a musician, too?' asked Peter.

'A conductor and composer. We're all looking forward to finding out what he thinks of our *Pendle*.' Max gave them all a tired smile. 'So you don't know any more about what the inspector thinks than we do?'

'No, only that he noticed Pete's nose twitching,' said Harry.

'Eh?' Max and Owen looked confused.

'Pete's a freelance journalist. He said his journalistic nose was twitching,' explained Libby.

'What – about Paddy?' Max looked even more puzzled.

'He thought he might be spying,' said Harry, digging his beloved in the ribs.

'*Paddy*?' echoed Max and Owen together.

'Never in a million years,' added Owen. 'And what for, for fuck's sake?'

'I don't know.' Peter shrugged. 'I just home in on unusual behaviour patterns.'

'Paddy is the nicest, quietest bloke you could ever wish to meet. In fact, I was a bit surprised when he got spooked by those threats,' said Max. 'He's always seemed so calm, so balanced.'

'I suppose,' said Libby suddenly, 'he did go back in after the interval? Did anyone see him?'

'No, I didn't. I wasn't looking for him,' said Owen.

'I was backstage, so I didn't,' said Max.

'I wonder if Damian did. He had a good overview from the box,' said Peter.

'I expect Ian will have asked him,' said Libby. 'Meanwhile, I think I need to go home and go to bed. I hope Ben won't be too long.'

On cue, her phone rang.

'Where are you?' asked Ben.

'I'm still at the caff. Owen and Max are here, too.'

'Stay there. I'll be back in a minute. They've found him.'

Libby's stomach did something peculiar.

'They've called an ambulance. You'd better tell the others – they'll see the blue light.'

'He's –?'

'Still alive, but only just. See you in a minute.'

Libby turned a shocked face to the others.

'Oh, no!' groaned Max.

'He's not dead,' said Libby and sank back on to her chair just as the blue light approached and turned up the Manor drive.

'Where was he?' asked Owen.

'I don't know. Ben's coming back here. He said to wait for him.'

'I'd better get supplies, then,' said Harry.

'I'll replace it tomorrow,' said Max.

'No you won't.' Harry gave him a friendly buffet on the shoulder as he passed. 'You've got enough to think about.'

Minutes later, Ben arrived and was besieged by questions.

'Quiet!' He yelled. 'I can't hear myself think. Thanks, Hal.' He accepted a whisky. 'We opened the theatre and searched. They're very through these policemen. Then we went outside and there he was.'

'Where?' asked Libby.

'Just round the side in the hedge. Very little attempt to hide him. Just looked as though he'd been quickly shoved out of sight.' Ben swallowed half his glass of whisky. 'God, I needed that. I'm not up to all this finding bodies.'

'At least this one was alive,' said Harry. 'How was he …?'

'As far as I could tell, another bash on the head.' Ben smiled wryly. 'He doesn't vary much, our murderer.'

'Do you think he knew Paddy wasn't dead?' Even to herself Libby's voice sounded quavery.

'How do I know?' Ben shrugged. 'I'd rather not think about it.'

Owen stood up. 'We'd better get back to the pub. I expect the police will want to talk to us again.'

Max stood like an old man. 'I suppose so.' He turned to

Harry. 'Thanks for the hospitality.'

'Come on, Lib, we might as well go, too,' said Ben. He turned to Peter and Harry. 'We'll let you know tomorrow what developments there are.'

'You know,' said Libby a few minutes later as they walked along the deserted high street, 'this is ridiculous. It should be so easy to work out. Doesn't it strike you as completely amateur and panic-driven?'

'I was thinking that earlier,' said Ben. 'As if there was something hidden that the murderer wanted to conceal, and everything that's happened is to stop it coming out.'

'Exactly,' said Libby, 'especially this last one. But it doesn't fit with the incidents in London.'

'Unless it's those the murderer wants to hide,' said Ben.

'But would you commit murder to hide them? No, it's got to be more serious than that. Another murder? One that hasn't been discovered?'

They turned the corner into Allhallow's Lane.

'The attacks on Stan and Max were definitely linked to *Pendle*,' said Ben, 'but Paddy had left. So what was his connection?'

'It must be something that happened before they came down here,' said Libby.

Ben unlocked the door of number seventeen. 'Well, if we've worked it out that far, so will Ian and his minions. I suspect there's a good deal of work going on we know nothing about.'

'I know.' Libby sighed. 'I wish he'd hurry up about it, though. This has all got a bit out of hand.'

Ben laughed. 'Slight understatement!'

'You know what I mean. I wish we hadn't asked them down here, now.'

'It wasn't us, it was Andrew. Now, come on, it's bedtime. Get up those stairs, woman.'

The following morning, Libby was unsurprised to receive a call from one of Ian's officers asking if she and Ben could possibly meet DCI Connell at the theatre.

'How did he get in there?' she asked Ben as she ended the call.

'I left the keys with the officers who found Paddy.' Ben drained his coffee mug. 'We'd better get up there. I don't want them messing up the set or the lighting.'

'I'll follow you,' said Libby. 'I must call Fran.'

Fran was suitably impressed by the news of Paddy's attack, and the prescience of Peter, Libby and Ian in suspecting something was wrong. Libby concluded the call by saying she would let Fran know if they needed any help in the theatre that night and, throwing her cape round her shoulders, said goodbye to Sidney and left.

# Chapter Thirty-one

The foyer was crowded. Max and Owen sat at one of the little white tables, Ian was talking to Ben and Peter by the spiral staircase and various police officials appeared to be inspecting every inch of the floors and walls. Ian beckoned Libby over.

'I know you didn't know Paddy Milburn, but you did speak to him, didn't you?'

'Yes, I told you last night. He just said now he'd seen the theatre he wished he'd stayed with the company.'

'And he didn't appear to be distracted – or angry?'

'I don't know what he was like normally, but he seemed perfectly cheerful. Not harbouring any great secret, or anything.'

Ian narrowed his eyes at her. 'What do you mean by that?'

Libby was taken aback. 'Well, if he was attacked to stop something from coming out, he must have known something. A secret.'

'And presumably didn't know he knew it,' said Ian.

'Oh, do you think so?'

'Ian's been thinking along the same lines as we were,' said Ben. 'I said he would be.'

'This murderer is careless,' said Ian. 'That said, we should have caught him by now. I got sidetracked by the incidents in London and trying to work out motives.'

'And?' Libby prompted.

Ian's half-smile appeared. 'You don't catch me out like that. Now, would you like to see if Max wants to use the theatre today?'

'Can they open tonight?' asked Peter.

'I don't see why not. It doesn't appear that the attack took place in here.'

'But there are people going over everywhere with a

toothcomb!' said Libby.

'Standard procedure,' said Ian. 'And yes, if you wanted to know, Mr Milburn is, as they, say, holding his own.'

'Oh.' Libby felt the colour rush into her face. 'Oh, dear. Sorry.'

She crossed to Max and Owen and put her question.

'As long as we can get in this evening,' said Max, 'I don't mind what happens. I suppose I'd better go over and speak to the boys.'

'I'm going over, too,' said Libby. 'Poor Hetty must be wondering what on earth has been going on.'

In the Manor sitting-room, the dancers were draped over the furniture in the manner Libby had come to expect. In a group near the coffee urns sat Jonathan, Tom, Will and Damian.

'Have you heard anything?' called Jonathan.

'He's still alive,' said Max, perching on the edge of a table. 'Look, everyone, I know how bad this has been for us all, and I honestly couldn't blame you if you wanted to stop now. I really thought that the worst was over, and last night was such a success – but now I have to face the fact that whoever is doing this isn't going to stop until we do. So, what do you all think?'

The dancers exchanged glances.

'It's got to be someone here, hasn't it?' said Dan. The others turned to him in surprise. 'Well, it has. Unless Libby or Ben or Hetty has suddenly decided to have a vendetta against us. I don't believe it's got anything to do with the stuff that happened in London either.' He shook his head. 'It seems quite unbelievable to me – all of it – but we've had one murder and two attacks. So which one of us doesn't want to go on?' He looked round at the rest of the room. 'Come on. Because if anyone doesn't want to go on, I think I might be a bit suspicious.'

The others regarded him uneasily, but Owen threw back his head and laughed. 'Well said, Dan! Unless a majority want to pull the plug I suggest we leave it to Max.'

'I think it's an unlucky show,' said Paul from where he sat on his own near the door. 'I think you've offended them.'

All eyes turned to him in shock.

'Who's "them"?' asked Libby.

'Do you mean the witches?' said Lee. 'Like the ones you were looking for when we went to see that grotto?'

Colour had risen into Paul's face. 'It isn't wise to mock,' he said.

'I can't make out whether he's a Christian fanatic or a pagan one,' said Libby under her breath to Owen.

'Sounds as if he's into witchcraft to me,' whispered back Owen.

'Well, if Paul's the only one who doesn't want to go on,' said Max, 'we'll go on. Paul, if you want to go back to London, I'm sure we can cover for you.'

Paul, now the centre of censorious attention, was the colour of beetroot. He shook his head and retreated further into his corner.

'Show of hands, then,' said Max, raising his own. Slowly hands went up all over the room. A few people were reluctant, including Damian, but in the end all hands were up and Libby led a round of applause.

'Could I add, please,' she said, as the atmosphere brightened, 'that I believe Dan was right. The murder and the two attacks were perpetrated by a member of the company, which means – someone in this room.' A murmur of disbelief greeted the statement. 'I know that's uncomfortable to think about, but the police are getting closer because of the careless nature of these crimes.' She crossed her fingers behind her back. 'And any more attempts will only confirm their suspicions, so whoever you are, please just stop now. I don't ask you to give yourself up, because I know you won't. I've met murderers before.' She looked round at the shocked faces. 'Now I'm going to see if Hetty needs a hand in the kitchen.'

She left a silent sitting-room behind her, hoping she'd done the right thing. Ian probably wouldn't like it, but she hoped whoever the murderer was, he would be too scared to do anything else.

'I dunno why they don't pack up and go home,' muttered Hetty when Libby told her what had happened. 'Less trouble for us.'

'You know what they say – the show must go on,' said Libby.

'You do,' said Hetty. 'I wouldn't. They want more coffee?'

'They've got coffee in their rooms, haven't they? Leave them to it for a bit,' said Libby. 'Is there anything I can do?'

There wasn't, so Libby went back to the theatre. Ian had disappeared with most of his officers and the SOCOs, although a uniformed policeman stood on duty at the door. Ben called down from the FX box.

'Everybody all right over there?'

'Yes. They've just taken a vote to see if they pull the plug or not. Again. They're not.'

'I could have guessed that,' said Ben. 'Let's just hope the idiot behind all this stops now.'

'I think he might,' said Libby slowly, 'if he listened to what I said in there.'

'Why? What did you say?' Ben was looking suspicious.

'Nothing, really. Just asked whoever was doing it to stop it. Now,' she said hastily, 'I must get back.'

'Libby.' Ben was coming down the stairs. 'What exactly did you say?'

'Um …' Libby felt the colour rising into her cheeks once more. 'I said – I said – well, I actually said the police were getting close and as it was certain to be someone in the company they'd better stop now.'

Ben looked at her hard for a long moment. 'I don't suppose that could do much harm. You didn't say you knew who'd done it, did you?'

'No, of course not – I don't. But if anything else happens, it simply must point the finger. We can't have people being laid out right and left, can we? I bet there's a really simple answer staring us in the face if only we could stand back and see it.'

'Perhaps the students will have something to say tonight. They're all coming down, aren't they?'

'Yes. Somebody's taking the minibus to meet the train at Canterbury. And come to think of it,' Libby added, 'I don't suppose they'll be able to stay for long after the performance as they'll have to get back for a train home.'

The students, however, arrived early. Sebastian, having been added hastily to the insurance by Owen, went to collect them in the minibus and they descended on the pub for an early dinner. When Libby and Ben arrived at the theatre, they found Max sitting at one of the white tables looking exhausted.

'I've left them with Owen,' he said. 'They're his pigeon. But they've got so much *energy*!'

'What did they have to say about the murder? And the attacks?'

'They only knew about the murder, nothing about the attacks on me or Paddy. Owen's filled them in. Sadly, they seem more excited about it than anything else.'

Libby was amused. 'Youth!'

'I suppose so. They're nearly all late teens, except for one or two who are twenty. The juniors aren't coming.'

'Let's hope they enjoy it,' said Libby. 'Paddy's still alive, isn't he? So let's forget all the unpleasantness and enjoy the rest of the week.'

'It occurred to me,' said Max, standing up and stretching, 'that when Paddy comes out of his coma –'

'Coma?' interrupted Libby, startled.

'Medically induced to allow the brain swelling to go down,' Max explained. 'Anyway, when he comes round he'll be able to tell us who attacked him.'

'You couldn't,' said Libby dubiously.

Damian and Sebastian arrived together, neither looking overjoyed at the prospect of another performance.

'Cheer up, boys,' said Libby. 'First night's over and you all know what you're doing.'

'I've never had anything to do with the students before,' grumbled Sebastian. 'Boisterous, aren't they?'

'You won't have to have anything to do with them, though, unless you're driving back to the station,' said Libby.

'I'll come with you,' said Damian. 'Then you won't have to drive back on your own.'

Sebastian looked at him in surprise. 'Really? Thanks – much appreciated.'

'Also,' added Damian going faintly pink, 'to be fair, I don't

239

think any of us should be on our own for any longer than necessary at the moment.'

Sebastian grinned. 'You'll be safe with me!'

'Quite honestly,' Max said quietly to Libby, 'if they had voted to pull out this morning I would have been almost relieved. I shall need a month off after this.'

The performance went as well as the previous one, if not slightly better. Libby had two members of the Oast Theatre's company manning the bar, so was free to watch, which she did, cramming into the lighting box with Peter.

'No Damian?' she whispered.

'He said he'd sit this one out. He's around somewhere. All I have to do is start it off.' Peter adjusted his head phones and moved a couple of sliders on the control panel. 'Here we go.'

At the interval, Libby found Damian with Max and Owen surrounded by the students.

'Sound OK?' she mouthed at him, and received a thumbs up in return.

'He's cheered up, thank goodness,' said Owen as he went back into the auditorium. 'I was quite worried about him.'

'Yes, he did seem as if he might break down,' agreed Libby. 'But better now.'

Libby waited in the foyer after the performance to greet Patti and Anne and watched Damian and Sebastian, like reluctant sheepdogs, shepherding the little crowd of students out of the building.

'It was terrific,' said Anne, as she wheeled her chair over to Libby. 'So atmospheric. I wish I could go to more ballet.'

'We always go to The Marlowe for the Northern Ballet,' said Patti.

'Oh, I know, and they're wheelchair-friendly, too, but I still wish I could see more. Where's Max Tobin? Can I speak to him?' Anne looked round eagerly.

'You've seen him in the pub,' said Patti, amused at her friend's enthusiasm. She looked at Libby. 'Real fangirl, isn't she?'

Leaving Patti and Anne with Max, Libby went over to where Owen was talking to a few of the company.

'How did the students like it?'

'Loved it,' said Owen with a grin. 'Made a lot of suggestions as to how they would have done it, of course, but they actually asked if they could perform it next year.'

'Will they be able to?'

'Yes, unless the company is touring it. After all, you never know, it might take off in a big way.'

'It deserves to,' said Alan.

It was nearly eleven o'clock before Libby and Ben were able to lock the theatre and walk home.

'No accidents tonight,' said Libby. 'And only two more to go.' She shuddered. 'I'm beginning to look over my shoulder all the time. I seem to be in a perpetual state of nervousness. But surely, that'll be the end of it?'

Ben tucked her arm into his. 'Don't tempt fate,' he said.

# Chapter Thirty-two

Friday was a bit of an anti-climax. There was nothing to do in the theatre, no police to talk to, no questions to ask or be answered. Libby, feeling distinctly unsettled, decided to take herself off to Nethergate.

Fran was relieving Guy in the shop, so Libby sat on the big customer chair and kept her company.

'So everyone's quite happy now?' said Fran. 'No more tantrums, alarums or excursions?'

'Looks like it. Young Paul's still against it all, and I can't make up my mind about him, but I don't think he's guilty of anything but being a bit of a pain. Damian's nervous, doesn't want to be alone anywhere, but everyone else seems fine. Whatever the answer is, everything seems to be fine now. And when Paddy comes out of his medically induced coma we might get some answers.'

'And if Max could remember what he went into the lighting box for,' said Fran.

'Oh, yes. And Paddy might not remember, either.' Libby gazed unseeingly at a large painting of what looked like a malformed egg. 'I just want to forget about it all.'

'No, you don't,' said Fran shrewdly. 'You can't wait to find out what it was all about.'

'It doesn't look as though I will, though, does it?' Libby sighed. 'Do you fancy a sandwich from Mavis? I'll go and get them.'

'Good idea. I'll ask Guy what he wants.' Fran got up and went through to the studio, and Sophie appeared from the flat upstairs.

Libby was blown along Harbour Street to Mavis's Blue Anchor cafe and battled against the wind on the way back with a basket full of sandwiches, which the four of them ate together in the shop.

'That was really nice,' said Libby, licking her fingers and collecting up sandwich paper. 'Having lived and breathed dancers for the last couple of weeks it made a nice change to be normal.'

'Glad we provided respite,' said Guy. 'I'm looking forward to seeing it tomorrow.'

'Me, too,' said Sophie. 'All those lovely bodies.'

'They don't look very lovely,' said Libby. 'They're either ghoulish witches or forbidding seventeenth century men.'

'I don't care,' said Sophie. 'I shall meet some of them afterwards, won't I?'

'If you're staying for the after-show party, yes,' said Libby. 'Are you?'

'Yes, please.' Sophie looked down at her lap and Fran winked.

'Are you staying with us?' Libby asked her.

'Ben said so,' said Guy.

'So ...' Libby indicated Sophie, who still wasn't looking.

'Adam,' mouthed Fran.

'Ah.' Libby grinned. Adam and Sophie had been a couple for some time, but had broken it off. It seemed as though it was on again.

'Well, I'll get off and make sure nothing's gone wrong while I've been away. I'll see you tomorrow.'

Steeple Martin was just turning its lights on when Libby got back. She made tea and prepared supper, then sat down to wait for Ben. It was always the same when there was a performance in the evening, whether her own or one at which she was working, the whole day seemed to be holding its breath until the time to go.

It was, therefore, earlier than usual when she made her way up the Manor drive with Ben's keys. She'd barely opened the doors when Max arrived at her shoulder.

'Is Damian here?' he asked.

'I've no idea,' said Libby. 'I've only just got here. Did he have keys?'

'No, I'm sure he didn't.'

'Isn't he at the pub?'

'No. He isn't in with the boys, either.' Max shoved a hand through his hair. 'I can't believe it.'

Libby's stomach had swooped again.

'This,' she said shakily, 'is ridiculous. Come in and start looking, just in case. I'll call Ben.'

Phillip, Jonathan, Tom and Will all burst through the doors.

'Can we help?' asked Phillip, no trace of a wasp in evidence.

Libby shrugged. 'You can look over the theatre. Who saw him last?'

'I haven't seen him all day,' said Alan, 'but we often didn't unless he came in for lunch at the Manor.'

Max came down from the lighting box.

'No one's seen him at the pub, either. Seb said goodnight to him when they got back from the station last night and that was it.'

'He was terribly nervous about the show,' said Libby.

'Yes, he was,' Phillip looked thoughtful. 'Do you think he knew something?'

They all looked at each other and Libby saw her own foreboding mirrored in the other faces.

'Let's look,' said Jonathan and they went through the auditorium doors. Libby went back to the main doors as the Range Rover drew up and Ben climbed out.

'No sign?'

'No,' said Libby, 'and Max said no one's seen him at the pub, either. Oh, Ben, he was so scared about this production. He must have known something.'

'And you think that's why he's disappeared?'

'Or *been* disappeared,' said Libby.

'In that case we'd better call Ian,' said Ben, fishing his mobile out of his pocket.

'Oh, must we?' groaned Libby.

'If you think something's happened to him, in the light of Paddy and Max's attacks, we haven't got a choice. I'll call his work mobile first.'

Ben left a message on voicemail. 'I won't call his personal

one, just in case. Has anyone looked in the lighting box?'

'Yes, Max went up there.'

'I'll go and check. Remember what happened last time?'

'Oh, the equipment being damaged? But Damian was here then. It was nothing to do with –'

'It was an attempt to stop the production, wasn't it? I'm going up. Will you wait down here?'

'I'll open the bar,' said Libby.

The dancers reappeared from the auditorium.

'No sign,' said Jonathan.

Phillip looked grim, Tom and Will worried.

'This is bloody awful,' said Phillip. 'Damian was right. We should have stopped the fucking show. Another one! Stan, Max, Paddy – and now –'

Ben came down the spiral staircase.

'Nothing's been disturbed up there. But Ian just called.' He looked puzzled.

'And – what?' asked Libby.

'He said that we weren't to worry.' Ben looked at the anxious faces around him. 'Then he asked if the show could go on without Damian.'

'It did yesterday,' said Libby. 'The score's programmed in, now, and Peter started it off. Damian didn't come into the box.'

'Not worry?' Alan frowned. 'Does that mean they've found him?'

'I don't know. I asked him what he meant, and he just said leave it to them. He'd call later.'

'It sounds,' said Libby, 'as if they've found him somewhere. Hurt, perhaps.'

'Left for dead like Paddy,' said Jonathan.

'And if your policeman said not to worry, perhaps he's been able to tell them who did it?' suggested Will.

'Mmm.' Libby stared at her feet for a minute. 'Well, whatever's happened, if Ian said not to worry, we won't worry. It sounds as if he thinks the problems are over, doesn't it?'

Max, who had been sitting at one of the tables with his head in his hands saying nothing, looked up.

'That's it! We won't worry. I have great faith in your

policeman. We'll just get on and do the best we can for Damian's music.'

The other dancers were filtering in now, and Peter followed them in. When they had all been told the current position, the lightening of the atmosphere was noticeable, Libby thought, as she went over to the bar to open up. She didn't have to act as barman tonight, but she needed something to do.

Ian's words had made her think, and as she bottled up the bar from the store behind, decanted ice into buckets and fetched lemons from the fridge, she went back through all the events of the last two weeks. Ben found her scowling at the sink.

'What's up?' He took a can of soda water from the fridge. 'Stop worrying. If Ian says we can, we can.'

'I know, I know. I've just been thinking things through.'

'And?'

'I think we got it all wrong.'

Ben frowned. 'How do you mean?'

Libby shook her head. 'I'm not sure I've got it right, and every time we speculate it turns out to be wrong anyway, so I'm not saying anything. I haven't fitted all the pieces together yet.'

'Look, Lib. Leave it to Ian. He said he'll call later, and we'll probably get the whole story then.' He patted her shoulder.

'We might.' Libby regarded her beloved seriously. 'And then again, we might not.'

Ben smiled in loving exasperation. 'Have it your own way. I'm off to harry young Sebastian.'

Libby handed over to her bar staff and went up to join Peter in the lighting box. He regarded her quizzically.

'Come on, old trout, what's up?'

'Nothing. Ben just told me to leave it to Ian, and of course we have to, but I can't help thinking about it all.'

'Of course.' Peter patted her shoulder exactly as Ben had done and Libby scowled at him.

'Don't patronise.'

Peter looked amused. 'OK. And don't scowl.'

Libby smiled reluctantly. 'I'll just sit over here and keep quiet.'

They watched the audience filling the auditorium,

recognising a few regular patrons, including the former Chief Inspector Murray and his wife, but seeing far more unfamiliar faces.

'A whole new crowd,' murmured Peter. 'Wonder if we'll keep them?'

'I don't think they're local,' said Libby. 'Except the dance schools. And we haven't got one here. They'll come from Canterbury and Nethergate.'

'Maybe we'll recruit some dancers, then.'

'I'm not having any child dancers,' said Libby. 'They require chaperones who have to have police checks and all sorts. Nightmare. And we couldn't afford it.'

'Pity,' said Peter. 'Kids bring in the crowds.'

'Obviously, so does ballet.'

'Dance theatre, dear,' said Peter. 'Remember what Max said.'

Eventually, front of house notified Peter and Ben everyone was in, and the performance started.

Again, there was a slight difference in the performance. Libby thought they all seemed more relaxed, even little Paul, and Phillip, as Alizon Davies, was positively ebullient. When casting the spell on the pedlar John Law he was unpleasantly seductive, and actually raised a laugh from the audience.

At the interval, Libby asked Ben if Ian had called, but he hadn't. She fretted about the foyer getting in everybody's way, until Max told her to go back to the lighting box and stay there.

By the time the curtain had come down – virtually – and the company had taken multiple bows, which seemed to be the norm for ballet and dance theatre, she was in a fever of impatience, with a hard knot of apprehension in her solar plexus.

'Yes, he called.' Ben met her, smiling, at the bottom of the spiral staircase. 'He's coming over, and says can we keep everybody here, or over in the sitting-room. Do you think he's going to make an arrest?'

'No.' Libby shook her head. 'He wouldn't do that in public.'

'No, I suppose not. I'd better go and tell Max.'

Ian had arrived before the audience had finally drifted out, and signalled to Libby that he would be in the Manor. Eventually they were clear, and Libby shepherded everyone over to the big sitting-room. She fetched Ian from the kitchen, where he was sitting comfortably with Hetty, whom he also invited into the sitting-room.

'You've had as much to do with this lot as anyone else,' he said. 'Why not come and hear all about it?'

The buzz in the sitting-room quieted as Libby preceded Ian into the room.

Max spoke first.

'Have you found Damian?'

'Yes, we have.' Ian smiled at him and a sigh went up from the whole room.

'And was he able to tell you ...?'

Ian looked round the room. 'Yes, we have the murderer in custody.'

Gasps and exclamations gradually died down, until Owen said, 'But who is it? We're all here.'

Into a tense silence, Libby spoke.

'Except Damian.'

# Chapter Thirty-three

The shocked silence held for a moment, then exploded, until Ian held up his hand.

'She's quite right, I'm afraid. It is Damian Singleton.'

'*Damian*?' Max sounded shell-shocked. 'But why? He's such a mild boy. And he seemed the most frightened of us all.'

'He had every reason to be, didn't he?' said Ian. 'As to why –'

'The music,' Libby butted in. Ian turned to her with raised eyebrows.

'Indeed it was. What made you suspect that?'

'The sound equipment was damaged and at one point he was trying to refuse to let them use the music.'

'I don't understand,' said Max. 'We workshopped it all together. The choreography and the score.'

'Not the finished score,' said Libby. She turned to Ian. 'Has he told you?'

'Oh, yes. He's scared stiff. None of this came easily to him.'

'So – what?' asked Jonathan. 'What about the music?'

'Libby?' said Ian, with a smile. 'Any theories?'

'Only one. Could the music have been written by someone else?' She turned to Max and Owen, standing close together. 'Your friend Sergio, for instance?'

There was another collective gasp and Ian nodded approvingly.

'Spot on. What made Damian run last night was he found out that Sergio was coming to see the performance on Saturday.'

'The letter!' Max suddenly shouted. Everyone looked at him in surprise. 'That's why I went into the box that night. Sergio's letter. He was asking how I liked the piece he'd sent over, and I didn't know what he meant. So I went to the box to see if … well, I suppose I began to suspect Damian then. Did he come in after me?'

'He did. If only you'd remembered what it was you went there for, we'd have got him a lot earlier. But he didn't know Sergio was coming. Paddy told him that the night before, and the students confirmed it yesterday, apparently. He hadn't known until then. So he ran.'

'Where did he go?' asked Ben. 'How did you find him?'

'We had someone watching the pub. He was followed.'

'Watching the –' Max shook his head.

'And the Manor, of course. Sadly only after Wednesday, or we might have found him a lot earlier.'

'But how –?'

'Why –?'

'When did he –?'

The questions were coming thick and fast.

'Not now,' said Ian. 'I'll be able to tell you a lot more later, but meanwhile, enjoy your last night tomorrow dancing to Sergio Padista's music.'

Libby and Ben followed him out into the hall.

'Thank you, Ian, that was nice of you to drive all the way out here,' said Libby.

'I had to collect something from his room, anyway,' said Ian. 'The original score that Sergio had sent Max a year ago.'

'How would Max have not recognised it, then?' asked Ben.

'He never saw it,' said Ian. 'Oh, yes it's all come pouring out, now. And the fact that he actually saw Stan Willis putting the cockerel in Tom Matthews' locker in London and threatened to tell Max. He says he was actually going to, but Stan countered by knowing about the music. Stan was a snoop, apparently, and poked his nose in everywhere. He found the score and recognised it and that was that.'

Ian opened the door. 'I'll tell you as much as I can when I can. Meanwhile go and calm those boys down.'

Fran and Guy, with Sophie, arrived in time for an early dinner the following evening with Ben and Libby.

'So it was Damian all along. Nothing to do with witches or

black magic,' said Fran, sipping a glass of Sancerre.

'Not in Damian's case, although it was in Stan's,' said Libby, placing an enormous bowl of chilli on the table. 'And, of course, young Paul's. He was a member of a witch cult, as we thought he might be, not a religious cult. He was terribly muddled about it, but even so, he had nothing to do with the incidents in London or the attacks down here. Stan, though, was, as we thought, completely against the whole witchcraft thing after his father's involvement with the fake Medmenham movement. Damian was scathing about Stan, Ian said. He blamed him for not facing up to his sexuality and for hating his father, yet using him.'

'Using him?' asked Guy.

'Yes, to get people off young Sebastian's back after he got into trouble over drugs,' said Ben. 'They kept tabs on each other, Stan and Wally Willis.'

'So what about the rat?' asked Fran.

'And the knife in the curtain?' said Guy.

'That was Damian. Max forgot to tell us he'd lent keys to Damian to "pop back" to the theatre on Sunday evening.' Libby shook her head. 'He completely fooled us, yet Ian said each attack was completely unplanned and panic-driven.'

'What was the reason for Max's attack?' asked Guy.

'Damian had got paranoid by this time, and was expecting to be found out and exposed all the time. When Max went to the theatre on Sunday and up into the box he was sure he'd found something. So he followed him in, hit him over the head and damaged the equipment, hoping they wouldn't be able to use the music.' Libby poured herself more Merlot.

'But I thought Sebastian had breakfast with Damian that morning?' said Fran.

'Damian was already there, and left almost as soon as Max had gone. That was one of the things Seb was hiding. He'd begun to suspect Damian. Why he didn't say anything, heaven knows. I suppose he was scared,' said Ben.

'And as far as Paddy was concerned,' said Libby, 'they were talking in the interval on Wednesday – I saw them. Paddy told him Sergio had been supposed to come down with him and commented how like Sergio's compositions the score was. That was enough for Damian. Complete panic again. How he lured Paddy outside we'll never know.'

'Cigarette?' suggested Sophie.

'I don't think either of them smoked, but maybe,' said Libby. 'Anyway, again it was a spur of the moment thing.'

'And by Thursday night he was in a complete funk,' Ben went on. 'If Paddy came round he'd identify him, unlike Max who never saw him, and on Saturday Sergio would identify the score. So he ran.'

'Where did he run to?' asked Fran.

'The bus stop on the Canterbury road.' Ben looked amused. 'He was apparently going to curl up in the shelter until the first bus came. He thought no one would notice he'd gone.'

'But Ian was already suspicious of him, and the officer set to watch the pub called it in and followed. A patrol car came and collected them and that was that.'

'So he was safe in police custody all day and you didn't know?' said Fran. 'That was a bit mean of Ian, wasn't it?'

'I suppose there was no need to let us know. He said he would have told us before the performance, but we called him first.'

'But he still didn't tell you.'

'He didn't want to worry anybody, he said.' Libby snorted. 'I think he just wanted his dramatic moment.'

'So that's that,' said Guy. 'Another adventure over.'

Libby sat back in her chair and lifted her glass. 'And I'm –'

'Never going to get involved again,' chanted everybody else.

**END**

Other titles in the Libby Sarjeant Series
by
**Lesley Cookman**

LESLEY COOKMAN
Murder in Steeple Martin

LESLEY COOKMAN
Murder at the Laurels

LESLEY COOKMAN
Murder in Midwinter

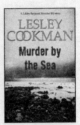
LESLEY COOKMAN
Murder by the Sea

LESLEY COOKMAN
Murder in Bloom

LESLEY COOKMAN
Murder in the Green

LESLEY COOKMAN
Murder Imperfect

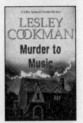
LESLEY COOKMAN
Murder to Music

LESLEY COOKMAN
Murder at the Manor

LESLEY COOKMAN
Murder by Magic

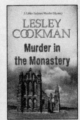
LESLEY COOKMAN
Murder in the Monastery

LESLEY COOKMAN
Murder in the Dark

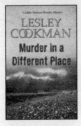
LESLEY COOKMAN
Murder in a Different Place

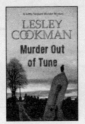
LESLEY COOKMAN
Murder Out of Tune

LESLEY COOKMAN
Murder in the Blood

# Shadows and Sins
by
## Andrea Frazer

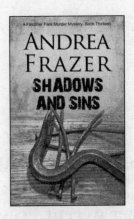

The thirteenth in the best-selling Falconer Files by Andrea Frazer.

The body of a woman has been discovered in Castle Farthing Woods, and it appears that although she had been dead for years, nobody had ever reported her missing. DI Harry Falconer of the Market Darley police is perplexed – and not only in his working life. He has recently resumed his relationship with Dr Honey Dubois – but in the course of his investigations, unsettling memories of a former love are revived.

Then the bodies start to come thick and fast...

As Falconer's sidekick DS Carmichael is coping with the early birth of his twins, the DI is forced to form a closer bond with his new constable, as they try to solve a nightmare conundrum. For Falconer is forced to confront the fact that someone has been committing these murders his very nose: he is forced to acknowledge that, in the midst of beautiful countryside and quaint market towns, there is a serial killer on the loose...

For more information on **Lesley Cookman**

and other **Accent Press** titles,

please visit

**www.accentpress.co.uk**